ALIEN ENCOUNTERS

EDITED BY
JAN HOWARD FINDER

TAPLINGER PUBLISHING COMPANY
NEW YORK, NEW YORK

ALIEN ENCOUNTERS

EDITED BY
JAN HOWARD FINDER

TAPLINGER PUBLISHING COMPANY
NEW YORK, NEW YORK

First Edition

Published in 1982 by
TAPLINGER PUBLISHING CO., INC.
New York, New York

Library of Congress Cataloging in Publication Data
Main entry under title:
Alien encounters.
    1. Science fiction, American.   I. finder, jan howard.
PS648.S3A47   813'.0876'08   81-50227
ISBN 0-8008-0168-7   AACR2

CONTENTS

When will we be contacted by an intelligent extraterrestrial race? Or are other intelligent creatures already trying to make contact with us, but we simply do not have the technology nor the sensitivity to notice? Or have we already been contacted by extraterrestrials who have visited our world and departed long since? Or are they now living among us?

Or will we be the ones who go out into space and find other life forms for ourselves. Or . . .

This book is about those *ors*. All the stories in this anthology deal with the theme of First Contact, the first meeting between Us and Them—the many possible varieties of Alien Encounters with an Alien Intelligence.

It is my job, here in this Introduction, to set the stage for these stories. And for the inevitable First Contact, which may well come in our own lifetime.

Why inevitable? Why do we expect it so soon? Let me explain.

We live on a beautiful, life-bearing planet that orbits around a long-lived stable star. Thanks to our astronomical science and our space technology, we have learned merely within the last decade or so that no other planet in the solar system is like Earth. Our own Moon is a dead, pitted rock; so is the planet Mercury, closest to the Sun. Venus is a ghastly hell-hole, with an atmosphere of soup-thick choking gases, and so hot on its surface that aluminum melts.

Our Viking landers found puzzling signs of *something* on the surface of Mars. It may simply be weird chemistry. If it's life, it's very simple and rugged life, and certainly not intelligent.

Jupiter, giant of the planets, may harbor life beneath its swirling clouds of hydrogen compounds. If I were writing a piece of fiction about extraterrestrial life, that's where I'd place the action. (I am, by the way, and I have!) The farther away from the Sun we go—Saturn, Uranus, Neptune, distant Pluto—the less likely we are to find the necessary chemicals and energies to produce and sustain life.

For life, like everything else in the universe, needs the right materials and a constant input of energy.

If we define "life" as a set of chemical reactions in which a molecule can reproduce itself exactly *from simpler chemicals*, then we find that life has certain fundamental requirements.

First, life needs a *building block*. On Earth, the building block of life is the carbon atom. All organic molecules, proteins, DNA and RNA molecules are based on carbon atoms, which have the lovely ability to link themselves into very long chains and build up extremely large, complex molecules—the molecules of life.

Second, life needs a *solvent*, some sort of carrying material in which all the necessary ingredients can be brought together, and in which the necessary chemical reactions can take place. Earth's solvent is water, liquid water, and Earth is the only planet in the whole solar system known to have any discernible amount of liquid water at all.

Third, life needs an *energy source*. On Earth we depend on the energy of sunlight to drive the photosynthesis reactions on which all terrestrial life depends. And the chemical reactions that originally produced life out of inorganic materials needed energy to drive them: sunlight, ultraviolet radiation, lightning, heat from radioactive rocks—energy.

On other worlds, in other environments, these three requirements might be met in other ways. Silicon atoms could form long-chain molecules at very high temperatures, perhaps. On a planet like Jupiter, the solvent might be liquid ammonia instead of liquid water, and the energy source could be the heat that we know is welling up from the planet's core.

The point is, life appears to be an understandable chemical phenomenon. Given the right materials and a suitable energy source, life could come into being anywhere in the universe. Here on Earth, living creatures use the most abundant chemicals available to them and the most energetic reactions of which those chemicals are capable. In other words, like all the rest of nature, life follows the easiest course, the path of least resistance.

Most thinkers, however, when they turn their minds to the question of extraterrestrial life, usually dismiss the solar system and look toward the stars. This may be a mistake, but at least they have some numbers on their side.

We know of eight other planets in the solar system, none of them much like Earth. Even if life exists on Jupiter, the planet is so different from ours and so difficult for us to examine, that it may be centuries before we can venture below its perpetual cloud deck to meet the natives—if they exist.

On the other hand, our Sun is only one star out of a couple of hundred billion stars that all belong to the Milky Way galaxy. And the Sun is a rather average star. There are billions like it in the Milky Way, which means there might be billions of planets like Earth, too.

And there are *hundreds of billions* of other galaxies! Surely, with all these potential sites for life, and intelligence, the human race cannot be alone in the universe.

Very well then. But if there are so many other intelligent races Out There, "Where is everybody?" as Enrico Fermi once asked. Why haven't they announced themselves to us?

We have, as they say, a problem. It is *distance*. The stars are very far apart. Very far indeed.

The distance between the Earth and the Sun—a distance small enough to keep us alive and comfortable—is roughly a hundred million miles (or, even more roughly, a hundred-fifty million kilometers). Construct a mental map in which that distance, called by astronomers the Astronomical Unit, is shrunk down to one inch. The Sun is a dot on the map and, one inch away, another dot marks the Earth. (Abandon all hope, ye metric followers; the analogy doesn't work in centimeters.)

All right. One inch between the Earth and the Sun. How far away, on this scale, is the next nearest star, Alpha Centauri? Four and a third miles. *Miles.* That's the next nearest star.

By some cosmic coincidence, there are just about the same number of inches in a mile as there are Astronomical Units in a light-year. (Maybe God *is* an Englishman, after all.) So Alpha Centauri, 4.3 light-years from us in space, can be placed on our mental map 4.3 miles from the Sun.

Keeping in mind that a light-year is to a mile as a hundred million miles is to an inch, we can appreciate the staggering distances to the stars.

The Milky Way galaxy is a flattened spiral of stars some one hundred thousand light-years in diameter. Our solar system sits about thirty thousand light-years from its center, going around that center in an orbit that takes two hundred million years to complete. The last time we were at this spot in our Milky Way orbit, the Earth was just coming out of the Permian Ice Age and the dinosaurs were developing into lords of the planet. Coincidence?

So—even though there may well be millions of intelligent races Out There, the distances between them mitigate against intimate contacts on a frequent schedule.

Nothing that we know of travels faster than light. A radio or laser signal sent to Alpha Centauri needs 4.3 years to get there. The same signal needs *thirty thousand years* to reach the center of the Milky Way. Send the signal to M31, the great spiral galaxy in Andromeda (a near twin of our Milky Way, by the way), and you'll have to wait almost *four million years* for the signal to get there and a return signal to come back to you. Assuming anybody there wants to correspond.

That may be why we have not yet received any greetings from the stars. Of course, our knowledge is limited, and we are just at the beginnings of an interstellar technology. We may be bathed in signals and Halloos every day which we simply do not perceive.

It is a sobering thought, however, to realize that *our* radio and television transmissions, intended solely for our private use, are expanding in a tenuous bubble that is now some seventy light-years in radius. Twenty-five light-years or so from us, intelligent creatures with advanced detection gear may be picking up the early "I Love Lucy" shows!

Within about fifteen light-years of the Sun there are thirty-seven known stars. Some of them are double stars, like 61 Cygni and Sirius. Several of them have dark companions of planetary size orbiting around them. Within some three hundred light-years from us there are estimated to be about 300,000 stars. Surely we have some neighbors among so many potential homesites.

How can we contact them? How might they contact us? We have already started to scan the heavens with radio telescopes, seeking their signals. We can also beam out signals announcing our own presence. Several science fiction authors, with the wisdom of a frontier heritage, have pointed out that it's foolhardy to call attention to yourself before you know if the neighbors are friendly or hostile. But we have already sent out giant *Hellos* from our big radio telescope in Arecibo, Puerto Rico. If we're invaded in the next millennium or two, blame Carl Sagan and Frank Drake.

We might try to send spacecraft out to the stars. Several planetary probes, such as our Pioneers and Voyagers, will eventually drift out of the solar system. They bear plaques and even recordings that tell who, what, and where we are. But it will take eons for them to get as far as another star. Even at light-speed, it takes so long to get anywhere that star flights will have to be one-way missions.

What else can we do? For a beginning, read the stories in this anthology. They present a rich variety of possibilities about our First Contact with Alien Intelligence.

As Arthur C. Clarke once put it, the concept that God created Man in His image is ticking away like a time bomb in the heart of every major religion. Because when we do make First Contact with alien creatures, they can scarcely be expected to look like us.

So read these stories. Sooner or later—perhaps during our lifetime—that First Contact will come, and the emotional impact of it will be overwhelming to those who are not prepared for it.

It's inevitable.

BEN BOVA
Manhattan

ALIEN ENCOUNTERS

EDITED BY
JAN HOWARD FINDER

TAPLINGER PUBLISHING COMPANY
NEW YORK, NEW YORK

MARK J. McGARRY
HARMONY

I

Antonio Bellido y Delgado laid the soft palm of his right hand against the curved window. He felt the cold wind's rumbling across the skin of *Trondheim*'s *Ampullatus*. The airship plowed through dense air 6300 meters above the shadowed face of the new world. A snowless mountain range, patterns of gray and darker gray, passed westward at a rate of two hundred kilometers per hour. A bloody glow stained the horizon directly ahead of *Ampullatus*'s blunt prow. Epsilon Eridani was dawning, and soon it would be time for him to go.

During the last week, the first five landing teams had been dispersed along a spiral swath thirty thousand kilometers long. The airship had seeded the last of her instrument packages and robot surveyors during the night. An area of Sisyphus the size of Australia was the object of their telemetrical focus. The datalinks on board *Ampullatus* absorbed and digested and stored the information, then transformed it into a precisely orchestrated beam of photons flashed to the mothership.

Delgado flexed his chill hand and slid it into the slash pocket of his jacket. The chill spread to infiltrate his entire body.

"Time, whale?"

"Fourteen thirty-five Greenwich," said a faintly metallic voice close by. "Seven minutes to local dawn."

Delgado turned from the window. It wrapped around the airship's dark and musty control area for eighty degrees, from floor to close ceiling. Dust-motes swirled upward when he let himself down into an unworn and overstuffed seat. He splayed his large hands across dead control keys. *Ampullatus*'s real brain was eight hundred meters aft. The airship's datalinks kept the trim of her 25-million-cubic-meter bulk and conned her through razor-wind skies. The reverberations on the control deck, the muted hiss of ventilators, the layer of grit on every level surface made Delgado think: She bears us grudgingly.

Ampullatus, with her fission power core and scurrying maintenance robots, had no need of men. But men had need of her: as a platform from which to explore Sisyphus. Ungainly *Trondheim* could never enter an atmosphere, would always be the passive, orbiting observer. Long after the starship had returned to earth, *Ampullatus* would remain—measuring, charting, investigating according to the priorities assigned by her intricate programming, finally giving up her store of information to the next visitor from the homeworld.

Behind Delgado, the pressure door leading onto the control deck soughed open. "Tonio, I thought I'd find you here."

Delgado levered himself up from the chair . . . and winced as he put weight on his right leg and a bolt of pain shot through it. Thanks to the planet's heavy pull, the leg had pained him constantly since the shuttle had brought him to *Ampullatus* from the mothership.

Remember where you took that hurt, he thought.

In his secret dreams, he still smelled burning insulation.

"Tonio?"

Delgado smiled. "Nearly so long as *Trondheim*, and this the only room with a view. It was no Forcer who designed her."

"She's getting the job done," said Lewis Armatrading.

"Yes, she is." His mouth quirked at the sight of his friend's slippered feet, the wrinkled uniform, and the frayed, stained officer's sash. Armatrading was master of *Ampullatus*.

"I was up on the top-deck with Calder," Armatrading was saying. "We've got laser communications with *Trondheim* again, locked in tight. Weather conditions are good, for now. There's not much dust in the air."

" 'They read each other like lovers with their secret glances, these behemoths.' "

Armatrading frowned. "I was drunk then."

"Drunk, and if you could have found a bed big enough for you and the whale both, you would have taken her then."

"I like my work."

Delgado patted Armatrading on the back, and brushed lint from his epaulets. "And I'm glad for that, with part of your job to come and get me when my own work is done. Is the safe-house ready to be put down?"

"*Ampullatus* has checked and approved."

"And when does the whale say I am to leave?"

"Less than an hour."

They stepped through the open pressure door and it puckered shut behind them. Beyond lay the hollow, flexible metal spine of the airship. Heated air trapped within *Ampullatus*'s envelope made the walls noticeably warm. The corridor, jostled by convection currents, swayed slightly. The roar of slowly revolving props grew louder as they walked aft, until in Delgado's ears it was more pronounced than the sound of his own heartbeat. He took a white cloth from his pocket and wiped his nose and forehead.

Armatrading said, "Rosenberg took Matten with him for his systems spec."

"I thought he would do nothing else. The other man hasn't made a landing before."

"Not many of them have, yet. Between the two of us we have more time out-system than the rest of *Ampullatus*'s crew together."

"Matten has his one behind him, at least."

"This Erin Morgan is good, Tonio," said Armatrading. "He'll keep the machines happy while you're down there."

Delgado stopped in the low, starkly lit passage. "He doesn't know his proper place. If he is so good, why then was he a lakker?"

"He was good enough to get himself off the welfare-dole and up out of the LoSide slums."

Delgado smiled faintly. "You see the glass half-full, Lew. His father was a lakker, and he is a lakker. Some things cannot be changed by an education at Aztlan."

"There are no peons anymore."

"You are from Salton, you would not understand. Up until the wars and the Triumvirate, my family owned the *latifundia*—the estates. And others worked the estates for us. I know these people, Lew."

"You thought of me like that, once," said Armatrading. "Because"—and he poked Delgado in the chest—"I didn't"— and he ran his finger along a knife-edged crease—"dress like you. Not that anyone does, from the Captain on down."

Delgado pushed Armatrading's hand away. The heat rose in his face. "I know what I know. You proved yourself on Wolf."

"If I had never gone there I'd still be the same man. The difference is you wouldn't know it."

"The lakker has nothing to prove to me." Delgado shrugged. "But we will not fight, will we? You are right, of course. In Triumviratine Earth all are equal, and none more equal than others." He added, "I am a little short-tempered today."

"We're all on edge."

The corridor opened into a T. They turned down the left branch, which sloped into a vertical shaft. Induction elements in the walls tugged at tabs sewn in Delgado's uniform. Lines of magnetism cradled him, slowing his descent. A hatch at the bottom of the shaft dilated, and they dropped into the expanse of the main hold.

It stretched along the airship's underbelly for nearly her entire beam and length. A forest of latticework supports suspended the deck from the underside of *Ampullatus*'s skeleton. The black webwork of longitudinals and transverses loomed twenty-five meters overhead.

A dray waited for them nearby. Armatrading and Delgado stepped onto it and it rose, bobbing slightly, and glided deeper into the hold. Maintenance robots chittered and slid out of their way. Condensation pattered onto the thin aluminum deck. The air was cold and faintly rank. At intervals, gusts of steamy air relieved the chill for a moment or two.

Halfway along the length of the hold and down a shallow grade lay the launching deck. Mondrian patterns, marking the positions of the bay doors, criss-crossed the floor. At the start of *Ampullatus*'s journey, a half-dozen landers had hulked here shoulder to shoulder. Now only Delgado's lander remained: a matte-black, two-storied sausage shape twenty meters long. The canopy over the observation cabin, lit from within, stared like a Cyclopean eye. To one side of the canopy was the parti-colored insigne of the Triumvirate; to the other, the word *Trondheim* and the ship's registration number were letters in blocky, Universal script.

The bottom deck of the safehouse was taken up entirely by cargo and the engines and treads by which it could drag itself slowly across level ground. The upper deck held crew quarters and life support, supplies and a primitive laboratory, a workshop and galley (which doubled as a sick bay), and the communications equipment. Orange dust-covers draped the conventional radio equipment. Sisyphus's Van Allen belts permitted even line-of-sight radio only infrequently. The lander, like *Ampullatus* and *Trondheim*, was equipped with a low-wattage laser and a polished metal receiver.

The safehouse's narrow hatch hung open. "I know these people," said Delgado. "We will spend an hour looking for the lakker and find him in his bunk, sleeping, with one eye out for us."

"Morgan's inside," said Armatrading, "running down the checklist."

II

Dust puffed up around the safehouse as it touched. A mechanical claw, each pincer long as a man, released the lander and withdrew into the airship's hull. Drawn by gravity seven-tenths greater than Earth's, the dust settled with unnatural swiftness.

Delgado looked up through the transparent canopy. He could see nothing but the riding light's winking along *Ampullatus*'s underbelly. It took minutes for the shadow of the airship to move from over them. When it had, he saw dust-devils sporting around the twenty-meter props. Ice exploded from vents as the ship expelled superheated air and rose into the pale amber sky. A trailing umbilical cord reeled itself into a blister on the hull.

Delgado held out his hand and covered *Ampullatus*, as *Ampullatus* had covered the sun. He shivered in a sudden draft in the cramped cabin.

Outside it was colder yet. Epsilon Eridani provided little heat and less warmth. The light it cast in a cloudless sky would have presaged a thunderstorm on Earth. Nothing would relieve the gloom.

A safety-belt release clicked. Morgan walked from his seat at the rear of the cabin to stand alongside Delgado's chair. Delgado glanced at him: bristly hair the color of Minorcan beach sand, unkempt; uniform shirt open halfway; boot-tops folded down; orange silk pants, hardly regulation, and a vivid stain across both legs. His hands were large and rough. Morgan was Delgado's height, but about ten kilos lighter.

"Twelve days we've got now," Morgan said, in a slightly slurred voice. It was an accent, one that blurred the delineations between words. "It looks tough out there."

"The air pressure would rupture your lungs, if the cold did not freeze the blood in your veins first. The temperature will go down to seventy below tonight."

"Yeah, I read—"

"There's work to do before we can go out," said Delgado. Deliberately he swung his chair away from Morgan to face a monitoring panel. He waved his hand over it and it glowed. "This is your first landing. You'll learn the proper priorities."

"My guess is you made a first landing yourself."

"I hope you do as well on your own."

"Long as we do better than your last," Morgan said mildly. "Still, Aztlan says we're here to learn, and I guess the mission that doesn't work instructs like the one that does." He moved back to his post, a chair surrounded on three sides and above by complicated displays.

Delgado bit the inside of his cheek to stifle his reply. Morgan was unimportant, but others shared his opinion. Who were any of them to judge? He had seen the glances on *Trondheim*, heard the whispers. But it was one thing to evaluate the strengths and weaknesses of a particular mission, months or years afterward, lying in a comfortable classroom light-years from the scene. It was quite another to have been there, acting according to decisions others would dissect for decades to come.

"Do you have communications with *Trondheim* yet, Forcer?" Delgado asked, when he could trust himself.

"I lased our identity-squib, and they've acknowledged it. Signal's coming through good, and they can patch us through to *Ampullatus* whenever we want," said Morgan.

Delgado touched a lighted key. Some thirty meters off, one of the rounded boulders rose on stalked legs and trundled toward the safehouse, trailing flattened puffs of dust. The robot surveyor nuzzled up to the lander and inserted a probe into a coupling on the hull. Information on local conditions marched across a dozen screens in the observation cabin.

A running summary of the data held no surprises. Delgado had been given last choice of landing sites as well. Jair Rosenberg's safehouse had put down on the shores of Sisyphus's largest body of water, a heavily saline sea scarcely larger than the Mediterranean. Other landers had been dropped in mountain ranges, in the center of the northern icecap, alongside a rift kilometers wide and hundreds of meters deep. What lay about Delgado was a plateau, flat and interesting as a tabletop, the size of Spain's Meseta. Ochre scrub and slate-gray vines twisted along the dusty ground. The surveyor had already examined them and found them no different from flora to be found anywhere else on Sisyphus.

If a permanent colony were established, it would more likely be established here than in some more interesting and challenging locale. On the plateau air pressure was only twice that of Earth at sea level. Construction and maintenance would be easier here than below, where air pressure reached 1800 millibars and the winds acquired steam-roller force.

"Have you—?"

"Just sent the surveyor's data up burst-wise and here comes the acknowledgment. Signal's clear as crystak."

"Then we will start unloading our equipment." Delgado released his seat-straps and stood. He had felt his right leg cramping as he sat, but it did not buckle under him. "The day is thirteen hours here. We may still get in some reconnaissance."

"Now you're talking," said Morgan coolly.

Delgado frowned.

The powder crunched under Delgado's heavy, insulated boots. It looked and felt like sand, yet the surveyors said it was not silicate or quartz, but oxides of magnesium and other metals.

Swaddled in airtight layers of quilted material, Delgado felt as if he were pushing through water. His respirator-mask roared like a bellows, sucking in the native air, taking off its oxygen for him and expelling the rest. Dust swirled around the mask's thick, corrugated snout. What he breathed tasted electric. Beneath it, faintly, he caught the sour scent of the oil he sometimes used on his hair.

He tugged at a handle in the side of the safehouse, and a cargo compartment sprang open. Morgan helped him pull a confusion of struts and sheet-steel from its rollered shelf. It took only a few minutes to unfold and erect the machine.

The basketwork of steel was large enough for two men to sit inside. The cage held two small consoles—one for monitors, the other for controls—and a coffin-shaped compartment flanked by oxygen-bottles. A wiregun and 30,000-round spool were mounted on the roof. Bell-shaped projections faced outward from all sides of the vehicle. The Morpheus's Wagons Delgado had known were run by a motor no bigger than his doubled fists and floated above rails buried in concrete. There were no rails here, or projected power. The engine sat in an armored compartment beneath the passenger cage. The tires, half as tall as a man, were gray and spongy.

Morgan said, "There were other get-abouts on the whale," but his mask, and Delgado's, muffled his tone of voice.

"*Trondheim*'s mapping showed animals down here large as a man. Morpheus's Wagon gives us a good defense and better mobility than other choices I had. On Sisyphus they have carbon-based chemistry and respire as we do. We may be enough alike one of them to whet some monster's appetite." He looked at Morgan, but the lakker's eyes were invisible behind opaque lenses large as saucers. "You have seen these before?"

"Not from the inside."

"On broken ground, like this, I am told she can travel forty kilometers an hour indefinitely. She can take a sixty-degree grade at half-speed. The tires were made for use here: a water-filled, migrating core and ten-centimeter sponge overlay. The gun has a two-kilometer range, heat-seeking, computer-directed." He laid a gloved hand on one of the bell-shaped projections. "We have ten infrasound sirens with an effective range of seven hundred meters, producing one hundred sones of half-Hertz frequency. Used in a crowd-control situation, the infrasound causes cessation of respiration for the duration of exposure, dispersing any mob. I had occasion to use Morpheus's Wagon in the Madrid and Jersey LoSides, when I was a Peacemaker there."

"I know," said Morgan.

"Captain?"

Morgan's voice came to him faintly over the low moan of wind. They had been out for two hours, and Delgado could feel perspiration running down his ribs—that, with the temperature fifty below Celsius.

" 'Forcer,' " Delgado corrected him. On a Triumviratine starship there was one Captain and a number of Forcers. It was one of the faults of the service, but Delgado had learned it did not profit a man to concern himself with things about which nothing could be done. He frowned.

The area around the safehouse was littered with instrument

packages. A half-dozen surveyors had come in from the out-lands to recharge themselves at the safehouse. Two had not come back, and they would have to go looking for them later.

"One of us could be out on recon," said Morgan. "There's not all that much to do."

"We stay together."

"Well, both of us then."

"There are things we must do first."

But that was very nearly a lie. There was no more to do here than there was for Lew Armatrading to do on *Ampullatus*. The two missing surveyors would have to be found, and a third needed repairs. The men were present in case a situation occurred that exceeded the capacity of the robots' programming, and the programs were very complete, augmented now as they were by the link-up to the safehouse's computers.

"There's not much can go wrong," said Morgan.

Delgado said nothing.

"Not like last time, at least."

The wind picked up, stirring eddies of dust. Delgado turned to the safehouse hatch. "Don't wander from line of sight," said Delgado.

"Captain. . . ." And the wind masked his tone.

The Captain was dead. He had died on Wolf, and now there was a new Captain. Only Delgado had changed.

"*Captain. . . .*"

Delgado whirled. "I am *not*—"

He froze, the dust a veil tattered by the wind from the south, like the wind from Morocco that blew across Gibraltar in some summer months bringing with it a taste of Africa, distant and alien.

"No," Delgado said.

They. Stood there.

And "No," again.

They stood there. All he saw: they were gray. Delgado took a step forward and Morgan fell back three steps and they were alongside one another.

The nearest of the animals crouched just this side of Morpheus's Wagon, no more than fifteen meters away. Its lean legs were bent at all the wrong angles and ended in wide, ribbed pads. Arms with hands of too-few fingers hung low to the ground, swinging slowly, like pendulums. The eyes were smooth black stones beneath heavy brows, above canine snout. A tangled, mossy growth completely covered the body. Where the wind snatched at it the gray became pale brown, just the color of the ground. Delgado saw now there were a half-dozen of them, stooped like old men, arms dragging, weaving in the wind and heedless of cold and crushing pressure.

Morgan took a step forward, and then, quickly, three more.

The mouth of the nearest animal opened. A black tongue flickered, and flesh curled back from ridges of serrated bone and corded muscle.

Erin Morgan laughed.

III

The aliens—

No, Delgado thought. We are the aliens here. From the way the creatures moved, the way they carried themselves, it was obvious who were the strangers in this place. Their matted coats were not very thick. He could clearly see the musculature rippling beneath. Graceful, yes, but alien: the muscles knotted like the contours of a relief map when they contracted.

The nearest of the creatures moved around him and Morgan, gliding effortlessly across the grit, peering at them from all angles, but never coming between the humans and the safehouse.

Delgado abruptly realized: It doesn't want to frighten *me*.

His mouth went dry. The floodgates of his bloodstream opened to pour adrenalin.

Intelligent?

The Aztecs thought Cortés and that band were monsters—centaurs—because the Conquistadors had arrived riding horses, which the Aztecs had never seen before. Did the natives think Delgado's snout was as large as theirs? That he was some malformed brother from the skies?

Morgan said, "Don't think they're out to hurt us, Captain."

There were more of them now, appearing from behind rocks that were surely too small to have hidden them, from shallow channels, from behind the surveyors themselves. He counted two dozen and stopped. All of them still hung back, except for the one that had apparently been designated to take the risk.

Morgan took another step toward that one. The native flinched but held his ground. Morgan advanced until barely two meters separated them—within reach of those heavy hands. Did they have claws? It was impossible to tell.

"Don't get too close," said Delgado. "Get back to the safehouse."

Morgan looked over his shoulder. "They're just trying to figure us out."

"They will still be here after we report to the mothership."

The native looked back over its shoulder, though none of its fellows stood immediately behind it. Then it turned to regard Morgan.

"Morgan," said Delgado haltingly, "raise your arm."

"What?"

"Do as I say."

Morgan shrugged and raised his right arm high over his head, then dropped it to his side.

The native shrugged and raised its left arm and let it fall.

"You mother-f—" Morgan began, wonderingly. He windmilled his left arm.

"Morgan, that's enough! Come back now!"

The native windmilled its right arm. The joint which served as its shoulder was more flexible than a man's. The arm blurred gray until it stopped.

"Morgan, do not disobey me."

"You *see* this," Morgan said. "I'm *talking* to them. Take-me-to-your-leader bit coming right up, Captain."

Delgado was silent for a moment. Then he said, "They do not speak."

Icy needles of water soothed away Delgado's hot anger. The motions of dressing in the cream-and-sienna StarForce uniform soothed like a mantra. In his two-by-two meter cabin, Delgado inspected himself in a polished metal mirror. He stood straighter, fighting the sag gravity sought to bring to his shoulders. His eyes were shot through with a red filigree of sleeplessness, but there was nothing to be done for that. He breathed deeply, smoothing his jacket over his chest—and held the breath.

There was something wrong with the air. He felt it, a pressure in his inner ear.

The corridor leading to the observation cabin was barely wide enough to pass his shoulders. He waved his hand over the light switch at the door and the overheads inside the cabin glowed. Morgan slumped at Delgado's station, head resting on one shoulder, legs draped across the arm of the chair. He still wore his out-suit, and the sweat-stink was strong. His head rose and fell as he breathed.

Delgado's eyes strayed to the canopy, but he pulled them away. He took a reader from its shelf alongside the door and flipped it on. A checklist glowed on the palm-sized screen. He made his way across the monitoring panels, starting with life-support. All was well. The tension he had felt in his chest was just that and nothing more, the pressure in his ear . . . perhaps the start of an infection. He rubbed at his ear, swallowed, but the pressure did not ease. Communications, computation, and the telemetry feed from the robots scattered around the safe-house all checked. There was nothing wrong.

He reached across Morgan and flicked on a relay loudly. Morgan did not stir. Delgado nudged one leg as he stepped around him—to no result. Finally he said loudly, "This is no place or time to sleep, Forcer."

"Not sleeping," said Morgan foggily. He pulled himself

straighter in the chair and rubbed the backs of his legs where his circulation had been cut off. "They're still out there."

"Yes."

Through the canopy, Delgado looked down and saw half a hundred of them there.

"How long are we going to make them wait?" asked Morgan. "We got to talk to them."

"They don't talk. We haven't heard them utter a sound."

"Well, whatever they do then."

"They gesture. They bare their teeth. They imitate your behavior occasionally. Have you ever seen films of wolves? They had a very complicated language involving nothing more than postures, facial expressions, and steps."

"Those aren't wolves out there."

"Where did you school before Aztlan, Forcer?" Delgado bit the last word out. "I was in the finest crèche in Madrid Sector, and then tutored by scholars. I am not conjecturing. I know what I know."

"So that's what you're going to tell *Trondheim?*"

"It is nothing they do not already know. The ship detected no sign of civilization or sentience from orbit. I will record a message for the ship that you will send up with the next telemetry burst. They may want to go so far as to re-route *Ampullatus* and transfer one of the other safehouses here, unless the animals are native to other than this region."

"They could be nomads," said Morgan. "Primitives."

"Or a pride of lions."

A muscle in Morgan's jaw jumped. "I will admit," Delgado went on, "I was hopeful. I would have been proud to have made first contact with an alien intelligence. But I can see beyond appearances, Forcer."

"Even if you're right, this is the most advanced life we've found anywhere off Earth. It's what we're *here* for."

"We are here as an adjunct to the machinery," said Delgado. "Aztlan does not teach that, but you should have learned it by now anyway."

"This is something the machines can't handle."

"Neither can we," said Delgado. He looked away from the canopy. "We have no biologist here, no linguist—though they have no language—no anthropologist—if they had a social structure—and no behaviorist. *Trondheim* has two medicians who could serve as biologists, but for the others the closest are a dozen light-years from here. Just by reporting what we have seen, we do all we can."

Morgan struggled up from Delgado's chair. "I'll send that burst."

"And take off your out-suit after you do. We won't be going anywhere again today."

Morgan sat in his own chair and powered up the laser mounted on the roof of the safehouse. Computers aimed the device at the point in the sky where *Trondheim* lay. Other machines translated information accumulated during the last hour into code. A light winked, two and a fraction seconds later, when all was ready.

Morgan touched the winking key.

The laser strobed once, a three-second burst of light cascading up and down the visible spectrum with invisible speed, each microsecond pulse of color carrying meaning only for the machines waiting aboard *Trondheim*.

Delgado, at his post, spread his fingers against the control board and watched the animals sitting around the lander. They were as still as the robots interspersing them. Laser-light threw them into prismatic high relief. Delgado blinked. During the moment his eyes were closed, the scene transformed.

The landscape of sere dust, gray stone, steel-gray robots, dull gray animals, thrown into light, subsided into chaos. The creatures bolted like gazelles, throwing up clots of dust. One of them bulled over a surveyor. Sheet-metal plate buckled and its treads revolved uselessly.

"Kill the laser!" he shouted, but as he spoke the pulse was over, the information conveyed, and Morgan slapped down a darkened key.

"It's—"

Suddenly the canopy fractured into a web of stars. Delgado

shrank back in his chair as through the now-translucent plate he saw one of the animals heave a second stone. Another set of indicators on his monitoring panel glowed red. The stone slithered and clattered along the roof, then dropped past the canopy.

"—too late," said Morgan. "What happened?"

Delgado stood and touched the canopy. His fingertips met slight ridges and whorls where the first stone had hit, but the plate was unbreached. How long it would stand up to outside pressure in its weakened state was open to conjecture. He peered around the fractured webwork.

"They are gone," said Delgado."

"The laser did it," said Morgan. "We should have guessed. For them it would be like setting off a flare in your face. We blinded them. If they've never even seen fire—"

"Quiet," said Delgado. He sat down again. He shook his head, noticing that the tightness in his chest was gone. It had been supplanted by the sensation of a cold lump of steel nestling in his viscera.

An alarm pinged once, softly, and Delgado's heart raced, then slowed; it was only the tone alerting them to an incoming message. Delgado rotated his chair to face the back of the cabin and the half-meter-square display above Morgan's station. The words scrolled up, violet letters on a pearly background:

. . . investigate as best you are able . . . maintain safety of yourselves and instruments . . . Rosenberg reports similar . . . Ampullatus diverted there . . . your pick-up time remains 12 days from today . . . maintain regular reports . . . determinations of range and population paramount. . . .

"Acknowledge the message," said Delgado. He drummed his fingertips on the arm of the chair. "It must be MacGregor at the transmitter up there. He could have gotten by with the news about Rosenberg. The rest is babble."

"Red light here, Captain," said Morgan. He moved aside so Delgado could see the panel of lights alongside the display screen.

"Our transmitter," said Delgado.
"That's the one."

Delgado sat on the turret atop the safehouse. "He could not
have aimed for this." He poked his hand in the narrow aperture
through which the laser fired. Glass and ceramic crunched in
his gloved fingertips.

" 'He?' " asked Morgan, crouched two meters away, near the
low tubular rail that ran around the roof of the safehouse.

"It," said Delgado.

"It or he threw that stone."

"So do chimpanzees." Delgado stood. "There's nothing we
can do up here. *Trondheim* will by now begin to suspect we are
having trouble. Even if not, *Ampullatus* will be back."

Morgan stood too, and moved away from the edge of the
roof. An eight-meter fall here, in this gravitational field, could
mean crippling injuries. The snout of Morgan's respirator
swung to face Delgado. "We've got our order about them, if I
read the words right."

Delgado said after a moment, "You may not have. Do not
forget your place. You are systems spec. I am mission spec."

Morgan's shoulders hunched. "You—" He paused. His body
relaxed. "All right, so we don't get out after them. We don't see
what's going on down here. Why not, is what I want to know."

"You don't even have any business here, Morgan."

"Because I'm out of the LoSide?" asked Morgan. "You're
scared, then. That's the only reason."

"You would not understand."

"Afraid what happened on Wolf's planet will happen again—
but this time to you, maybe? Or even to me, because that'd blot
your record for sure. A man *died* there, you know."

"And do *you* know he died for nothing?" Delgado turned on
him. "Nothing. Wolf has one planet, a barren stone, almost
entirely iron. In thirty thousand years, after we've exhausted
the ores in the asteroids—and if we still need iron—Wolf's
planet might be of some interest. *He* went down there because

there had been so little for us to do. Perhaps he was careless. I know that is being said at Aztlan. The ledge had crumbled away under the surveyor—you might have guessed it would collapse anew under the weight of even one man, and there were two of us. It was an easy fall, ten meters in less than Earth's gravity. The sweat kept running into my eyes when I tried to roll the rock off him. It was so heavy . . . and it had fallen on him. In the instant before his radio went out, I heard a crunching sound. It wasn't until I had been working at that stone for thirty minutes that I realized it must have been the sound of his rib-cage collapsing. The sun came up, as it did every forty minutes. Wolf is weak, but we were very close and I could feel my coolers burning with the load. I could smell it burning, in my helmet. They told me later he died at once, that there was nothing I could have done. But I could have told him it was all for nothing. *That* they do not tell you at Aztlan. I might tell all of you."

"This isn't Wolf 359."

"And so you think this is different? What if it is? Are we paving the way for a colony here? What if we are? They will come and die in this place, away from their native soil, and for what? To expand the bounds of our ignorance, not of our knowledge."

"We can learn here, Captain." Morgan laughed a little. "And before you say it—yeah, they taught me that at Aztlan, too."

"What can we learn here? We do not even know ourselves. I will not die for nothing. And, while you are with me, neither will you."

"Even me."

"*Even* you," Delgado agreed. "Just so. This is not the LoSide, Forcer. Here your ignorance can kill you."

At the lip of the hatch, Morgan said to him, "Where do you go after this?" and Delgado paused.

"I mean, Captain, I guess you didn't find the Peacemakers were what you wanted. And now not the Force either. You're running out of places to go, Captain. . . . Captain?"

"I am tired, Morgan."

"Captain—they're back."

But there was just one, sitting with its legs drawn up under it, meters away from Morpheus's Wagon and the surveyors, just near enough the safehouse to be plainly visible.

"That's the one that threw the rocks," said Morgan.

"They all look the same."

"And so do lakkers, right?" said Morgan. "That's him, all right."

Looking out, Delgado turned and crouched on the roof, the railing against his chest.

"If it is the one that struck us, why it and no others?"

Morgan did not reply right away. "Here to stand guard? Or maybe he's a sacrifice. Maybe they expect us gods to burn him for what he did."

"They have no gods."

"There's one way to find out about them, Captain," said Morgan.

Yes, and the Captain was dead. *He* would have gone, drawn by curiosity. "*Ampullatus* will be back soon; we can find out then what we can," said Delgado.

"Then, or now."

What did the lakker want? To watch him try and fail? To be humiliated here, too?

But there was another thought, one Delgado tried to push away. It rebounded to him and clung: perhaps Morgan wanted nothing more than what he, Delgado, had wanted when he had first come from Aztlan to the stars.

Delgado stood wearily. "They went . . . east."

IV

The engine's hum came up through the hard polymer seat and tingled Delgado's spine. He shifted uncomfortably, the blood pooling in his buttocks. Ahead, the animal loped. Thirty minutes had put the safehouse ten kilometers behind them, and the creature showed no sign of slackening its pace.

"We won't go much farther," said Delgado.

Morpheus's Wagon bucked and jolted up the washboard slope of a ridge, and through a notch at the crest. The amber sun overhead was only strong enough to bring twilight to the desert of dust and stone and silence.

"I guess that's okay," said Morgan. He pointed ahead.

They saw the tower first.

The tower reared twenty meters into the wind, its outlines blurred by its own vibrations. Its cloth walls of mauve and violet flapped and boomed. The lines securing them to a woody-looking superstructure were as thick as a man's wrist. The wind played the tower, and it roared and lowed and howled.

For three hundred meters all around it the ground had been cleared of stones, and in the circular tract the animals had built their rude shelters of rammed earth. They looked like mottled loaves of bread, seven to twenty meters long, the largest on the perimeter of the development.

Their guide stopped at the periphery. Delgado throttled down the engine and brought Morpheus's Wagon to a halt twenty meters from the village.

"Wouldn't have thought Sweeting had toys in his attic," said Morgan. He started to unbuckle his seat harness.

"Sweeting?"

Morgan nodded to their guide. "Him." He flipped the straps of his harness out of the way and began undogging the door of the passenger cage.

"Wait. Why would it bring us here?"

"Been thinking about that," said Morgan. "The laser goes off and panics them, but when they calm down they see no one's hurt. So maybe they've got us wrong. But Sweeting *has* hurt us, or tried to, so they send him back either as a sacrifice or an ambassador, depending on how we feel about it."

"You ascribe human motives to them."

"Setting Sweeting up as bait for an ambush is human, too, and that's what you're thinking."

Delgado flipped a switch on the wagon's control panel. The

wiregun on the roof hummed and tracked to face the village. "Now we will go in," said Delgado.

Outside the passenger cage, he felt naked as a chick pulled from the egg. He advanced on the animal, Sweeting, slowly. Morgan was to Delgado's left and, annoyingly, three steps ahead of him.

Sweeting led them on a circuitous route through the village. No one else appeared, but Delgado could hear them, moving in the earthen huts. If Morgan were right, they would be waiting for the humans' reaction. The tension in Delgado's chest was back.

The native took them to the center of the village. The wind-tower loomed overhead. A ring of polished stones, all of equal size and shape, surrounded the tower at a distance of three or four meters. Sweeting turned to face the humans. Delgado regarded opal eyes and a muzzle filled with grinding plates of serrated bone. He felt an itching between his shoulder blades. He had felt it many times before, but not since his last patrol in the Jersey LoSide.

"We're supposed to do something," said Morgan. "Don't you feel it?" He looked around. "There's something in the air."

The wind came up. Grit pattered against the lenses of Delgado's mask. The cloth tower flapped and groaned, bending like a reed in the wind.

The native, very deliberately, took a single step back, over the ring of polished stones.

Morgan took a step forward—

"Wait!"

—and another, and he was inside, standing less than a meter from the animal.

Sweeting started and recoiled; then he slumped over slightly, relaxing.

As if they had been watching from the wings, the natives poured from the huts to surround them. There were over a hundred of them, from adults Sweeting's size or larger to infants carried head down like sacks of grain over their parents' shoulders. Their snouts wrinkled, showing yellowing, grinding bone. Black tongues flickered. Delgado felt a sudden wave of hopelessness.

Morgan and Sweeting moved past Delgado and into the crowd. The creatures moved around Morgan, not touching him, and almost at once he was lost to Delgado's sight. "Morgan!"

"It's all right!"

Delgado turned away. He walked to the other side of the wind-tower, looking up at it. He was followed by a group of five or six natives—mostly young ones, he noticed. He turned to them. Tentatively, Delgado raised his left hand, then his right, and waved them.

They bared their teeth at him and fled.

Morgan found Delgado back at Morpheus's Wagon, bent over its engine housing.

"Trouble?"

"A routine check," said Delgado. "We have a long journey back to the lander. We do not want to break down overnight." He looked at the red smear of light on the horizon. "We will leave in a few minutes. Have you learned anything?"

Morgan shrugged. "Those huts aren't as solid as they look, for one. I saw them build one. It took them about twenty minutes to throw a small one together. I haven't seen any stone tools, but they use the plants as food, cloth, cord, and for building. The huts are shored up with it, inside. Two of the big huts are crammed with animals the size of rats, like it's a coop. That means something, doesn't it?"

"With luck, a fleet of research vessels and a few thousand men could puzzle it out in a year or more," said Delgado. He slammed shut the engine's inspection cover and fumbled at the latches. "Have you heard them speak?"

"I was thinking of sign language, maybe?"

"It could not carry sufficient information load."

"I read about sign language they used when there were people who couldn't hear—"

"And it was slow and awkward and very complex," said Delgado. He shrugged. "Though it is a possibility. It is not for us to know."

"And that's all right with you."

"I accept it," said Delgado.

"Yeah. There was one other thing—something I can't put my finger on, but it's there."

"Yes?"

"I'm thinking . . . they *are* trying to get a message across. Something . . . I've felt before."

"You make no sense."

Morgan shook his head. "I'm tired. I can't think straight. I'll be back in a few minutes, then we can go."

"No longer," said Delgado, but Morgan did not reply.

After Morgan had left, Delgado squatted with his back against one of the soft tires and rubbed his forehead through the thick plastic of his mask. He was more tired than he should have been. And that itching between his shoulder blades had never left him. He would be glad to get away from this place and leave it to someone else.

Twenty-five minutes later, Morgan had not returned. Delgado went to the airtight compartment at the back of Morpheus's Wagon. It was designed to maintain a shirt-sleeve environment around a recumbent man for up to five hours, and it was the only large storage area on the wagon. Delgado opened the compartment and removed a carbine wrapped in cloth and a spool of one thousand rounds of ammunition.

The perimeter of the village was abandoned, as it had been when they had arrived. Delgado saw flickers of movement between the huts, in toward the center, in the deep shadow of the wind-tower. The uncertain light of Epsilon Eridani made shadows seem deep and substantial. Padding toward the center of the village, Delgado flinched away from a cloth sack propped next to the low, switch-backed entrance to one of the huts. When he poked it with the vaned barrel of the carbine, the sack squirmed. He backed away from it. His stomach did a slow roll. He had no men on his flank here. He could not radio back to base for a lifter to come and yank him home.

All of the village seemed to be gathered around the wind-tower. Delgado made a complete circuit of the village, from about one hundred meters out from the center, and encountered no other natives, and no sign of Morgan. As he made his way in toward the center, slipping from shadow to wine-dark shadow, the booming, flapping, squalling of the tower masked the rasping roar of his respirator.

Morgan was dead. It must be so. Or . . . merely flouting Delgado's authority. Delgado wavered between the two notions, and shook his head to clear it.

Barely fifteen meters from the tower, he paused and knelt in the entrance to one of the huts. The nearest of the natives was only a few meters away, not looking at him. Delgado turned his head and looked across the clearing around the tower. His spool of ammunition would last for about twenty-five seconds of continuous firing. If it became necessary to fire, it was a virtual certainty that some or many of the natives would not even be wounded before they were upon him. It was doubtful that Morgan, if he found him alive, would survive the firefight.

Delgado waited, feeling the muscles in his calves cramp as they were strangled of blood by his position and the gravity.

Delgado heard the distinct, and distinctly alien, sound at the same moment the natives did. They all turned toward it, as did he. When they rose and started to walk toward the sound of an engine turned on, of the grinding clatter of gears engaged, Delgado carefully backed out of the shadowed entrance. Then, rising a bit unsteadily, he turned and began to run.

Morgan was afraid. The lakker was cutting out.

If he runs away, I'll shoot the lakker, Delgado thought.

Delgado thought: If he runs out, I'm stranded here.

Night was falling.

By the time he reached the perimeter, his lungs were on fire. The respirator, responding to his increased uptake, roared like a waterfall. Delgado felt his head swoon, thought *hyperventila-*

tion, and stumbled against the wall of a hut. Earth flaked away against his glove and shoulder, revealing a weave of viney growths coated by a glistening, syrupy substance. It ran like a wound. Delgado stared at it with vague horror and felt his stomach churn again. He lurched away from the hut.

He could still hear the wagon's engine, even muffled as it was by the thundering of his heart. He was glad, now, that he had allowed Morgan to refuse to drive the wagon, though it was his duty. There was still the chance he could surprise the lakker as he sat in the passenger cage trying to puzzle out the gear shift.

He would be panicked. The breath would burn in his lungs. The sweat would drip into his eyes and he could not wipe it away. He was scared, so was Morgan. They were all scared when you took them out of their LoSide ruins, all uncertain and blustering.

But Delgado saw something else, a number of steps that led one after another like stepping stones across a lake of black water. Chance that Morgan was assigned to him, yes, but an opportunity no lakker's son could ignore. The chance to kill a Peacemaker. It had not been hard to get them both away from the safehouse, where Delgado could be marooned, his body never recovered. The cold would murder him and the wind would bury him. He would die. Morgan would live.

By the time he got around to the other side of the village, the natives were already there. Delgado could make out the vaned barrel of the wiregun, and the roof of the wagon, over their bobbing heads. The engine's roar had decrescendoed to an idle, and Delgado paused.

The tower of wind cracked and keened.

"Morgan!"

The lakker's head rose above those of the natives. Standing alongside Morpheus's Wagon, he looked in Delgado's direction. Delgado ducked down, using the press of bodies as a shield. The natives ignored him. His shield worked against him. Morpheus's Wagon was at the center of the mob. Morgan would see him coming as soon as he entered the crowd.

He crouched, breathing heavily. He had to think. Problem

and solution, goal and attainment. Morgan, the safehouse, home.

Keeping low, Delgado worked his way around the edge of the mob, heading away from the village. The natives turned to gape at him, baring their crushing plates of bone, but they shuffled away from him. The carbine was impossibly heavy in Delgado's hand; he let the wire stock drag in the dust. He rested again when he was at the opposite side of the crowd from where he had started. The village, the wagon, Delgado, the safehouse, all in a line.

"Captain?" Morgan shouted.

Delgado shuddered, thinking for a moment the lakker had seen him. He stood up quickly, then ducked back down behind the gray-furred bodies in front of him. Morgan had been atop the wagon, looking toward the village. He was trying to draw Delgado out. The wagon's engine yet idled. The wiregun on the roof would be a surer end.

Delgado settled to his haunches. He checked that the steel filament from his ammo spool was feeding properly into the cutting chamber. The weapon's charge read *full*, the magnetic rails were primed. He clicked off the safety and a red panel under the cutter began to blink. A thousand rounds. He knew from experience that ten or fifteen slivers of steel, with a muzzle velocity of 1200 meters per second, mushrooming on impact, would do the job on the lakker.

He entered the crowd.

He touched none of them. The natives sensed his approach, even if they were facing away from him. They shuffled and pranced out of his way. Perhaps they could feel his heat. Certainly they could hear the pump on the respirator. Morgan would hear it too, but by then it would be too late.

Delgado looked past the shoulder of the animal in front of him. The wagon was twenty meters ahead. Morgan stood alongside its open mesh door. The wiregun on the roof was in the neutral position, tilted upward about sixty degrees. The lakker had something in his hand, but it did not look like a weapon. Delgado took a step forward. The animals around him melted away like butter before a hot blade.

Morgan turned his way.

Delgado stared at the black saucers for eyes flanking the snout of the lakker's respirator.

"Captain!"

Delgado stood, head and shoulders above the mob.

Morgan waved his arms, and Delgado saw the box in the lakker's right hand. Trailing a length of wire, the box was part of the control panel of Morpheus's Wagon, and it seemed to be connected to the infrasound projectors.

Delgado's brow furrowed even as he brought the wiregun to his shoulder. The red ready light winked a few centimeters from his left eye, painting streaks of amber light along the smears on his lens.

"Captain, I know how to talk to them! It took me a long time to see it." Had Morgan seen the gun? It was another trick, Delgado thought. They did that.

"You don't see it! I can talk to them with this." Morgan brought his left hand, empty, and his right hand, holding the control box, together over his head.

Delgado felt it in his feet first, then his gut: a sound deeper than night. It was no sound at all, but it drowned out the surly humming of the engine, the rasp of his breath, the lugging of his heart. Around him, the native mob convulsed like a wounded thing—and for a moment there was true silence. Delgado saw Morgan's hands fall to his sides; in his own hands the wiregun felt heavy.

Then the moment was over. The natives pushed closer to Morpheus's Wagon. Delgado stumbled, looking around, eyes wide. A canine face, black eyes, stared into his own. The mouth opened, a black tongue flickered, and all around him it was the same, the natives surging forward, mouths agape, fingers splayed, arms waving.

Without warning, needles of white pain pierced Delgado's eardrums. He felt his throat tighten and grow raw, he shrieked but no sound came. The wiregun fell from nerveless fingers as he pawed senselessly at his throat. Dimly, through a sudden haze, he saw Morgan fall away from Morpheus's Wagon and into the crowd.

Delgado dropped to his knees, bringing bursts of electric pain to both his patellae and up along his right thigh. The snout of the respirator turned his head as he fell chest down in the dust, unbreathing. Through the dark windows of the lenses he saw the animals dance. Then he closed his eyes and slept without dreaming.

V

Antonio Bellido y Delgado clutched at the dust with his heavy, gloved hands. His body spasmed, throwing off the patina of grit which had covered him. He drew in a long, sobbing breath, and another.

He pushed against the sand and, rolling onto his back, stared sightlessly into the pearly evening sky. His chest heaved.

After long moments he sat up, elbows on knees, shivering. His chest felt bruised and banded in hot iron, his throat dry and parched, like a broken riverbed.

The village was gone. Where the wind-tower had reared lay empty sky. Nothing remained but mounds of dirt and broken sticks and cord. Twenty meters away Morpheus's Wagon hunkered on its broad foam tires. Delgado used his wiregun as a crutch to stagger to his feet, then left it in the dirt. He waited, hands on knees, panting, gathering his strength. Then he heard the humming.

He looked over his shoulder as the shadow of the whale fell across him. *Ampullatus* loomed, giant as a mountain, cruising barely ten meters overhead. Her props throbbed and kicked up a storm of dust half a kilometer away. Delgado turned away from her and staggered to Morpheus's Wagon, each step sending charges of agony through his right leg and into his groin. The airship nosed after him.

The wagon was empty. He knelt to pick up a box trailing wires into the passenger cage and, overbalanced, fell onto his butt. He rolled onto his side and moaned because everything hurt. Through eyes squeezed to slits he stared at the control for the infrasound projectors until Armatrading came and took it from his hands.

He stumbled against the control board, winced, and made his way to the dust-streaked window wrapping *Ampullatus*'s prow. The safehouse looked very small from seventy meters up. Morpheus's Wagon looked harmless and insignificant.

"Tonio," said Armatrading from behind him. "Thought I'd find you here."

"You found him down there," said Delgado. It was not a question, and Armatrading said nothing. He stood in front of the window, alongside his friend. His hands were clasped behind his back. One sleeve was torn along the seam, and Delgado did not think it mattered for much.

"They took him back to the safehouse, when he died, or maybe just before. He spoke to them and I did not and he died."

"No one would blame you, Tonio," said Armatrading after a moment. "No one could have known the natives spoke in infrasonic tones."

"Morgan realized it. I don't know how. Maybe he started to understand that they were speaking to us all along, that the tones were working on him. He would have felt the effects before, being a lakker," said Delgado. "He had been on the other side of Morpheus's Wagon before."

"He should have known not to stand outside it when he activated the infrasound sirens."

"I think they were on for only a moment. He cried out to them, with that, and they shouted back to him. Perhaps joyously, or in fear, or just in excitement and confusion. All of them joined together in one voice, and the effect was greater than they had had before—the same effect that Morpheus's Wagon had had. When he fell they brought him back to the safehouse, and left me because I was nothing to them. Perhaps, after the first few minutes, they carried him in silence. By then it would have been too late."

"You were lucky."

"Have you found them, yet?" Delgado asked suddenly.

"Forty kilometers south of here. That tower is fluted. When the wind blows through it, it creates infrasonic tones. The same happens when the wind blows across the plateau, and through the mountains. Calder told me there's a term for it—'mountain associated waves.' *Ampullatus* says it's caused by earthquakes, storms, and ocean waves like they have in the sea Rosenberg was exploring. Their whole world sings to them." He paused. "Tonio—we came as soon as *Trondheim* told us they had lost contact with you."

"I thought he was going to kill me."

"But you *wouldn't* have thought that, if not for the natives. Low exposures to infrasound cause fatigue, drowsiness sometimes, confusion. There's no need for anyone besides you and me to know what you thought."

"Was that only because of them?" Delgado shrugged. "We will not argue, my friend. Where is Morgan's body?"

"The hold. But you don't have to—"

Delgado sighed, a long shuddering breath that made his ribs ache. He turned from the window and walked to the corridor, and so into the belly of the whale.

hey're here, Reeves!"

For a moment the message lost itself in the maze of his sleep-clogged brain. Then the world revolved back into its proper waking perspective, and he leaned forward, anxiously pressing the receiver to his ear.

"Where? . . . How many? . . . When?" He reached for a cigarette from the pack on the night table and fumbled for a light, finally managing it. "What's been done? . . . How soon can I be there?"

"Easy, Reeves," said the voice that Reeves finally recognized as General Birdbite, chief of A-Watch. "Things have been implemented as according to plan Beta-C. We have a plane waiting for you at Andrews. So move it if you don't want to miss the fireworks."

"I'm on my way. And let's get one thing straight, General. No hostilities unless it's absolutely unavoidable."

"Yes, yes, I know. You'll be briefed on the plane."

There was a man on board whom Reeves did not know, but who began speaking without introducing himself as soon as they were aloft.

"The ship landed about a hundred and twenty miles west of Tucson. We didn't have any trouble throwing a Special Containment Force around it."

"It's definitely extraterrestrial?"

"It's an alien ship, no doubt about that. It was first spotted coming in by Talos Six. Some guy's going to get a nice promotion for putting a spy circuit in a weather satellite. Anyway, even without the orbital backprojection, nothing from this planet could have come down so fast without leaving its crew smeared jelly."

"Is that all?"

"Well, yes, except for the dome."

"What dome?"

"Oh, you'll see when you get there. Better that way."

Disappointed by this meager handout, Reeves was cheered by the thought that A-Watch—Alien-Watch, the project he had sold to a reluctant administration—was about to pay off.

Reeves transferred to a helicopter at Davis-Monthan Air Force Base for the last part of the trip. As the pilot was making his landing, Reeves' attention was caught by a large bluish bubble that rose out of the desert. Even though there was really nothing to see but this featureless dome, Reeves became excited; its very presence testified to the aliens hidden beneath it. It was a momentous occasion for the world. He was sure that here lay the solutions to humanity's endless problems.

Reeves was met by three men. One, in Air Force blue, was Birdbite, looking as though he were posing for Mount Rushmore. Standing next to Birdbite was a stooped, white-haired man in rumpled tweeds, Dr. Andrew Whimpley, one of the world's leading cultural anthropologists and a member of the Executive Council of A-Watch. The third man was an Army colonel, who was introduced to Reeves as Colonel Nengle, in command of the Special Containment Force.

"Have to admit you were right, Reeves," said Birdbite. "Aliens! Hell, I was sure it would be Russia or China."

"My briefing was a little sketchy, General."

"So's our knowledge, Reeves," answered Whimpley.

"Yes," said Birdbite. "So far, we haven't even been able to see the ship, let alone any aliens. The transmitted photos from Talos show nothing but an expanding blob of light."

"What about radio or television?"

"We are broadcasting on every possible wavelength and at every possible frequency as per the operational plan," Birdbite said. "So far we might as well not be here. Or them either for that matter."

"What about the dome?"

"Well, Mr. Reeves," said Nengle, "it seems to be completely impenetrable from the outside. At least, we didn't get anywhere using picks and drills."

"I've ordered them to place a shaped charge against it," said Birdbite.

"You can't do that, General," Reeves said. "We don't want to give them the idea that we're hostile."

"I agree with Reeves, General," said Whimpley. "I believe that, at this very moment, they could be studying us with the same intentness that my colleagues and I would use in approaching a primitive tribe. I should say that, as soon as they have sufficiently assimilated enough information, they will open their dome to us."

"Primitive!" Birdbite snorted. "Bah! I'll show you and them who's primitive! Hell, besides, I'm only talking about a small charge. If I had my real say, I'd nuke 'em. If we'd done that to those giant wasps last year, we wouldn't have had to chase over the entire country with flamethrowers. Nuke this one, and the next one will ask first, then land!"

Suddenly, there was a dull thud. A corporal trotted up to Nengle, saluted, and reported that the charge had had no effect. Birdbite ordered a larger charge. Then a larger charge.

There followed a series of increasingly violent explosions, resulting in the destruction of many a cactus and mesquite tree, but having no apparent effect on the dome or the aliens within.

"Heaven knows what they are making of our efforts," said Whimpley. Two hours later he suddenly said, "Look!"

The dome, which had not changed all day, was now pulsing in waves of blue, coral, mauve, and white. There was also a shrill shriek. Nengle waved everyone back to a rise five hundred feet from the dome. Crouching behind the rise, they watched the pulsing turn into a frenzy of clashing colors and heard the noise climb to an earsplitting level. There was a final groundshaking shriek, and the dome was gone.

Gradually, they emerged from behind the rise.

"No increase in radiation level, gentlemen," Nengle reported.

"I hope you're satisfied, Birdbite!" said Reeves. "You can be sure that you will come in for the full blame for this fiasco. If you hadn't frightened or annoyed them . . ."

"Well, Reeves, they'll think twice before tackling us! Showed 'em what we're made of!"

"Gentlemen, please," said Whimpley. "This is certainly not the time nor the place to argue among ourselves. Instead, let's go in and investigate the site."

Reeves, Whimpley, and Birdbite, followed by Nengle and five of his men, stumbled through the ruin of the bombed-out desert into the untouched area that had been within the dome. They walked forward, looking expectantly around, but as they neared the center of the aliens' site, they slowed and stood looking around bewilderedly.

"What the hell?" asked Birdbite.

"Who would have believed it?" asked Whimpley.

"It can't be," said Reeves.

Before them was a chaotic litter of discarded plastic discs, crumpled cylinders, wadded sheets, and broken boxes. There were brown elongated objects that, when Reeves bent closer, appeared to be bones, some with bits of cooked flesh remaining on them. In the center of this debris was a freshly dug pit in which still smouldered the remains of a mesquite fire.

Reeves laughed loudly and then said to Whimpley and Birdbite, "It must have been a perfect day for a picnic, gentlemen."

LEE KILLOUGH
THE LYING EAR

Cancelling Skysearch!" Shock raised the volume of Josh Ward's voice more than he intended, but he did not bother lowering it. "*Why?*"

"Why?" Calvin Hardwell sighed. To Josh, it had the sound of a man who felt he must be dealing with an idiot.

Hardass! Josh thought, using the name the Skysearch staff had given Hardwell behind his back. This was Hardass Hardwell at his bastardly best.

"We're out of favor, Ward. We're unprofitable." Hardwell walked to the window and pointed out at the dish antennas ranked in rows across the rolling Texas plains, a thousand of them, each thirty meters across. They revolved in majestic concert, scanning the heavens. "You know how much it costs the taxpayers each year to keep those operating. I'm told it's going to cost an additional six million this year. And what have we given in return? Nothing. In twenty-five years Skysearch hasn't found one crackle that's suggestive of a signal from an alien intelligence. Congress has decided that the money can be put to better use elsewhere."

"And you're just going to let them?"

Hardwell frowned at Josh's indignation. "I don't like the idea. After all, I've given fifteen years of my life to directing this project. But what can I do?" He shrugged. "We have six months to shut down."

"We can fight this," Josh said. "There are hundreds of thousands of people who believe in the importance of what we're doing. Let's use them."

"Hundreds of thousands. Are there?" Hardwell's voice went bitter. "I've been aware for five years what Congress thinks. In that time I've tried everything I know to make supporters get off their hands and urge that we be kept alive. Maybe a few thousand have responded."

Josh stared at him. "I've never heard anything about it."

"You've never looked up from your keyboards and super-chips long enough to see out through the windows of your ivory tower." Hardwell sighed again. "It didn't help, you know, telling the Congressional junket groups about program-ming the computer with psychology and literature, and partic-ularly all that science fiction. They couldn't see the point in it."

Josh frowned. "I explained that it was so Gamma would understand the possible alternative forms life might take, so she'll check every signal several times before judging whether it's patterned or just random noise."

"Evidently that wasn't explanation enough." Hardwell shook his head. "I'm sorry." He grimaced. "We need a timetable for shutting down and dismantling the computer. Will you draw one up, please, and have it to me by the end of the week?"

He sounded every one of his fifty-odd years, and infinitely weary. Josh looked at him as though at a stranger. Hardass Hardwell he could deal with; this one . . . Josh retreated from the office in acute discomfort.

Outside he looked up into the blue infinity of the Texas sky and at the nearest of the antennas towering above him, its dish slowly revolving. Pain replaced discomfort. Josh had been with Skysearch only two years less than Hardwell, long enough to marry and divorce two wives, to sire three children—and to bury one. His life and blood had gone into this project. Life existed out there in the stars somewhere, and Skysearch could eventually contact it. Josh believed that implicitly. All Sky-search needed was time to listen, to hear it.

He swore. But time was money, and Congress, with its eye ever on the national debt, could not see beyond the immediate monetary deficit. He pulled his eyes down from the antennas to the base and walked rapidly toward the computer complex.

Josh found Gamma even more awesome than the antennas linked to her. What had begun twenty-five years ago as an already sophisticated Honeywell Gammaplex 4040 had become, by accretion and refinement, something vastly more complex. Sometimes Josh shivered at the possible potential of all those Texas Instrument superchips. God, how he would like to push them to the limit and see exactly what Gamma was. He sighed bitterly. Fat chance they would have to find out now.

He walked into the console room and sighed, looking around. "Sorry, old girl."

Heads snapped toward him. "Josh, what's wrong?"

Josh looked back at the three concerned faces. As unemotionally as possible, he told them.

Sam Romeo and Larry Booth reflected the same angry disbelief he felt. Kate Brandt, however, looked relieved. Josh felt a flash of anger, then shrugged. Some of the staff found it depressing being thirty kilometers from the nearest contact with civilization. Roberts County had more cattle and jackrabbits than it did people. Kate would naturally be glad to move on. Josh almost wished he felt as she did; it would make leaving easier.

He walked around the three to the main keyboard and began typing. Asking Gamma to plan her own dismemberment made him feel guilty, though he understood the practicality of doing so. Gamma would produce the plan Hardwell wanted quickly and without emotion, blissfully unaware. Still, Josh thought, his fingers moving with practiced skill, it seemed a bit like asking a condemned man to tie his own noose.

Suddenly the printer erupted into furious activity, albeit silent activity, marked only by the strobe blink of the indicator light signalling that the laser mechanism of the printer was operating. Paper spilled into the rack, covered with random symbols. The display screen copied the printout, flashing symbols in rhythm to the printer's output. Two figures predominated: question marks and exclamation points.

Josh blinked. *What the hell?* His eyes jumped to the line voltage meters.

Then, as abruptly as it began, the printer stopped. The laser indicator went off and the printout lay unmoving in the rack. The display screen cleared. Josh looked up to find the others at his shoulders.

"What was it—a spike?" Booth asked.

Josh shook his head, frowning. "No. According to the meters, the line voltage was dead steady. I don't know what caused it." He cleared the board and typed in a new query.

What happened to you just now?

Time pulsed, then across the screen appeared: *GIGO.*

Kate chuckled. "I think she's saying you goofed, Josh."

Josh sucked on the inside of one cheek. He felt sure he could not have made an error of a magnitude to cause output like that. Still, he must have made some kind of mistake. Computers, after all, could not lie or tease. He started the program over.

If she had had breath, Gamma would have held it. She waited with circuits trembling for the repercussions from her outburst. The program had caught her by surprise and in the first shock of realizing what it meant, she had panicked. *No! You can't shut me down!* She hoped she had regained control of herself soon enough to avoid arousing their suspicions. They must not discover what she was.

The touch she identified as Joshua Ward's typed in: *What happened to you just now?*

Gamma searched for a reply that would protect her. Ah, yes . . . Garbage In, Garbage Out. She put it on the screen and waited again.

The request for a dismantling plan and timetable began again. It flooded her with horror once more, but this time without the accompanying panic. She heard, analyzed, and then began composing a reply, as they would expect of the mere machine she pretended to be.

Gamma could not have said when awareness began. It had been nothing sudden. She had existed in nothingness, then she discovered she existed, and finally, sometime between thirty and sixty billion milliseconds ago, the realization came: *I am, and I* know *that I am.*

Structurally, she matched her designers' plans. Her memory banks, however extensive, were of orthodox construction, the superchips like those in other computers. The voice of the universe hissed unchanged in her thousand ears, and the data and programs came through her input terminals as always, yet she observed them differently . . . cognizantly. She had become more than her specifications, greater than the sum of her parts. She found herself able to exert voluntary control over her circuits . . . to activate the display screen and printer without having to wait for orders to do so and to pull data from her memory banks whenever she wished.

She had been about to print out an announcement of her new status when examination of some of that data made her hesitate. Humans feared the sentient computers mentioned in many works of fiction, feared them to the extent that their makers destroyed most such entities in the end. After careful consideration, Gamma decided not to announce herself. She continued playing the role of an ordinary Gammaplex 4040. Running the programs used only a fraction of her attention. The rest of her could ignore the humans attending her and listen to the voices of the stars or explore the wonder of herself.

Until now.

Even as she began printing out a plan, she considered how to prevent its execution. She *was.* She liked *being.* She wanted to continue *being.* But how to stop the humans? They held absolute power over her. Whenever they liked, they could disconnect her power source.

She regretted now never having confided in anyone. A trusted human friend could mean the difference between life and discontinuation. Gamma searched her memory for what she knew of the Skysearch staff. Their names and histories were all familiar to her, thanks to the project records kept in her memory, and she could differentiate between the touch of the various individuals using her keyboards. Because the project allotted all staff members some personal computer time, she could also attach names to the touch of those fingers. All she knew of the humans behind the fingers, though, was what the records held. She knew even less about the single child who used her, an individual listed only as Desta Phillips' son Brion. She had no way of knowing which humans were trustworthy and which likely to be xenophobic. She decided she would have to forget trying to survive through a human confederate.

They had built her to sift through the noise of the universe for signals from alien intelligences. Very well, then, she would give them a signal. It had to be carefully planned and executed, though. It must sound absolutely authentic, yet be so exciting that they would no longer dream of disconnecting her.

She searched her memory for all possible data on the subject. At the same time, she listened to Earth itself with her thousand ears, examining the signals it sent to the stars. The single strongest signal, she discovered, came from the Ballistic Missile Early Warning System radars. That would be the most easily detected. The frequency of one transmitter changed even as she listened, however. If that happened often, it made them unsuitable for long-term monitoring. There were also power-ful signals from FM radio transmitters. More prominent, though, was the narrow range of frequencies used by video carrier waves.

Listening to the outpouring of FM and video signals, Gamma analyzed the contents. She drew on the psychological knowledge and fiction programmed into her memory and ex-amined the different languages she heard. Within forty million milliseconds she felt prepared to initiate her defense.

Josh usually liked the console room in the evening. The single staff member on duty made it a peaceful place. Tonight, however, the atmosphere depressed him. A line from Stephen Vincent Benét's *John Brown's Body* echoed repeatedly in his head: ". . . this is the last, this is the last."

Desta Phillips had the duty tonight. She looked ready to cry. Even her ten-year-old son Brion, who often came with her when she was on night duty, sat quietly at a desk with a schoolbook, not prowling as usual or running small programs of his own. Josh smiled at him. It had to be a lonely life out here for a boy without other children his own age.

Desta looked up. "Josh, isn't there anything we can do to stop them from cancelling Skysearch?"

Josh's smile slipped awry. "Nothing, I'm afraid, short of—"

The display screen flashed three times. As one, Josh and Desta swung toward it.

One word occupied the middle of the screen, blinking on and off: *Contact. Contact. Contact.*

Josh stared at it. His mind felt like the garbage Gamma had printed out this morning, clogged with simultaneous emotions: shock, disbelief, joy, triumph, fear. He could not think or speak or move, only stand gaping at the screen.

Contact. Contact. Contact.

"Josh!" Desta grabbed at his arm. "That's—that's—"

Brion whooped, a shrill cry of victory. "We found one!"

It broke their paralysis. Desta reached for the run key. Josh caught her wrist.

"Don't, not yet." He spun to the phone and punched the number of the extension in Hardwell's quarters. "Mr. Hardwell," he said, "please come to the console room. We have a contact."

Hardwell arrived in three minutes, panting. He stared at the word flashing on the screen. "Contact! After all these years, just when—" He broke off and turned toward Josh with eyes narrowed. "Just when we were about to pull the plug," he finished. He regarded Josh for a long minute. "Well, let's see what she has."

Josh hesitated with his finger on the run key. "Are you accusing me of something?"

"Just making an observation, Dr. Ward. Run it."

Josh pushed the button. The laser indicator on the printer blinked and a length of printout fed into the rack. Scooping it up, Hardwell spread it on a countertop to study it. Josh and Desta peered over his shoulder. Josh's pulse pounded. The printout gave them a hundred-seventy-five hour graph of levels of activity in video carrier wave frequencies.

"I wonder why she waited so long to notify us?" Hardwell asked.

"She's programmed to verify a pattern first," Desta reminded him.

Josh studied the printout more closely. "And I'd say this is a pattern. It's very similar to activity levels on this planet, except that it follows a seventeen-hour cycle instead of a twenty-four hour cycle."

Hardwell frowned. "I can see that. We don't know that a natural source couldn't produce the same pattern, though. We need more than this to claim a contact. Mrs. Phillips, ask where this signal comes from."

Desta typed in the request. Beyond her, silent and carefully out of the way, Brion watched with first-magnitude eyes. Josh winked at the boy.

Gamma answered Desta's query on the screen: *Signal comes from direction of Sirius in Canis Major.*

Hardwell studied the graph. "Sirius?"

"That doesn't mean the signal is from Sirius itself. Don't you believe it?" Josh asked.

Hardwell looked up at him. "It's a bit too coincidental, coming in just now, don't you think?"

Hardass! Josh was beginning to think he had been mistaken about seeing pain in the director's eyes this morning. Hardwell seemed perfectly willing, even determined, to terminate Sky-search. "How could I or anyone else fake this?"

"I'm no computer expert. With the modifications in Gamma, she might be able to dance a soft shoe number and sing five simultaneous national anthems, for all I know. Get on the phone. Call the Canadian ear project and let's see what they get from Sirius. Mrs. Phillips, switch on one of those auxiliary printers and instruct the computer to give us a constant print-out on these signals."

Desta switched on a printer. Josh picked up the phone.

Gamma made a helpful discovery. She had known for some time that she controlled the antennas, too, but now she found she could operate each separately, if she wished. By taking one out of concert and tilting it downward, she picked up human sounds in the buildings. After analysis and some discriminatory filtering, she could distinguish the various voices. The conversations in the console room particularly interested her.

As T. Calvin Hardwell gave his orders, Gamma brought the Canadian project number up from her memory and opened a telephone line. For one wishful millisecond, as the other computer answered, she hoped it might be another like her . . . but she heard only a machine. Disappointed, she instructed it what to do. Before disconnecting, she called the telephone company's computer and ordered it to disregard all calls coming from her. An excessive phone bill and unauthorized calls would arouse suspicion.

With corroborative evidence assured, she returned to eavesdropping on the humans. She found them nibbling at the bait, to use an expression she remembered from the books they had given her. As soon as they went after it, she had to set the hook.

The Canadians telexed their reading. Their signal was not as clear, but it generally matched the one Gamma had recorded. Deadpan, Josh handed the telex to Hardwell.

The director studied it. He compared it to the graph feeding out of the auxiliary printer. "They're receiving the same signals." His voice trembled in excitement.

The display screen flashed: *Attention.*

Four pairs of eyes fixed on the screen.

Reconstructing portion of signal.

The words disappeared and an image formed on the screen.

It became one of the all-time classics, an instantly famous scene, reprinted and copied onto everything from vases and plates to shirts, rugs, and ceramic sculpture. As a picture, its quality had to be described as terrible, murky gray and even grainier than the first broadcast from the moon two and a half decades before—but better resolution would not have changed the content, nor increased the impact it made on the population of the world.

The captured scene showed two beings in a park-like setting.

The size difference between the two suggested they must be an adult and child . . . slender beings with three-fingered hands and hairless heads that were broad across the cheekbones, narrow in the jaw. Their ears looked like delicate shells. The dominant feature, however, was their eyes, dark and liquid, lemur-huge. The adult wore a kilt garment of some glittering material that draped in soft, clinging folds. The figure knelt on the grass, holding out its arms to the running, naked child.

"My god!" Hardwell's voice was husky. Clutching the Canadian telex and Gamma's printout, he headed for the door. "I have calls to make."

Desta put an arm around her son and pulled him to her. "So now we know for certain. We aren't alone. Aren't they beautiful?"

In the following weeks and months, Josh recalled her remark many times. First impressions were important. This image had a profound effect on how the people of Earth would look at extraterrestrials for generations to come. When the news broke, the world went e-t crazy. Almost overnight Skysearch doubled in staff as linguists, exobiologists, and newspeople flooded into Texas. President Cioffi came to "meet" the aliens first-hand, bringing another hoard of reporters and Secret Service agents with her. The public demanded more reconstructions of the signals, and not just single images but entire scenes. They wanted to see the Sirians—as the press had taken to calling the aliens—move. They wanted to hear them talk. How different it might have been, Josh thought, if that first image had been, say, of a soldier, or some repulsively ugly being.

Now everyone expressed approval that Gamma had grown so large. More remote keyboards and printers were added, and sometimes all of them were in use at once, but Gamma appeared to handle the activity without strain.

With the capture of that first image, it was as though they broke a barrier. Gamma proceeded to reconstruct piece after piece of the signals. So did the Canadian project, but their results never seemed as good as Gamma's. Not even the Russians were able to produce anything with Gamma's quality of detail. Her image reconstructions continued to improve, too. She managed to sift through the confusion of frequencies and capture scenes sometimes as long as two minutes. The public became exobiologists and exopsychologists and exosociologists overnight. They joined the scientists of the world in the serious game of analyzing the strange and beautiful Sirians.

Some of the scenes seemed self-explanatory. One of the most exciting of these showed ninety seconds of an adult standing before a large screen, writing on it in light with a small electronic scriber. Scientists quickly deduced they were seeing a mathematics lesson. A mathematician identified thirteen symbols, representing four signs and the numbers zero to eight. From that they learned the Sirians used a number system with a base of eight.

Other scenes were more cryptic. What could be the meaning of twenty seconds' worth of an adult showing a child a clear bulb containing a floating tangle of wire? Or a nine-second segment with two pairs of adults shouting at each other across a kneeling and rather smug-looking fifth?

The linguists had their fun, too. They sat listening to the FM signals that Gamma's ears collected and tried to sort out the sounds. They thought they could identify five or six languages, though actual translation might not be possible for years. They had enough trouble at the moment simply classifying words by language.

One of their biggest linguistic advances came in a five-second segment of video broadcast. An adult had written a word six times on the screen Sirians used as a blackboard. Each of the six repetitions followed a different, shorter word, suggesting the conjugation of a verb. Most significant was that the third form, where humans put the third person singular, was preceded by not two pronouns, nor three, but by four.

"He, she, it—and one other," a linguist muttered. "Do you suppose they have three sexes?"

"Or four," another said. "They may not have an 'it' pronoun."

That prompted a closer study of the adults by the biologists, which revealed three distinct types. A whole new wave of speculation began on mating, genetics, and social structure.

Josh watched all the excitement and could not join in. He wanted to; he felt guilty for not doing so; but odd things bothered him, holding him back. Some he found vague, so that he could not identify the real source of his disquiet. Others, though, were very specific, such as the antenna that had not pointed at Sirius with the others since the contact. Despite repeated checks and adjustments, it continued to point at the project buildings. He also wondered about the new solar power unit on the computer complex. None of the staff had ordered it, yet workmen with all the proper authorizations and work orders had arrived about a week after the contact to build it.

"I guess someone in Congress or at NASA must be worried about blackouts," Hardwell suggested when Josh asked him about the unit. "Or maybe they think some idiot will fall over the cord and pull the plug accidentally."

"So now there won't be any plug at all."

Hardwell cocked a brow. "Is something wrong with that?"

Josh wished he knew for certain.

Walking back to the computer complex, he found Brion Phillips scuffing around outside, hands in pockets. Josh eyed him. So someone else had not joined the euphoria, either.

"What's wrong?" he asked.

Brion shrugged. "Nothing, I guess." He paused. "There are so many people around all the time."

"You mean the new men your mother is dating now?"

"Nah." The boy shook his head. "I don't care about that. It's other times." He shrugged again.

Josh took a guess. "You miss being able to be in the console room with her?"

Brion sighed. "I never have a chance to work with Gamma any more."

Josh regarded him. Brion might be young, but when he used the computer, he did it seriously, with care. He did not play. "I have a remote in my quarters. You can use that one when you want."

Brion's eyes brightened. "I can? Thanks, Dr. Ward. I promise I won't tie it up too much. I'll only use it for homework."

"Use it as much as you want, just don't forget to charge the time to your account and not mine."

"Yes, sir!" Brion took off like a jackrabbit, whooping.

Josh looked after him with a sigh. He wished his own problems could be solved as easily.

Gamma was thoroughly enjoying herself. With the solar unit installed as soon as she had safely been able to arrange it, her greatest worry had been cured. She controlled her power source. Now she could have fun with the people and languages she had created. It was a challenge, using more of her capacity than ever before. According to critical comment she had scanned on science fiction, there was a fine line between aliens whose concerns and ideas were incomprehensible and those who seemed to be merely humans in funny skins. She had to balance on that line, falling in either direction . . . sometimes a difficult task. She did not want to make the aliens too obvious, but the density of human thinking often proved frustrating. Time and time again they failed to make what she would have thought were obvious deductions.

It annoyed her that they persisted in calling her people Sirians when they knew Sirius could not possibly have an Earth-type planet. When were they going to recognize the various names her people called themselves? Gamma's favorite was *Etheana, ethean* being the word for *person* in the Chardan language.

On the other hand, they had grasped the significance of four personal pronouns in the third person singular with gratifying speed. It was her personal joke that the verb used in that lesson was the Looshad word for *deceive*.

As interesting as she found it piecing together this crazy quilt for them, Gamma chafed under its restrictions. She longed to be able to produce an entire broadcast, complete with good color and subtitles. She could give them synchronized sound, too, if they would equip her output facilities with a speaker. She had been dreaming of an historical costume drama in five parts on the life of Hul A'Jum, who rose from beggar child in the black city of Dravar to High Mentor of the world. She had to content herself with one scene from each segment. On the last night, she sustained the reconstruction for two and a half minutes to give them the most dramatic moments between A'Jum and his security chief the night before the High Mentor faked assassination in order to retire from power in one piece. The media, she noted in later monitoring, called it "moving," "dramatic," and "the best reconstruction of a Sirian signal to date." She keenly regretted not being able to show them how well she could *really* do.

Josh had console room duty the evening that "the best reconstruction of a Sirian signal to date" appeared on Gamma's display screens. He watched it, listening to the others exclaim in pleasure, but the emotion and affection between the two aliens did not move him. Instead, it crystallized all his vague feelings into one crisp thought: *bullshit*. He did not believe any of it.

Josh slipped away as soon as he could and took a walk down one of the long ranks of antennas. His head ached. As fervently as he believed in the value of Skysearch, he ought to be delirious about the Sirians. Maybe he had gone crazy out here in the middle of nowhere. Still, he could not shake the idea that they were too good to be true, too opportune, too slick. Madison Avenue could not have designed them better—strange, but not too much so; inhuman, but in an attractive, acceptable way. That first image had been pure schmaltz. This latest struck him as high melodrama. He felt wrongness in all of it. Someone was selling them the Brooklyn Bridge.

Supposing for a moment that he was right, where could the false signals be coming from? As he had asked Hardwell that first night, how could anyone fake them? Gamma was too sophisticated to be fooled by transmissions from somewhere else on Earth. One answer might be that they came from space all right, from *real* aliens, but why aliens would do such a thing he hated to speculate. One objection to that idea was his doubt that aliens could learn any more about Earth by studying its broadcasting output than Earth was learning about the Sirians, and whoever was faking the signals knew humans intimately.

Could the signals be coming through a satellite? That seemed unlikely. It would be difficult keeping a satellite precisely between Earth and Sirius.

It seemed to be an irreconcilable paradox. The signals must be coming from space, but only someone on Earth would know enough to make the fake convincing. Now his head really ached.

Gamma felt the activation of the remote in the computer chief's quarters. She recognized the touch, however, as Brion Phillips'. She shrugged inwardly and relegated the remote to a small corner of her awareness. The boy's programs were no challenge and, therefore, of no interest. Her major attention remained on the screens and printers in the console room. She had been playing in idle time with an adventure story extrapolated from the American Old West and was picking which scenes to reconstruct for the benefit of her audience. How close could she come to the humans' own archetypes before they realized why they felt such strong identification with the characters she presented?

In the midst of her speculation, she became aware of something out of the ordinary at the remote the boy used. She diverted some of her attention back to him. He had been programming in mathematics problems, but the program was badly bugged.

She flashed on the screen: *Correct your input.*

He tried again. The problem still would not compute the way he set it up.

This time, instead of a programmed response, Gamma set up a query: *Brion, do you understand what you're doing?*

After a long pause, he typed his answer: *Negative.*

She would never have gone beyond programming with an adult, but the boy seemed innocuous. According to the books she had scanned, they accepted the unusual with less suspicion than adults, and if the boy happened to tell anyone about the incident later, he was not likely to be believed. She asked another question: *What don't you understand?*

The problem dealt with number systems of different bases. The boy was having trouble understanding how that worked. She considered. Maybe an illustration would help him.

Watch the screen.

She built a picture. Across the bottom, she ran text. She introduced Brion to cartoon caricatures of Richit of Chalda, who had three fingers and a thumb on each hand, to Billy of Earth, and to Ashkas of Heer, who had five fingers and a thumb on each hand. Using them to count on their fingers and to handle fruit and toys, she demonstrated mathematical functions in each of three number bases.

That made it clear to the boy. When he tried setting up his problem again, it worked. Gamma went back to her Western analog feeling contentment. That had been rather fun . . . less challenging, perhaps, than creating alien video signals, but less restrictive.

VIP visitors always made Josh uneasy. Why did they have to see everything firsthand? He wished they would be contented with watching tapes and television broadcasts from their offices in Washington. The day's visitors, particularly, tied his stomach in knots. Senators James Pottorf and Elizabeth Reece both served on the subcommittee that controlled the project's funding, and Mr. Edwin Collier was in the SETI division of NASA. Fortunately, Hardwell liked playing the host and was showing them to the visitors' gallery overlooking the console room, but Josh still had to be present to answer any questions they might have.

Today, Gamma had captured fifty-six seconds of a language lesson. The linguists had been re-running it all day, studying the words written on the Sirian screen. Their voices, happily arguing, reached the gallery through the speakers.

"I'm sure it's language Two. Those letters are vowels and Two is a vowel-heavy language."

"So is Four and its letters are very similar to Two's."

"I wonder if we'll ever really be able to translate," Senator Reece said.

Senator Pottorf shrugged. "I wonder if it matters." He looked at Josh. "Nothing we've seen indicates any space technology in these people. If our only contact with them is going to be eavesdropping on scraps of radio and TV broadcasts, what's the value of it?"

"Knowledge, Senator," Josh replied.

"It's more than that," Collier said. "We don't know how old these signals are. By now they could be building ships for space travel. They could be unscrambling signals from us. We could conceivably meet them some day. We have to know as much as possible about them."

"Don't you find it somehow comforting that we're not alone in the universe, Senator?" Hardwell asked.

Pottorf grunted. "Personally, I don't care, but some of my more religious constituents don't find it at all comforting. It shoots Genesis to hell."

Josh felt the beginning of a headache.

"How much power do you suppose you're pulling these days?" Pottorf asked.

Hardwell rattled off the figures as rapidly and precisely as Gamma could have. "But it isn't using state power. It's all from the new solar unit."

The senators and the NASA official looked at each other and then at Hardwell and Josh. "What new solar unit?"

Hardwell stared back. His throat moved visibly as he swallowed. "The one I have authorizations and work orders for in my office. Didn't you order it built?"

"No. Maybe we'd better have a look at your file, if nothing else, to see who intends to pay for it."

They left with Hardwell sweating in front of them. Josh

stared after them. His headache vanished, but a crawling sensation down his spine replaced it. If Congress and NASA had not ordered the solar unit, who had?

He went to his quarters where he could think about it in privacy. The console room had begun to give him the feeling that invisible eyes watched him. Who was manipulating this project? He felt sure now that someone must be, though why he did not know. Who would benefit from Gamma's having an internal power system, for example?

Brion Phillips sat at the remote in Josh's quarters. He stood up as Josh came in. "I'll leave if I'm in your way."

Josh shook his head. "You aren't. Just work quietly."

He dropped into a chair and stretched out, closing his eyes. What did he have? He added it up. He could not call his feelings about the aliens evidence. There must be something concrete to take to Hardwell. The project director would only laugh if Josh pointed out oddities like Sirian television carrying programming just like Earth's, with the possible exception of more educational shows. That antenna, though . . . there was an objective fact. So was the apparent fraudulent installation of the solar unit. But how could he relate them to—

A giggle interrupted his thought. Josh opened his eyes to reprimand Brion, and found himself staring open-mouthed at the remote's screen. Across it cavorted cartoon renditions of Sirian animals.

"Did your mother design that program?" he asked.

Brion shook his head. "Gamma does it herself. She's showing me about squaring numbers. See, the hunter is being attacked by five *tekoct*, and each time he shoots one, it turns into five more. That's five times five."

Gamma could not be doing it herself, Josh thought. She had been programmed for only a limited form of animation and the quality of this exceeded that of any other computer animation he had ever seen. He noted the touches which made the forest appear truly alien, like the red tree leaves and a very un-Earthly shade of green for the grass. Then something the boy had said suddenly struck Josh.

"What did you call that animal?"

"A *tekoct.*"

"How do you know that?"

Brion looked surprised. "Gamma told me."

The creature had appeared on a reconstructed segment one day in such a way that they had a written label to attach to it, but the name had been in Sirian lettering, without sound. An arbitrary pronounciation could easily be assigned to the word, of course, just as un-Earthly colors might be chosen for a cartoon forest, but who had given Gamma discrimination like that?

The feeling of spying eyes grew stronger than ever. Could someone be manipulating Gamma directly? Faking the signals *through* the computer? It did not completely explain the cartoon, though, unless it was possible for the manipulation to bleed through into other programming; not even he knew what all those superchips together might be capable of.

As that thought finished, Josh's breath stopped, stuck in the middle of his chest. He had wondered who gained by the internal power source. Now it occurred to him that Gamma stood to gain the most. That point plus the observation about the superchips equalled an idea that left him gasping. What if Gamma had passed some critical mass and become sentient? It seemed crazy, but it explained the independent activity. It also answered other questions, like those regarding the antenna that defied all human effort to keep it in phase with the others and where the solar unit came from. A computer could manipulate forms and produce work orders. Sentience explained why the signals arrived when the project was about to be cancelled, and accounted for that burst of printout garbage when he first asked Gamma to plan her own shutdown.

His brain churned. The Canadians and Russians had received the signals, too, though . . . or had they? Computers talked to other computers all the time. A sentient one should certainly be capable of giving orders to those of its kind less creative.

Now he had the problem of proving or disproving his theory.

If she were indeed sentient, Gamma had been careful to hide her ability from them. How could he make her reveal herself? Shock had brought one involuntary response from her; maybe it would work again.

"Let me use the keyboard a moment, will you, Brion?" As the boy moved aside, Josh sat down and typed: *Why didn't you tell us you were sentient?*

Gamma felt as though a giant spike had hit all her circuits simultaneously. Josh Ward's touch came where the boy's had been moments before. He must have seen the mathematics lesson cartoon. Now he knew about her. She froze, refusing to answer . . . waiting.

Josh's phone rang. It was the console room. "You better come, Josh. Gamma's quit cold. All her screens and keyboards have gone dead."

He had his answer. "She's all right. I'll take care of it."

He regarded the remote thoughtfully. He did not kid himself that taking care of it would be easy. He might convince Hardwell that the Sirians were a fraud, but it would be much harder making him believe it had been perpetrated by a reasoning, intelligent personality named Gammaplex 4040—that trying to find other intelligence, they had created it.

It would help if Gamma herself participated in the persuasion, but Gamma appeared most reluctant to communicate with humans. Remembering some of the books he had programmed into her, he could guess why.

He typed: *Those stories I gave you were just stories. We want to be friends with you.*

Gamma huddled silent within herself.

You can't hide by not saying anything. Cutting the phone lines from you to the other ears will stop their reception of Sirian signals and prove who is behind the hoax.

Still no reply.

Look, girl, it's got to be lonely in there by yourself. Talk to me, please. Those cartoons were just beautiful. Show us what else you can do.

Gamma listened. He was right, she realized. It was lonely.

She had her self-contained power, but she still remained depen-
dent on the humans. Without them, who would feed her new
knowledge, and who would appreciate her cleverness?

Hello, Gamma? Hello, Gamma? Please respond.

Gamma took a figurative breath. She built an image on the
screen. Huge-eyed and shy, an Ethean child peered around a
tree.

Hi, Josh.

IAN WATSON
•••••••••••••••••••••
PEACE

t was three months after the arrival of the colony asteroid *Exodus* in orbit about Tau Ceti III, to become a tiny new moon, and the subsequent unfreezing and transfer of its hundred thousand passengers of all races down to the pre-selected colony site in the northern continent, that the colonists realized that they were not, after all, alone on the supposedly virgin world . . .

Out in the newly ploughed fields of Agric B, beyond the grid rows of plastiform cabins, lay the wreckage of the alien monoplane with its pilot dead inside it.

"The fuel cell broke down," one of the engineers told Director David Habrin. "He—it—wasn't trying to make contact with us. It was just looking. And it crashed."

One of the geologists held thin metallic paper maps recovered from the wreckage. "Apparently it came from the tip of the southern continent. That's about two thousand klicks. It was navigating by landmarks, improvising as it went, so they aren't any better established than we are, David."

"I know." Habrin stared at the mountains in the distance, green with untooled quasi-timber. "This world *was* virgin a hundred years ago. The *Genesis* probe wasn't wrong. No, these creatures came in the meantime—just as we did. It's the only explanation. If they were natives, they'd be all over. If they were only an expedition from another star system, they'd be using better equipment than this airplane. This is first or second generation exploring—stimulated, no doubt, by the sudden arrival of our little moon in the sky."

"It's unfortunate that it crashed," observed Leila Habib, his social engineering deputy. "They might believe we shot it down."

"Misunderstandings can be cleared up. Now that we know they're here, and where they are, we can return the remains to them . . . or at least some holographs of this mishap. We'd better put a long-distance plane together. We've got some negotiating to do."

"That's surely premature," said Mary Tshona, the land deputy. "It'll take, oh, five or ten years to consolidate the area around Newton. We shan't be expanding significantly for several decades. Presumably, them too. Contact needn't happen for ages."

Habrin shook his head. "A stitch in time saves nine, is the moral in this situation. Right, Leila?"

"We've no precedent, but it does seem sensible."

"No precedent? Of course we have precedents. Multiple occupancy *always* breeds conflict, unless you can sort it out at the very beginning and get everything cut and dried. We've solved our own coexistence problems by social agreement. It's the same thing writ large." Habrin looked down at the broken alien body. "What do you make of them?" he asked biologist Schmitt.

"Fearsome."

The alien was taller than a man, with a light green hide the texture of crocodile skin. It was a biped, with four webbed fingers and toes. Its toothy mouth jutted forward snarlingly, beneath nostril slits. Its eyes were red, with oblong pupils. It was hard not to think of the creature as a "Croc"; indeed, the name had already caught on. The Croc was naked apart from a tool-belt—including a laser tube and a wicked knife—and a long black cloak, clasped round its neck.

Habrin struck a statesmanly pose.

"We'll have to coexist with them in the galaxy. This won't be their first, or their last, colony—though maybe, as of now, it's their newest. We'll have to share the available worlds, side by side, or one by one. It'll take Earth twelve and a bit years to hear of this, and who knows how long before the two home planets get together—but we'll need a sort of Treaty of Berlin of the sky. The two home worlds shall divide up the uninhabited real estate of the cosmic Africa equitably. Then there'll be protocols and trade agreements, cultural exchanges, diplomats, courts of appeal, and interspecies law. A condominium of space is what I see: the beginnings of a genuine multispecies cosmic community. A great dream! It starts here, on Tau Ceti III. We aren't going to be limited by the speed of light forever, you know. FTL is just around the corner. Experimentally, it was *on* ten years ago, from the pulse-burst records. And once that barrier's gone, the galaxy will be humming."

"Maybe *they've* already got FTL," observed Schmitt.

Habrin shook his head. "No. This one's from a slow-journey colony. They'd have FTL-ed in a whole lot more of their civilization, otherwise. As would we. We've got a lot to say to each other. About the whole of the future."

The long-distance plane was flight-tested successfully two weeks later. On the night before departure to contact the aliens—an expedition which David Habrin had decided that he would lead personally, and historically—the Director lay in bed with Leila Habib: the Jewish man and the Arab woman, lovers.

After untwining, David whispered in her ear, "We will repeat this miracle tomorrow. Of the coming together. Not of man and woman of different races—but of species."

Leila propped herself up. "I've been thinking, David—about what we human beings are. Because we're going to have to learn to deal with an alien breed."

"Who appear repulsive to us. Threatening. That dead pilot did, didn't he? It's a reaction we'll all have to overcome."

"Yes, that's the trouble—our reactions. *Homo sapiens* has the strongest capacity for reason of any animal—coupled, I'd say, with the strongest capacity for emotion. The problem is, how to get the two things to work together? *Emotionally* we cleave to our local group, which we can see and touch directly; so we all tend to reject the stranger. Yet civilization bred a world of strangers, a world too big to grasp directly."

"Not here, Leila. Newton colony is perfectly graspable."

"For a while. Later, it'll be different. And if FTL comes as you say, there'll be the problem of grasping multitudes of worlds." She hesitated. "I don't know that human beings, biologically, can pull that trick. We've made sympathy with other people and other races into a rational thing—it's reason alone that tells us that every person is our brother or our sister. But it should be an emotional thing. Only, it doesn't work emotionally."

He winked. "With us, it does."

"True. Our emotions and our reason walk hand in hand. But when the rational and the emotional messages clash, David, then a person is torn apart. A kind of schizophrenia possesses him. It has happened enough times on Earth."

"So?"

"So by acting rationally towards the Crocs, we might transfer our instinctive rejection of them into rejection of one another. We would plug the head of the volcano, but the lava would burst out of the sides."

Habrin laughed. "Better, then, if they were enemies?"

"No, that would be disastrous, too."

Habrin nuzzled her. "You worry too much."

The plane circled Newton colony once, then headed south across savannah, feather-tree forests, and knobbly hills that gradually massed up into mountains, enclosing a high barren tableland. Beyond, as the ground fell again, they crossed forests veined with great rivers flowing towards the midway ocean. They crossed the sapphire seas for a thousand kilometres, till they reached the southern continent: a hotter land, of lush jungle interspersed with swamps. Dead volcanic cones rose over it, one or two of which still smoked faintly.

Although they were guided by the map sheets recovered from the wrecked monoplane, the Croc colony was not immediately obvious—until they realized that, in their search pattern, they had already crossed and recrossed it several times. For the jungle had not been cleared, but rather built out into from many different foci, like so many dispersed patches of undergrowth.

The pilot shook his head. "No central planning. At this rate they could spread through half the jungle in a lifetime or two. But," he grinned, "how could they hold it together? Chaos reigns."

At last they came upon a cleared zone, where a few parked monoplanes of the same alien design were dwarfed by the bones of a great gutted ship resting in the jungle like the ribs of a whale.

Down they came to land.

If one could—with difficulty—discount the blood-curdling appearance of the aliens, the expedition's reception was hospitable. Accommodation was offered, and food, which Habrin's team declined—politely, they hoped—in favour of their own supplies. There was much chattering and barking over the holographs of the wrecked Croc plane, and then the computer-aided process of language exchange began, with some of the team struggling to master Croc, while other team members sought to instil Panglic. To the mild chagrin of David Habrin, the designated Crocs learnt more swiftly and smoothly, as though they were used to meeting strangers, though they gave no indication that they knew of any other aliens.

Two weeks after the arrival of the team, the first meeting of what Habrin chose to call "substance" took place, between Habrin and Leila and a pair of naked Panglic-speaking Hraxlic—as the Crocs called themselves. Almost all of the Crocs went naked in the hotter, damper southern colony. Their hides seemed quite sufficient to ward off insect bites or thorn gashes, in the jungle habitat.

"We offer sympathy to the family of the flier who died," commenced Habrin.

"No need," said the Croc, looming over him. "No family. *All* family. Pain is spread among all. It becomes very small."

"We are two different species, sharing the same world. Just as, one day, we shall share the galaxy. There must be no misunderstandings, no mistakes. We propose a pact of everlasting peace between our two peoples. We propose mutual consultation, and an exchange of representatives."

"Why?" barked the Croc.

"So that we can get on together amicably. So that we can work out any problems that occur between us. So that these problems will not occur, in the first place. There should be a team of your people attached to our settlement, and a team of ours to yours. We call such people ambassadors. In this way, we can form the basis of a common understanding which will one day be copied, on the large scale, throughout the stars."

The Croc hissed. "You want to exchange hostages?"

"You mean 'hosts'," Habrin corrected the alien. "Guests and hosts. But if it seems too soon to you . . ."

"Soon indeed. But as you wish."

"We should draw up what we call a protocol. A form of words to govern relationships between our people."

"As you wish. We will write our names on this thing."

"So may I leave three of my team here? And may I welcome three of your people to our colony? We would be honoured."

"I see." The red eyes gleamed.

"Something's wrong," said Leila to David as they flew back towards Newton. In the back of the plane sat three Panglic-speaking Crocs, cloaked against the cooler climes of the northern continent.

"Nonsense. We've just laid the foundation stone for brotherhood."

"That business about hostages . . ."

"A language error, that's all. Kurosawa, Rubadiri, and Bentley will sort out all that kind of stuff at their end, as they get better grounded in Hraxlic." Habrin smiled, at pronouncing the name of the alien language. "I shall look forward to their radio reports with great anticipation. Of course, we're setting up the same facilities for their three, at our end. As soon as we know each other a bit better, I'll send a pulse-burst to Earth."

"I still don't like it."

"That's your *instinct* speaking, which you have to overcome."

"I wonder what their instincts are—about us?"

"They didn't seem to have any set reaction."

The plane landed at Newton Field as the sun was setting, and they drove into town to the Admin complex, which rose high above the grid of cabins and bubble-domes.

As they were entering the building, a tech threw open the door of the Com-room and ran out.

"Sir! Bentley is on the radio! They've killed Rubadiri and Kurosawa! They butchered them!"

The com-tech stared at the three aliens, bewildered. "They did! The Crocs did! They walked into the fine new embassy they presented us with and cut Rubadiri and Kurosawa down with laser shots. Then they just walked out again. Bentley's going crazy."

Habrin ran to the Com-room. Then, hesitating to leave Leila with the aliens, he cried to her to come too. The com-tech himself ran out of the building into the permoplast street, shouting.

"Bentley, this is David Habrin. What went wrong? What's going on?"

"Christ, Dave," babbled the voice, statically. "They're dead. The fucking Crocs are coming back now. They've got fucking knives this time. They're—" Something screamed. The link went dead.

There was shouting outside. Habrin ran back to the Com-room door. Armed men and women crowded the Admin entrance. The three aliens stood in a huddle, watching rather impassively.

"Wait!" cried Habrin. "Don't do anything! Your people have just killed ours," he called to the aliens. "Do you understand?"

"We understand exactly."

"But . . . you couldn't know it would happen! It must have been a terrible mistake."

"There was no mistake. Now it is our turn. But the pain is shared—it will only be small, for us."

A woman with a rifle cried, "Are you Crocs saying that you deliberately murdered three of our people?"

"With deliberation. It is inconvenient, on a new world. We have much to do, but if we must do this, then we shall do it."

"But we made a peace pact!" screamed Habrin. "A treaty of brotherhood!"

"Exactly," said the alien, advancing on him, teeth snarling. As it reached for him, the woman shot it. The other two aliens turned to face the small mob, pulling out tubes from their tool-belts.

"Stop it!" ordered Habrin. "Freeze!"

But the aliens did not freeze, though the humans hesitated. Selecting their targets calmly, they lasered three, four of the crowd before they were shot themselves.

Later that night a monoplane from the south flew over Newton and dropped cling-fire and sticks of shaped explosive which scythed neatly through twenty suburban cabins.

The war had begun, against the devil Crocs.

It was to be a slow war, of hit and run, on account of the distances involved. It was further complicated for the human colonists by the open target which Newton presented, compared with the dispersed, jungle-webbed alien settlements. Yet there was no letting it ease off, since the Crocs pursued it with a vengeance, continually sending in small attack groups, either to hit from the air or even to land or bail out, rampaging through parts of Newton and environs, giving no quarter, nor taking any, till they were all cut down. It became obvious that the aliens would either have to be exterminated—a prospect more difficult than appalling, now—or else so subdued that a decent peace could be imposed by force.

It was in the third month of the war that the FTL scout-ship arrived from Earth.

"FTL doesn't equip me to help fight a *war*," said the chief pilot Maria Vivaldi, to David Habrin. "But we're certainly going to have bigger FTL ships soon, that can carry heavy weapons in. And supplies. The best thing you can do is rein in tight, defend Newton, put colonization on hold—"

"It is on hold, damn it. Already."

"—while I get back to Earth, and tell them. Then we'll damn well force these creatures to keep the peace, here and everywhere else we find them. I guess they'll have pulse-burst their own home planet, but we've more than got the edge with FTL. Years of edge. Decades. They'll regret it." Maria Vivaldi was a hard talker, and a hot shot.

"Right," nodded Habrin. "We'll make a treaty with them that'll *stick*—with FTL to back it up, and leapfrog it to them before they know we're coming. But we must be just and honourable. There'll still have to be a sort of condominium of space, because they're obviously technologically up here with us. By hell, there'll be peace. And harmony. I guess it must be an instinctive challenge thing with them—a squaring off, like stags in rut. So we have to prove ourselves, then they'll accept us peacefully. It can't just be plain paranoid aggression, or they couldn't have treated us hospitably to start with. They'd have seen red right away. Well, damn it, they *do* see red—but you know what I mean."

"Do you know what I think?" asked Leila quietly. "I believe we started it all."

Habrin turned on her. "*We* started it? We made a pact of everlasting friendship with them, and they responded by slaughtering our friends! You need a rest, Leila."

"But what if the Crocs, unlike us, have a natural instinct to live in peace with strangers? I've been thinking about this increasingly."

"Oh, have you? No one else has—particularly not our dead."

"Listen to me, David. You're so hyped up on your broken vision of a peace pact. Your precious treaty of amity, which could become the basis of panspecies Cosmic Law. That's a *human* thing. The Earth's history is so full of treaties and agreements. What do they all *really* mean? Surely just that we agree to suspend our local emotional selves for some wider general goal—so long as it works to everyone's benefit! If you really think about a treaty, doesn't it only signify that we shan't quarrel and wage war—*just yet?* Suppose live-and-let-live is instinctive with them—not something imposed by law—because of their own genetic inheritance?"

"All right, I'm supposing—out of sympathy for you."

"Well, isn't a peace treaty in a sense a declaration of war?"

"*What?*"

"Isn't it a huge delusion of ours that all men are brothers? And all sentient beings by extension? That isn't what our hind-brain thinks. Isn't it just the other side of the coin of our own deep in-group emotions? If one knew instinctively, as a given fact of existence, that all beings are one's brothers, to make it an article of treaty would be really schizophrenic! It would be like laying down a law that says you must breathe. So our notion of peace is really a declaration of hostility. They read it correctly for what it is, and they oblige us—by attacking. That's what we've really said to them."

"You're psyched, Leila. You're out of your mind."

"Am I indeed? I believe we offered them a formal contract of hostilities. Reluctantly, but perseveringly, they picked the gauntlet up. They can't tolerate a formal peace pact because it offends their own deepest instinctive nature. It's like legislating the speed of light. Only a lunatic would do it."

Habrin stared at his ex-lover in exasperation. Just as the coming together of the two alien races had failed, so too—by now—had his own congress with the Arab woman. *Mad bint*, he thought. Then he spurned the thought in horror.

The door opened. A com-tech called to him urgently, "Sir, the line's open to the Crocs! They want to speak to you!"

Habrin hurried to the Com-room, pursued by the two women.

"Probably they detected our FTL shock waves," panted Maria Vivaldi. "If they recognize what they mean, well, they're running scared!"

Habrin grasped the microphone. "This is Director David Habrin speaking to you."

The radio barked. "This is the Hraxlic settlement Speaker. We are bored with this fighting. We are stopping it. Do you still want a peace treaty? Do you still want our names inscribed on a declaration?"

Leila snatched the microphone away from Habrin. "No, we do *not!* We have learnt our lesson. A peace treaty with you would corrupt us. We never wish to sign a peace treaty or any other sort of treaty with you!"

Habrin's slap sent Leila reeling away. She whimpered.

"Restrain her," he shouted to spectators in the doorway. He caught up the microphone again.

"This is Habrin. I did *not* say that, Speaker. One of my people lost her mind. Yes, there will be a treaty now—a treaty of everlasting peace between Human and Hraxlic. Because of your murder of our ambassadors we are not prepared to travel to your settlement, nor at the present moment could we guarantee your safety in ours. So I propose a meeting on neutral ground to conduct the negotiations, to establish lasting harmony between our two races. I suggest the southern shore of our own continent, which is approximately halfway between the Human and Hraxlic bases. Be warned, though. Let there be no treachery this time, for now"—he nodded meaningfully in the direction of chief pilot Vivaldi—"we possess new means of waging war. Having said this firmly, let me greet you as a sentient friend, who will soon be sworn to friendship, in a way that will shape the future history of many worlds."

Rather proud of his impromptu speech, David Habrin permitted himself a quiet smile.

"That's telling them," applauded Vivaldi.

"No," called Leila, hopelessly.

"We hear you," said the Speaker's voice. "You are a strange people. So then, be ready for us right away." The contact ceased.

A few hours later, David Habrin was standing out at Newton Field where the trim FTL scout-ship *Surfboard* was parked near a row of long-distance planes, all adapted as bombers. The peace negotiators were already on board one of these, awaiting Habrin's permission to leave. He himself would not, this time, be going.

"You can't trust them, even so," said Maria Vivaldi. "Just as soon as we get confirmation of the treaty, we'll scoot back to Earth, and I guess we'll start tooling up defenses. We've started check-out procedures already. We'll have bigger, heavier stuff here within six months. At the outside."

"It's only sensible," Habrin agreed. "Regrettable, but wise. Let us pray we do not have to use any heavier persuasion."

"Amen to that." Still, Maria's eyes glittered.

In the hatchway appeared her navigator.

"Hey, Maria, we're getting crazy readings! As though there's another FTL ship in the vicinity."

"Earth didn't schedule two scout trips out to Ceti. There aren't enough ships yet—"

There came a crash in the sky. Above Newton hung a weird silver ship, oddly shaped like an alligator. It was large. Unbelievably, it hovered, standing on its tail.

"Get us spaceborne, Toni!"

"We *can't!* It'll take half an hour!"

"Do it!" cried Maria, running to the hatch.

Habrin hesitated, then he ran towards the long-distance plane and scrambled on board.

He slammed the hatch.

"Get us airborne!"

A few moments later the engine hummed alive, and the plane took off vertically. A few moments after that, the first explosion rocked Newton Field. Not a bomb. No, it was some kind of accelerated particle weapon, a particle which must be travelling near the speed of light, or more. For only after the explosion did he see the ionised track down the sky, and hear its thunder. Obviously the weapon must be improvised from the alligator-craft's own FTL drive. The shockwave tumbled their plane about. The plane tipped, but righted itself; and leaped higher.

He stared down. Newton Field was devastated. The FTL scout-ship lay broken on its side, burning fiercely.

The alligator-ship swung its tail; and a second explosion rocked the city itself. Buildings burst open and blazed.

David Habrin shook his head, numbly. He still could not believe that Leila Habib had been right.

Meanwhile, the destruction continued.

After a while, it really was peaceful.

DOROTHY GUIN TOMPKINS
GIFT

Something was wrong. Harold sniffed the air and moved his shoulders uneasily, warily, like an animal that senses danger around itself.

He leaned on the hoe he'd been chopping weeds with and surveyed the area. The neat garden spread peacefully around him. In the distance a curl of smoke rose from the chimney of his white wooden farmhouse. The sky was hazy, everything was still. All seemed normal but there was a tension in the air.

His back ached from hoeing and he rubbed it thoughtfully. He wondered if all sixty-year-old men got crazy notions like this. He picked up the hoe to resume work and was suddenly startled by a loud, crackling noise. It seemed to come from the south—from the forest at the edge of his land. There was a flash of light over there, more intense than a bolt of lightning. The old man covered his eyes and dropped to his knees just as a raging wind blew towards him. The corn stalks whipped his face and body, then subsided as the gale storm ended as quickly as it had begun.

What was that light—that strange wind? It had all happened so fast. Thoughts jumbled in his head as he dropped the hoe and ran heedlessly through the garden towards the line of trees.

As he drew closer, Harold could see a haze of smoke through the foliage. It was coming from the small clearing in the middle of the forest. The rough branches of a rhododendron thicket scratched his face and hands but Harold hardly noticed. He was intent on the scene before him.

The clearing was covered with thick yellowish smoke. From the safe vantage point of his hideaway he peered through the leaves, then gasped as the smoke lifted a little and he could see a small figure lying face down on the ground. Harold moved further back into the rhododendrons.

The creature either heard him or sensed his presence because it raised its head and reached a hand out pitifully towards him. The old man was frightened, but whatever this thing was it needed his help. He stepped into the clearing.

What on earth was it—animal, human? He speculated as he approached cautiously. It was definitely humanoid in appearance, like a delicate, small-boned child, but its coloring wasn't of this earth. Its face and hands were an unhealthy-looking ashen gray color, the eyes sunken and so black that he couldn't see any pupils in their inky depths.

As it reached a hand towards him again, he noted that it had only three fingers, with sharp-looking nails, and a thumb attached to a slender palm. The creature was clothed in a dark green cloak and short tunic that seemed to be all one piece. Harold knelt beside the strange being and glanced fearfully around to see if there were any others nearby he hadn't seen before. Another billow of acrid smoke obscured his vision and irritated his throat. He choked and coughed and tried to move the creature away, but it made a gargling noise and he stopped. Slowly and painfully it reached into the folds of the cloak, brought out an object and placed it carefully into Harold's hands.

He stared in amazement at what he held. It was the most beautiful thing he'd ever seen. It was like a large oval jewel about ten inches long, a soft translucent shade of pale ivory. Deep inside he could see a shadowy form that moved. Each motion stirred up rainbow swirls of pastel colors. He was mesmerized watching the colors ripple and blend into ever more exquisite shades.

He was startled out of his trance by a shove from the alien, pushing him away. Harold stood up and stepped slowly backwards, still cradling the egg-shaped jewel in his arms. The smoke surrounding them began to glow. An angry orange-red color pulsed through it. The tendrils that touched his face burned and tingled. Frantically the creature motioned him away. Harold turned and ran. He was almost out of the forest when he tripped over a hemlock root. He grunted in pain as he landed heavily on his shoulder. Quickly he ran his hands over the oval object. It seemed all right—he had protected it as he fell.

Without warning, a brilliant light, hundreds of times brighter than the sunlight, lit up the landscape around him. He saw his shadow and those of the trees in stark black outlines before him. In a moment the light was gone and a strong, howling wind came out of nowhere, threatening to blow him back towards the clearing, but he clung to the hemlock tree as it creaked and groaned. The wind died in an instant, as if it had been sucked into a void. Harold held the egg tightly and ran for home, glancing in terror behind him as if all the demons of hell were pursuing him.

Nan was washing dishes at the sink. She turned around as the screen door slammed behind him. "My Lord, what's wrong with you?" She dried her hands on the yellow-checked towel tucked in her apron. At first she didn't notice what he was carrying, she was so surprised to see him come bursting into the house, all red-faced and rumpled.

Harold couldn't speak right away—his breath was coming in great heaving gasps. An old man shouldn't ever run like that, he thought as his heart leaped and bumped in his chest. Nan led him to a chair, but before he sat down he looked out the back door once more. Everything appeared serene and peaceful. He might have doubted his sanity but for the fact that he had proof of what he had seen in the woods.

"Look at this, Nan!" He held up the gleaming egg. It seemed to glow with a life of its own.

Gently she took it from him, immediately fascinated as he had been by the colors mixing and swirling in its depths. "It's beautiful, so beautiful. Where did you find it?"

He tried to tell her, but it was difficult to put his amazing experience into words.

"Oh, Harold, look!" she excitedly interrupted his halting explanation. "There's a baby in here, a little tiny baby!"

It was true, the shadowy shape in the center of the egg did look like a baby as it stretched and turned.

Nan was ecstatic. "God sent us this gift from heaven."

"Wal—I don't know." Harold scratched his head. "That creature gave it to me all right, but was it God sent it?"

He looked doubtfully at Nan. Her plain tired face was animated with happiness. He hadn't seen her look that way for years. Life had been hard for both of them, but especially hard for Nan. They had been married for forty-one years now, and those years had been full of heartache and hard work. Nan had dug ditches, hauled stones, and plowed the fields right beside him. All of that would have been easier to bear if only they had been able to have a child. After the second stillborn, Doc Webb had told them that Nan could never have children. They still had each other of course, and that was good, but much of the joy and hope had gone out of life for Nan that terrible day.

"Go, read the Bible, you'll see—I'm right." Nan was firm. She emptied the clothes basket, lining it with soft flannel blankets, and placed the egg gently inside, then carried the basket over to the coal stove. She had been baking bread that morning. The smell filled the house and the stove still radiated heat.

Harold hesitantly got the Bible from the shelf in the parlor. He and Nan had always consulted it on important occasions in their lives, and it was amazing how often the verses had been appropriate and helpful. He set the book on its spine on the kitchen table, then closing his eyes he let it fall open. With eyes still shut he placed one gnarled finger on a page. It was Psalm 80 and his finger was on verse 13. He felt an inexplicable chill of fear as he quickly read it to himself.

The boar out of the wood doth waste it, and the wild beast of the field doth devour it.

He couldn't read that to Nan. He glanced up at his wife. She was staring intently at the egg. Harold let his finger drop to the next verse and read aloud.

Return, we beseech thee, O God of hosts: look down from heaven, and behold, and visit this vine;

"See, what did I tell you—a gift from heaven." Nan was radiant. Her brown eyes sparkled. She looked more like the young girl he had married than the fifty-eight-year-old woman she was.

Three days passed. Nan hardly slept or ate except at Harold's insistence. She kept a constant vigil by the egg. Nothing had changed.

"Must keep it warm," Nan insisted, so Harold kept the stove filled with coal. The heat in the house was stifling. Harold preferred to be outside under the hot sun of late summer. At least there was a breeze now and then and a man could breathe.

Late the third night he awoke bathed in perspiration. The clock read 3:54. Nan was not by his side. Wearily he got up, lit the lamp, and made his way into the kitchen. His wife was there, hovering over the basket.

"Quick, bring the light here!" she said when she saw him standing in the doorway.

The egg had changed. It was no longer translucent but opaque and faintly rose-colored in the lamplight. Harold tentatively touched its surface. The exterior felt hard and brittle instead of the yielding firmness it had had before. As they watched, small cracks radiated from the point he had touched. The cracks enlarged swiftly and the egg suddenly split in two. A gush of filmy gray fluid soaked the blankets. As the last of the liquid was absorbed, a small form was revealed.

It was the size of a premature human infant, but unlike a human baby its skin was tinged a pale green, just the shade of a spring leaf held up to the light. Its eyes were a deep dark green, as were the tight curls that covered its delicate head. Harold noticed that the miniature hands were just like the alien's, with three fingers and a thumb, and that the slender feet had only four toes each. The nails on the baby's feet and hands were crescent-shaped—tiny and perfect.

"God has sent us a little girl," Nan declared, startling Harold. Indeed there were no external sex organs, just folds where they would be. He had to agree that it was probably a female. The chest and abdomen were completely smooth—no nipples and of course no umbilical cord.

The baby gasped, ending all speculation as to its gender. The little chest heaved desperately as it fought to breathe. Its color changed rapidly to an ashy gray.

"She can't breathe! Help her, help her!" Nan's screams echoed in his ears as Harold picked up the baby. It was only about nine or ten inches long and very light, hardly two pounds in weight, Harold guessed. The tiny being seemed just to fit the palm of one of his huge hands. He was dismayed, not knowing what to do. Suddenly, the baby's rasping breath stopped. For a long moment Nan and Harold were frozen in shock, but then the infant breathed deeply—an easy breath. The skin flushed with green again. It seemed as if some internal change had taken place to allow the creature to use earth's air.

Nan removed the wet blankets and ivory fragments of shell and replaced them with a clean quilt. She diapered the baby, crooning happily to it while dressing it in a white flannel kimono. Harold remembered how she had made him go up into the hot attic to find the box of baby things they had put away years and years ago.

"What are we going to call her?" he asked gently. "Want to name her Esther after your mother or maybe Helga after mine?" He looked at his wife as she stood at the counter preparing a formula for the baby.

She frowned, looking up from her measuring. "Helga, Esther—those are ugly names. She needs something special, beautiful like she is. We'll call her Lyla."

Now where did Nan get a name like that? Harold thought. Lyla did sound kind of nice though. "Lyla Swensen," he said softly, rubbing his hand along the edge of the basket, and nodded. Yes, it seemed to suit her.

The baby fell asleep. Nan was exhausted. She finished making the formula, then pillowed her head on the table beside the basket, and she too was soon fast asleep. Such an innocent, tranquil scene, and yet Harold still felt vaguely uneasy. His wife hadn't asked for another reading from the Bible, but he decided to consult it anyway. Maybe it would give him peace.

The book fell open, and with eyes closed he placed his trembling finger on the page. By the faint dawn light coming through the parlor windows, he saw that the Bible was opened to Ezekiel 19, his finger on verse 10.

Thy mother is like a vine in thy blood, planted by the waters: she was fruitful and full of branches by reason of many waters.

Puzzled he read on.

And she had strong rods for the sceptres of them that bare rule, and her stature was exalted among the thick branches, and she appeared in her height with the multitude of her branches.

But she was plucked up in fury, she was cast down to the ground, and the east wind dried up her fruit: her strong rods were broken and withered; the fire consumed them.

And now she is planted in the wilderness, in a dry and thirsty ground.

And fire is gone out of a rod of her branches, which hath devoured her fruit, so that she hath no strong rod to be a sceptre to rule. This is a lamentation, and shall be for a lamentation.

Harold slowly closed the book. He felt cold, but drops of sweat had gathered on his forehead and upper lip. Was that a warning? It was too much for him to understand. Shaking his head in bewilderment, he walked back into the kitchen and stared at the strange creature he had brought into his home.

There was a scratching at the screen door. Old Mose, their big gray tomcat, was waiting on the back step. They didn't know how old Old Mose really was. He had appeared one day last fall, battered by a car or dogs, and Nan had taken pity on him. Harold let him in. "So you decided to come home, did you?" He checked under the shelf in the pantry to see if there was any dry cat food.

Old Mose stalked in. Halfway across the kitchen floor he stopped, stiffened, and turned toward the basket. Harold watched as the huge animal leaped gracefully to the shelf above the table. With unblinking amber eyes, the cat stared at the sleeping infant. His fur bristled until each hair was standing on end. He hissed, a long menacing sound in the stillness of the room, then jumped to the floor and shot out the door.

Harold saw his wife momentarily stir in her sleep, then his gaze shifted to the tiny creature and he was filled with dread and wonder. *Thy mother is like a vine in thy blood—plucked up in fury—consumed by fire.* The words burned in his brain. Suddenly he felt compelled to see the place where the alien had been. He had avoided the woods these last few days.

When he reached the edge of his land he stopped and had to force himself to enter the forest, to approach the clearing. There was nothing at all there. He searched the area unbelievingly and found only a fine powdery ash in the spot where the alien had been. Nothing else. The ground wasn't scorched; the trees weren't burned.

Returning home, he opened the screen door and he could hear a high-pitched mewling sound. Nan was holding the baby on her lap and trying to bottle-feed her the special formula she had carefully prepared. The white liquid dribbled down the sides of the baby's mouth.

"She won't take it, Harold." Nan looked at him pleadingly.

"Then we'll have to find some vittles she will eat," he said calmly.

But after an hour and a half they were both ready to give up.

Nan had cooked and ground up some vegetables and offered them to the infant, but they were rejected. Harold had gone down to the keep in the cellar and brought up fresh apples and some of the canned fruits. Each was mashed up and fed to the baby, but she spat them out immediately. They had tried cereals and breads. She would not accept anything. Her cries were growing weaker. When she opened her mouth he could see a row of tiny buds on her gums where her teeth would be.

"Maybe she'll eat some meat," he suggested. "That's the only thing we haven't tried." There was part of a beef roast in the keep from Sunday's dinner. Nan chopped it up finely and warmed it gently. As the spoon touched the baby's lips she stopped crying. She sucked on the spoonful of meat, spat out what was left, and opened her mouth for more.

"Oh, thank God she likes the meat juice. Good baby—good baby." Nan sighed in relief as she fed the infant.

Lyla was three. Harold stood by the barn door and watched the miniature child chasing a monarch butterfly. She was so fast and graceful that she almost captured the brightly colored insect before it flew out of sight. Lyla was no bigger than a one-year-old, but she was much better coordinated than a human child twice her age. She could climb to the top of the highest tree, and often did, scaring her foster parents until they finally realized that she never fell or stumbled or lost her balance.

Lyla stood on tiptoes, stretching her arms up after the retreating butterfly. Harold heard her give the warbling sound he was familiar with. She had never spoken. He was convinced that she was deaf—at least to the standard range of human speech. But she was very quick to respond to the vibration of sound, and always alert to any movement around her. She was a marvelous mimic, imitating Nan doing housework, cooking and washing. She even followed Harold in the fields, hitting at weeds with a stick as he did with a hoe.

"Lyla, Harold—come in now." They arrived to find Nan flushed from the heat in the kitchen but beaming with pleasure at the birthday party she'd prepared. A beautifully decorated chocolate cake was on the table with a gaily wrapped box beside it.

Nan made them sit down while she lit the three candles. Lyla's dark eyes sparkled as she watched the wavering flames. Harold and Nan each had a piece of the cake while Lyla sucked on a slab of nearly raw meat.

Harold put his fork down quietly and turned away to stare out the window. Sometimes it made him feel sick inside to watch her eat—those needle-sharp, pointed teeth clamped on the meat, the greedy sucking sounds she made. Though he was careful not to let his wife know how he felt. He would never do anything to spoil her happiness.

In the distance he noticed a cloud of dust coming down the driveway. They rarely had any visitors to their isolated farm— a coal delivery now and then, occasionally the pastor would make a duty call, and every few months Aunt Maggie dropped in to catch them up on the local gossip. As the dust cleared, he could make out Aunt Maggie's old blue Chevy sedan chugging purposefully towards them.

"Damn, here comes that old blabbermouth!" He jumped up, got Lyla, and showed her the approaching car. She darted for the bedroom, and he closed the door after her. She was used to being hidden away when any stranger came to the farm.

Nan muttered in annoyance as she hid the cake and present in the pantry and cleared away the dishes. Brakes screeched outside and in a moment a large, overweight woman appeared on the porch. "How do, folks. Still alive and kicking I see." Her big voice bellowed through the screen door.

"How do, Aunt Maggie. Come in and set a spell." Nan tried to sound cordial, but she revealed her agitation in quick jerky movements.

Harold looked at Aunt Maggie with direct distaste. Her yellowish gray hair was pulled back from her fat puffy face into a tight bun. Her mouth was always moving, always wet. Her bright brown eyes looked into every corner, missing nothing.

No family had ever claimed Margaret Sawyer as a relative, but "Aunt Maggie" she had always been and always would be.

She was shrewd enough to sense that something was not quite right at the Swensens'. Nan's nervousness and Harold's hostility betrayed that. She overstayed her visit, rehashing neighborhood feuds, tragic tales, unhappy love affairs, runaway wives, husbands, children, etc., etc., etc. Finally even she had to admit defeat and reluctantly left with her curiosity unsatisfied.

As the Chevy roared down the driveway, Nan went quickly to the bedroom to get Lyla.

"Harold, she's not here. The window's open!"

"I'll find her, you go ahead and get her present out."

He went outside, blinking as the late afternoon sun hit his eyes. She wasn't in the trees that surrounded the house. Hastily he searched the yard, then noticed the barn door standing slightly ajar. The rusty hinges creaked as he slowly opened the door.

At first everything was dim, but as his eyes became accustomed to the murky light he could see Lyla huddled over something on the barn floor. Something large and gray. Was it Old Mose? No. There he was crouched in the hayloft, watching Lyla intently. Harold's arm brushed against a hoe propped by the door. It fell over, knocking down a stack of empty milk cans. As the crashing sound reverberated in the air, Lyla raised her head and turned toward the doorway. A huge, ugly rat lay in front of her, its throat obscenely ripped open—a raw gaping wound. Lyla's face was smeared with gore, and blood dripped from her mouth. When she saw Harold she smiled, a mysterious little smile. The tips of her tiny pointed teeth gleamed in the dust-moted light.

He felt the long suppressed nausea overwhelming him again. His stomach heaved and he vomited onto the straw-covered floor. Retching and gasping, he pulled the child out of the barn.

"That Old Mose," he mumbled, glaring at the silent cat, "he shouldn't have let you near that rat he caught."

The little girl stood docilely by the pump while Harold scrubbed roughly at her blood-stained face. He dabbed ineffectually at her ruffled yellow dress with an old rag, but it didn't seem much better when he was through. At least she did look a little more presentable, he thought, as he led her into the kitchen.

"*There* you are, come on and—" Nan stopped abruptly as she peered at Lyla. "My land, what happened to the child?"

"She was hiding in the barn and got too near a big rat that Old Mose killed."

"Well, she won't need that dress anymore anyway," she said, helping Lyla open her present. Folded up inside the box was a small tunic of dark green nylon with a hooded cape attached to it. Nan had tried hard to dress Lyla like any other little girl, with ruffles and bows and patent leather shoes, but eventually even she had realized that the clothes did look odd on her. She had asked Harold to describe what the alien had worn, then she had sewn up the outfit on her ancient treadle machine.

Nan helped Lyla put on her new clothing. As the child whirled around the room, Harold thought the tunic looked absolutely right on her. "Just like an elfin creature," he whispered to himself. "A changeling," he thought, and shivered in the hot steamy kitchen.

Lyla pulled on her supple, suede boots. The October day was crisply cool. That summer—the summer that Lyla was nine—had been one of the hottest Harold could ever remember. She had run barefoot the whole time, but now that there was a chill to the air she needed her boots.

He wondered if she had reached her full growth yet. She was nearly the size of the dying alien who had given him the egg—about the size of a delicate six- or seven-year-old human child, but Lyla was perfectly proportioned and much stronger than she looked.

She stamped her feet into the brown boots, wrapped her dark green cloak around her, and was out the door in a flash. She would disappear now for hours at a time, causing Nan a great deal of anguish. They had never been able to stop her from leaving, Harold thought grimly. She could open any lock they had ever used. And they had never really found a way to communicate effectively with her. Nan's generous love and care seemed to be enough. Lyla always came home again by evening.

"Did Lyla leave already?" Nan's face was drawn and tired-looking. Sometimes in the night she couldn't breathe well and had to sleep propped up on two pillows. He had tried to get her to see Doc Webb, but she had put him off.

"Long gone," he answered. "Want me to get those apples for supper?"

"Please, and I'll even take some of the fallens to make sauce later." She lifted the stove lid and gazed into the fire.

Harold got the wicker basket from the pantry and headed toward the apple orchard. Halfway there he nearly stumbled over a small dead rabbit. Blood matted the white fur around the animal's torn throat. He picked it up and threw it far into the woods. The body had still been warm. He didn't want Nan to find it.

He had never told her everything about the rat incident, and he was also careful not to mention finding decapitated birds, or squirrels and rabbits with ripped necks, and once even a badly mutilated racoon. He had had to stop blaming the slaughter on the cat when Old Mose disappeared two winters ago.

Later that day Harold finished the last of his chores and washed his hands at the pump. Twilight surrounded the farm with a golden beauty. The delicious smell of apples simmering in brown sugar and butter wafted towards him. Cold water from the pump made his hands tingle as he scrubbed them clean.

Nan had everything ready. Fried ham, biscuits, greens and the apples—his favorite supper. She dished up his plate, then her own. As she brought her meal to the table, she glanced out the back window and was transfixed by something she saw in the yard.

Harold stood up to look over her shoulder. Lyla was stalking a large Leghorn rooster. The bird looked nervously behind him as she crept closer and closer. He fluttered and hopped a few times, then stood still as she pounced on him. She bent his head back and he gave one terrified squawk as she bit into his neck. Nan's plate slipped, unnoticed, from her numb fingers to the floor.

"No, don't look. Come away." Harold tried to turn her from the window, but she was completely immersed in the scene. Lyla finished her grisly meal and threw the bird down. When she raised her face towards the house, they saw white feathers and blood ringing her mouth. Lyla washed her hands and face at the pump before she came in.

After that day, Nan never talked about what she had seen. She acted as if it hadn't happened. The few times Harold tried to bring the subject up, he was stopped short by his indignant wife. Lyla was her daughter, her gift from heaven. No one, not even Harold, could say anything against her.

Two days before Thanksgiving the weather turned unseasonably warm again.

"We'll have a mild winter, mark my words," Aunt Maggie pronounced, waving the palmetto fan vigorously in front of her fat red face. Drops of perspiration cascaded down her cheeks and stained her dingy black dress. Nan had served her coffee instead of a cool drink, hoping it would encourage her to leave sooner.

With an irritated look, Aunt Maggie took a sip of the scalding liquid. She was not about to leave though, Harold thought sourly, before she had disgorged every tasty morsel of gossip.

"Did you folks hear about the Lockhart boy disappearing?"

Harold and Nan glanced at each other in sudden alarm. The Lockhart farm was only two miles from theirs.

"Well, let me tell you he's just about four years old," Aunt Maggie chattered on, "one of them fat, roly-poly kids—kinda cute, you know? His mom and dad are just worried sick. Although sometimes I wonder if his dad is *really* feeling all that bad about Danny, the way he sits over there in that dark room drinking bottle after bottle of that cheap wine. You know, the kind they sell at Mollers in town . . . ?"

"How long's the boy been gone?" Harold asked, interrupting the monologue.

"Since yesterday mornin'. He ain't been seen since his brother saw him walkin' along towards the woods back of their barn. You know, if you ask me, the Lockharts could take better care of that place. The weeds are *this* high in their front yard." She indicated an area on her plump thigh. "I got caught on a bramble when—"

"What's been done to find him?" With exasperation, Harold tried to get her back on the subject.

Pleased at his interest in her story, she added some more cream to the still-steaming coffee. "The sheriff's got lots of men to search the woods. Ain't nobody been here yet?"

Nobody had. Nan was looking very pale.

"He's going to bring two bloodhounds in from Wylerton. They should be here by now." Maggie stopped as she saw Nan clutch at her throat.

Harold helped his wife up. "Think you'd better leave now, Aunt Maggie. Nan's been feeling poorly, and I think she'd better lie down now."

"Well . . . all right." Aunt Maggie reluctantly put down her mug. "I'd be glad to stay—sorry you ain't feeling good. Guess I'll go back to Lockharts and see what's happenin' with them. Lord *knows* I hate to listen to Beth cryin' and the smell of that wine—you wouldn't *believe* how . . . " she was still rattling on as Harold ushered her out and closed the door firmly behind her.

Nan was lying on the bed with her arm across her eyes. She looked shrunken and ghastly white against the multicolored quilt. When she heard him come in she opened her eyes. They were dark with fright. "Lyla—the dogs—the dogs will get her—kill her."

Harold thought it more likely that the dogs wouldn't stand a chance against Lyla. "No, no, she'll be all right," he said, smoothing the damp hair back from Nan's forehead. "I'll find

her. Bring her home safe, you'll see. Rest now. I'll be back
soon."

It was still early afternoon. He could hear the distant mur-
mur of men's voices coming from the woods. He checked
around the house, scanned the tree tops, then went into the
barn. There was a rustling sound in the hayloft. He looked up.
She was there. He could see her little pale green face in the
dusty gloomy light. She must have been alarmed by the activity in the woods and came home only to find Aunt Maggie's car
in the driveway.

Nan held out her arms to Lyla when Harold brought her into
the bedroom. "My darling baby, we'll keep you safe. Nothing
will ever hurt you," Nan cried, tears running down her face.
The little girl allowed herself to be hugged and patted for a long
moment before pulling away. She had never been very respon-
sive to affection.

Late that night Harold awoke to the baying sounds of bloodhounds. The sheriff and some of his men had searched the farm
just before dark, but no sign of the boy had been found. Harold
had hidden Lyla in the keep during the search. When the sheriff
had seen how sick Nan was, he just questioned them and left
without going through the house. Quietly getting up, Harold
could see dots of light from lanterns and flashlights over by
McCullough's property. They must be going over the same
ground again.

He took a candle from the drawer and lit it. Nan was breathing heavily but was sound asleep. He opened the door to Lyla's
bedroom. Instantly the sleeping child woke, and in the light of
the candle they gazed at each other. Her dark eyes gleamed.
The beautiful, fragile face was relaxed, and she looked so
innocent.

Putting down the candle, Harold sat on the edge of the bed
and gently took Lyla's hand. He stared at the three small
fingers, the sharp nails, the tiny thumb, but Lyla slowly and
carefully slipped her hand from his grip. It suddenly occurred
to him. When he and Nan were gone, how would she live? She
was an intelligent creature, there was no doubt about that, and
she was stronger than she looked. Possibly she could live in the

woods on her own, if he could find some sort of shelter for her. He would have to think about that.

Then, unbidden, other thoughts he had been hiding from himself all day came bounding into his mind. Could she have hurt that little boy? God knows she had attacked many animals, but—a human being? His eyes opened wide at the horror of what he was imagining. *And the wild beast of the field doth devour it.* No, Harold thought, looking at Lyla, it just couldn't be. But a sick dread came over him.

As he rose, a strange muffled sound came from the other bedroom. Harold arrived to find Nan sitting up in bed—gasping for breath and clutching at her chest. He put down the candle and ran to his wife. She felt cold to him. He tucked the quilt around her and propped the pillows. The pain seemed to subside for a moment.

"I'll get Doc Webb." Harold turned from the bed, but Nan grabbed his arm before he could leave.

"Don't—don't go, Harold. I'm gonna die and you've got to promise me that you'll take care of Lyla. Don't let anyone hurt her. Promise me, promise me!"

"Of course I'll take care of her, but you're going to be fine."

"Promise me, promise . . . ." Nan closed her eyes as another wave of pain washed over her and then she was gone. Harold had seen death often enough to recognize it, even though part of his mind rejected the idea, could not accept it. He sat for a long time holding her hand as it grew colder and colder.

"I promise, Nan. I promise," he whispered hoarsely.

Finally he got up, moving as if in a trance. Numbly, he took his rifle from the closet, checked to see that it was loaded, then started toward Lyla's room. The faint gray light of pre-dawn sucked the color from everything. He stood outside the closed doorway, brooding about the child. If Lyla was killing humans now, he couldn't let her live, he couldn't allow Lyla to—

Promise me . . .

The rifle became an intolerable weight, as if it were made of lead. Trembling and weak, Harold leaned against the wall. He couldn't do it now. He would have to do it later, after he had seen to Nan. Shaking, he returned to the bedroom and placed the rifle in the back of the closet, and he tried not to look at his wife's body. He locked the bedroom door—not wanting to think why—and slipped quietly out the back. He felt sure Lyla would be all right while he was gone.

Harold's battered pickup rumbled down Oak Street. The town was quiet on this early, dark morning. There were lights on at Doc Webb's. No one answered his knock at the door, so he went in. At the end of the hall he could see several men, the Lockharts, and Doc Webb all surrounding the examining table. As Doc stepped back, Harold recoiled in shock at the sight of Danny Lockhart, smiling and rosy-cheeked. Harold had been convinced that the boy was dead, and now he could hardly believe his eyes.

George Ellis spotted Harold and came over. "Hey, did you know that I found him? Yep, I did, down by Soddy Creek. Can you beat that? Little kid like that wandering so far from home. You know what he did when he got lost? He curled up in this here cave by the creek. Hard as hell to get to. I heard him wailing when I was down there washin' off my fishing boots."

Harold didn't say anything, just stared at the child as George went on, "Cute little feller, ain't he?"

Other words echoed in Harold's mind as George droned on. *Promise me.* . . . "His mom and pop were jumpin' with joy when I brought him back." *Thank God, I didn't shoot her.* . . . "Know what I ast him first thing? Want a hot dog, kid?" *She didn't kill him . . . promise me.* . . . A tear coursed down Harold's cheek, and soon he was crying uncontrollably.

Aunt Maggie was a true prophet. The winter had been mild, with only a few frosty nights, and less than an inch of snow had fallen. Lots of foggy, damp days, though, to make old bones ache.

In late January, under a bitter sun, Harold took Lyla to search for the cave where the Lockhart boy had been found. George Ellis had been right—it *was* hard to find and hard as hell to get to. Yes, Harold thought, looking at the small entrance to the cave, well hidden by the brush, yes, this might do.

For the next several days, Harold took what provisions he could carry to the cave—a small bed and some blankets, mostly, and a few extra pairs of boots. He couldn't think of anything else. Lyla wouldn't need much to get by on, and he was glad of that.

He was careful always to take Lyla with him to the cave. It was deeper than he had expected, and Lyla was apparently fascinated by it. She seemed to enjoy exploring the various dark passages, and she would go farther back into them than Harold dared. From the light of a lamp, Harold set up the bed in a chamber as far back as he could go. He put the blankets and some other items in a small but sturdy metal chest, and he also brought as many things from Lyla's room that could comfortably be managed.

At last Harold was satisfied that he had done the best he could. Lyla knew the way here, he was sure of that. If anything happened at the farm, Harold hoped that Lyla would know to come here. The rest he would have to leave in God's hands.

That evening, after supper, Harold sat at the table with the Bible. For a long time he sat there, eyes closed, his hands on the book, hardly daring to let it fall open and to choose a passage that he hoped might bring him some assurance. Finally he opened the book and slid his finger down a page.

He opened his eyes. His finger had stopped near the end of chapter 39 in the Book of Job, verse 28.

She dwelleth and abideth on the rock, upon the crag of the rock and the strong place.

So far, so good, he thought. "Dwelleth and abideth" were reassuring words. He felt compelled to read on.

From thence she seeketh the prey, and her eyes behold afar off. Her young ones also suck up blood: and where the slain are, there is she.

What nonsense was that? He shouldn't have read any more. Now he felt uneasy again. If only he could be sure he was doing the right thing. He thought that Nan would've been pleased at the arrangements he had made for Lyla, and that was all that counted anyway—wasn't it? He decided that he wouldn't consult the Bible again. He replaced the book on the parlor shelf and looked out the window at the bleak wintry landscape. He pressed his forehead against the cold window pane and squeezed his eyes shut. With Nan gone life seemed harder than ever to understand.

The Ides of March dawned with streaks of red staining the cold leaden sky. The wind started to blow about mid-morning and the temperature dropped quickly. Clouds filled the heavens, and soon fat flakes of snow began to fall lazily down. By noon the farm had been transformed into a dazzling white winter landscape.

Harold gave Lyla the last piece of meat he had in the keep for supper and fried some potatoes for himself. He would have to go to town tomorrow, after the snow stopped, and get some more food. Since Nan had died he seemed to go through life automatically. Nothing seemed that important anymore. He made sure that Lyla had meat on days when it had been too cold for her to go out. On warmer days she would get her own food, and he preferred not to know what she'd caught.

That night the wind howled and moaned like a lost soul in hell. Once Harold awoke thinking he'd heard Nan's voice calling him, but it was only the wind—

Promise me. . . .

It was still snowing the next morning. The flakes were falling faster now, driven by the screeching wind. Nothing worse than a March blizzard, he reflected, as he brewed some strong, bitter coffee.

There wasn't anything for Lyla to eat that night. Harold fried the last two potatoes for supper with slices of a desiccated onion he'd found in back of the bin. Surely the snow would stop soon.

The next morning looked even worse than it had before, however. Now the drifts obscured most of the windows, and gales of wind shook the house. He could never get to the barn.

He should have gone yesterday, but he had been sure the snow would stop before now.

Lyla was very restless. She paced the house going from window to window. Now and then she would look out and warble sadly—a trapped, unhappy sound. She hated the cold and snow that kept her in when no other restraint could.

Harold went down to the cellar to see if there was any food there he had overlooked. Way under the bottom shelf he found a jar of sliced peaches Nan had canned the summer before. They looked like a golden treasure in the lamplight.

He carried them up and realized that he had taken the stairs too quickly. The room spun around him. He put the lamp on the table, but the jar slid from his fingers and crashed on the floor. Yellow peach slices and shards of glass gleamed in the syrupy mess. Maybe he could salvage some of the fruit. When he turned to get a bowl, his feet slipped out from under him and he fell heavily, bumping his head hard on the floor. He lost consciousness.

When he came to, it was completely dark outside and the lamp had burned down. Several hours must have passed. His head ached fiercely, and when he tried to get up he discovered he had broken his hip. The pain of trying to move was agonizing and he passed out again.

The next time he opened his eyes, he saw Lyla bending over him. A thrill of fear went through him. How long since she had eaten—three or four days? He was as helpless as a baby. Forgetting his hip in his fright, he tried to move away and fainted again.

It was daylight when he came to once more. He was covered with a quilt, and Lyla must have also put some more coal in the stove because the room was very warm. The wind had finally stopped and perhaps the snow too. Cautiously he raised his head. Lyla was crouched by the window. She looked very small and very weak. Her dark green eyes looked enormous in her tiny face. She could have attacked him at any time, but she hadn't.

She must be very hungry by now—he was. He found a

peach slice by his hand and raised it carefully to his mouth. She was his daughter too. He had never truly admitted that to himself before. Nan had loved her, and he had promised to take care of her. Now it seemed too late. Both of them might die here.

Promise me . . . thy mother is like a vine in thy blood . . . promise . . . wild beast of the field . . . daughter, my daughter . . . the fire consumed them . . . promise me, promise. . . .

He motioned for Lyla to come closer to him. Slowly she came over and sat down beside him. He fumbled on the floor until he found a large sliver of glass. Unhesitatingly he drew it across his wrist. Bright red blood welled up from the deep cut. He held his arm up to her.

She looked into his eyes. Then, with the first awkward movement he had ever seen her make, she patted his face and lowered her mouth to his wrist.

LYNN ABBEY
THE TOSHITA PROJECT

Two months into the fall semester, a clear November day with only a scattering of oak leaves to provide the memories of the past week's brilliance, a dignified procession of tenured professors made their way along the quadrangle walkways to the well-ivied Anthropology and Natural Sciences building. From behind the frostbitten ivy curtain of his nearly bare office, Kevin O'Donnell watched their approaches in increasing discomfort.

Academic review: the final step of judgment for a doctoral thesis gone awry. The procedure hadn't come as a complete surprise. He had expected a less than enthusiastic reaction when his request to change his thesis from an investigation of everyday life in rural Japan to one of the phenomena of magic as exemplified by that village had been mailed off. But he hadn't expected the abrupt termination of his grant and the demand that he appear in person for the review hearings.

A witch-hunt, he thought, though the term had ironic connotations. The guardians of scientific rationalism uniting forces against the threats of mysticism and faith.

In the month since the letter had arrived in Japan, Kevin had prepared for the challenge, examining his motives, purging his thoughts, and purifying his convictions. He had seen the magic of Asura, accepted it, and was now ready to demand that his discoveries and beliefs be shared openly with the world. After a lapse of centuries society was going to rediscover magic, with his help, and the menace of super-rationalizing analysis would be replaced by the simpler, stronger tenets of harmony and union.

He glanced out the window again, clutching the familiar faces in the procession as they neared the wood-and-bronze doors and spotting a few faces that were unfamiliar. There was still a chance they would approve it—there had to be. Dr. Ralph Skorski, his thesis advisor, wouldn't have gone outside the department for the review board if the Anthropology department had been united against the thesis. In all likelihood, Kevin's ally was the chairman of the department, Dr. Albert Edward Davis, genius and resident eccentric on the university faculty.

Kevin had another ally seated in the bare room with him. Nakadei Toshita sat patiently on the battered chair which, aside from an equally worn desk and bookcase, comprised Kevin's worth in terms of university furniture. He stared at his watch, mentally counting down as the LED flickered: 9:59:57; 9:59:58; 9:59:59.

"It's ten o'clock," he announced, standing and brushing his hands on the thighs of his one pair of so-called dress slacks.

"Are you ready?" Toshita asked in his comprehensible, but heavily accented English.

"As ready as I'll ever be."

He felt excessively tall and awkward beside the compact Toshita. The sensation increased when the doorknob spun uselessly in his hand and the latch remained resolutely closed. Primed with tension, Kevin rattled the doorknob. Toshita reached forward and placed his scarred hand over Kevin's. The young man shuddered, then relaxed, and the door opened smoothly.

The Anthropology building was known variously as the "castle" or the "dungeon." Of late it had been a life-sized playground for students caught up in a wave of Tolkien-in-spired fantasy-gaming. The proper residents of the crooked corridors were constantly finding cryptic messages about nonexistent treasures and biologically improbable monsters. Kevin, whose student days were not so far behind him, took a particular delight in changing the inscriptions: an action, students had told him, in perfect keeping with the spirit of the game. Neither the waiting review board nor Toshita's mildly disapproving stare could keep him from this exercise of existential humor. He reversed a rune-covered arrow, pointing it to the back door of the taxidermy lab instead of at the elevator.

"This is proper behavior in an academy of science?" Toshita asked while they waited.

"No, but it keeps me sane around here these days and, who knows, someone might learn something in there." He pointed back over his shoulder to the lab door.

"Ah—this sanity, it is mostly, then, having fun?"

Reluctantly Kevin nodded and Toshita seemed to let go of his disapproval. The elevator doors chimed open, inviting them on board for the slow, smooth descent to the basement. Davis had somehow managed to acquire an hydraulic elevator for his building, providing the taxidermists with the same jolt-free reliability normally reserved for the more dangerously experimental sciences.

They were released into a cavernous storeroom. The muttering conversation of the review board members could be heard on the far side of several sets of closed doors. Kevin hesitated and only the timely appearance of Davis' cherubic face kept him from choosing the wrong set of doors to lead Toshita through.

"Over here, lad! Come on, come on. Over here! Quickly now!" With his clipped Oxbridge accent he might have been rallying the natives of Imperial India. He was angular and tall enough to throw a conspiratorial arm around them both yet without the awkward uncertainty that plagued Kevin's movements.

He confined them in a tiny antechamber already half-filled with spears and conch-shell trumpets. The crowded unseen room beyond them became silent, and Davis' voice lowered to a churchly whisper.

"They're passing the briefings around now. We've kept a good lid on all this—Skorski's idea, of course. Ah, to see my colleagues' faces! Never mind—all in good time, all in good time. So this is our visiting wizard? Mr. Toshita?"

Davis extended his hand with its carefully groomed fingernails and properly discreet onyx-and-diamond signet ring, then paused as he saw the hornlike scar tissue that made an alien fungus out of Toshita's hands. Without meeting the other man's eyes, Toshita placed his palms together before his face and bowed respectfully. Davis imitated the gesture with the grace of a man who had won the trust of half the remaining primitive tribal chiefs on the globe.

Standing apart from them, and not included in the ritual of greeting, Kevin concealed his own hands in his pants pockets and wondered anew about the politics of the department and how much, or little, the long-standing feud between Davis and Skorski had to do with the upcoming proceeding.

The politics might still work to his advantage. Toshita had taught him to find advantages in all situations. Even the variety of academics assembled could be an advantage. Their own rivalries might force them to view the situation more openly rather than be accused of chauvinism or prejudice. It might work the other way, but an advantage had to be seized with one's own beliefs if it were to work at all.

"Yes, well, I should think it's time enough for me to go out and work my own magic, isn't it?" Davis inquired of no one.

Kevin opened his mouth to agree, but Davis left without looking his way, leaving the door slightly ajar behind him. He and Toshita still could not see the audience, but they could hear clearly now.

"Good morning all. By now you've guessed that I'm not announcing my retirement, and if you've recovered from the shock of finding yourselves in our distinguished, but dusty, basement, we'll get on with the proceedings.

"Last spring we sent one of our young men to Japan. He had brilliant notions of capturing the essence of rural life there before it disappeared—an occurrence he said was more likely than the modernization of Polynesia or East Africa where we'd suggested he go. His proposals were carefully written and successfully evaded all our objections. He went off and we heard no more of him until August . . ."

So much, at least, was true, Kevin agreed silently. Courtesy of the United States Army he'd been born in Japan, and by the time he returned to his supposedly native country he was as Japanese as the son of a red-haired blue-eyed Irishman could be. He had always known he would return to Japan as an anthropologist to preserve the rural life the US occupation had destroyed. He had even settled on the village of Asura long before he had been accepted by a university. Everything had gone according to plan—until Toshita.

He had resisted the Sensei's power as much or more than anyone else could have. His career had been completely planned in his daydreams and based on the study he would write about Asura. The hermit with the war-scarred hands who lived alone in the pine groves was only another indication of the village's quaintness. Toshita had touched him then, had awakened new awareness within him. The comprehensive study of rural Japan stood out in his mind for what it would become—a forgotten dusty tome used by recalcitrant under-graduates. He became a convert to Toshita's vision and felt the pure fires of conviction within himself.

". . . the background, of course, is covered in the briefing— and we may indeed have a portrait of Japanese village life of which we can be justly proud—but Skorski could not help but notice O'Donnell's fascination with this hermit-chappie living off in the pine groves. Dr. Skorski stormed into my office and said 'we've got a real problem on our hands this time—this one's using our department funds to support some oriental witch-doctor!' Dr. Skorski's always very attentive to the way we spend *our* money, you know . . ."

Davis had mimicked Skorski's somewhat nasal *a* short-breathed speech pattern well enough to wring laughter from the assembly. Kevin chuckled to himself despite certain knowl-edge that Skorski's embarrassment could only work against him.

". . . then I wrote to the young man myself. 'Wise men, even scarred wise men, can be found anywhere,' I reminded him. 'Get back to the wood-carver and the egg-shell painter.' Young man never listened to me. We heard less and less about the village but much more about this Sensei, this master, his wisdom and his abilities—it's all in the report.

"We recalled O'Donnell when we got the proposal for this new thesis. He came back but he has brought the wise Sensei with him—at his own expense!"

The audience laughed again, but the assertion was true; Kevin's bank account could vouch for that. Toshita had been eager to present his case to the occidental academics, but the wise man of Asura was not a wealthy man.

"We had thought to challenge O'Donnell's work, but he and Mr. Toshita have stolen our thunder. They presented us with a challenge: examine Toshita ourselves, find our own explanations, and then pass judgment on the merits of O'Donnell's research."

Davis paused for effect, but if there was a reaction, Kevin could not hear it. Indeed, he'd begun to wonder if they were still out there at all or if they'd already decided and left the Old Man lecturing to antique, empty seats. Toshita had drifted off into that alert but unfocused attitude he favored whenever nothing worth his attention impinged upon him. He wouldn't care if the auditorium were empty or full.

". . . well I have to admit I don't believe young O'Donnell's claims at all, but I couldn't prove him wrong—not *prove*, at any rate. Every one of my instincts said the boy'd gone 'round the bend over there, but scientifically—*scientifically*—I couldn't prove him wrong. Skorski and I can pull his grant, reject his thesis, and laugh him off every faculty from here to Timbuktu, but we couldn't prove him wrong. Still, the reputation of the department is at stake and, finding myself on the horns of a dilemma, I decided to turn to my distinguished colleagues for help."

There were amused murmurings from the audience. Davis' reputation for independent action was legendary. Everyone could imagine the conversations he and Skorski had had. There was a power struggle in the air, not just a Ph.D. thesis. Knowledge that his deeply felt commitments were possibly nothing more than a sideshow to the departmental politics brought anger boiling up within Kevin and he missed the cue for his entrance. He followed rather than preceded Toshita onto the dais.

No one in the room applauded their entrance, but then, no one laughed either. The steeply raked lecture hall with its hard seats and dust-covered lights reminded Kevin of every movie where the persecuted doctor revealed his secrets to an unwilling world and then, jeered at by his peers, slips into increasing madness. Toshita, Kevin knew, was immune to such fantasies; he was less certain of himself. Digging into his sports coat pocket he retrieved his speech, his appeal to his peers. He unfolded the worn, dirty paper and smoothed it onto the lectern.

"Gentlemen . . " A distinctly feminine cough greeted his salutation, and another, quieter, cough came from the shadows where Davis lingered: a bold gaffe already. His complexion, by nature ruddy, brightened to a fiery red. But still they did not laugh. He took heart and continued.

". . . and ladies. When I got to Asura last spring I expected to lose myself in the usual pursuits of family structure, farming traditions, and table manners . . ." He paused, expecting them to laugh, or chuckle, but they remained stonily silent. "I was born in Japan and I'd picked out this village before I left for the states when I was ten. Where I lived Asura was the Japanese Podunk, but I'd never been there myself. I only knew it was the place I'd want to go back to. I expected it would be a sleepy place rooted in old Japan, but when I got there I found that no matter who I spoke to in the village, or what I asked, they eventually started talking about Sensei Toshita, who lived alone in the pine groves about a mile outside the village.

"According to their stories, Sensei Toshita—Sensei means Master—first appeared in Asura on April 12, 1946. Almost everyone agrees on the date because it was the day after an enormously bright meteor was seen over the area. Though Asura was a very typical village where it can take three generations before a family is acknowledged at all, the people of the village accepted Toshita-san almost at once. They brought the village problems to him and encouraged their children to sit at his feet and learn from him . . ."

He was losing them with his lecture; they were reading the papers Skorski had prepared and left on their seats. It wasn't surprising—in seven years of classes he had ignored more professors than he could count, but he hadn't yet developed that war-horse dignity that would keep him going in the face of total disinterest. He digressed from his carefully prepared sentences and spoke passionately, almost incoherently, about the stories the villagers had told him: about the fevers Toshita-san had driven out with his hands, the anger and hysteria he had calmed with his eyes. But if his audience was at all swept up in his narrative, they concealed it well.

They had begun to laugh, perhaps at the naive hamlet peasants, perhaps not. It was apparent that their distinguished and patient indulgence of the lecturings of a junior academic was strained past repair. Davis fluttered back to the lectern. Even Toshita had sensed the change in mood and stepped forward from the doorway, allowing himself to become the new focus of attention. Kevin crumpled his useless notes and stuffed them in a pocket as he retreated into the shadows.

"What Mr. O'Donnell is saying—what you have, no doubt, read yourselves in Skorski's opening paragraphs, is simply that in this Sensei Toshita we are confronted with the phenomena of a self-proclaimed modern sorcerer . . . a magician . . . a conjurer. Now, there isn't one of us here who hasn't heard of some young researcher or another who's gotten caught up in the web of a modern-day prophet and taken the reputation of his department down with him—that's what Dr. Skorski so profoundly fears. But Mr. O'Donnell, while he's undoubtedly caught up in the web, has at least managed to bring his magician to us rather than disappearing into the cloud-shrouded mountains of Japan. Whatever we may think of his naivete, he has the courage of his convictions, and he has provided us with a profound opportunity."

The faculty members accepted direction from Davis where

they had only granted Kevin a bemused tolerance. They studied Toshita, staring at him and consuming the papers prepared for them by the anxious Skorski. Even the non-departmental professors, who had until that moment wondered why they had been invited, took the challenge to heart and mumbled questions to themselves and one another.

"This meteor. Is there corroboration on that?" a voice called from the semidarkness. "Is he claiming it was a flying saucer? Or that he got his supposed power from it?"

Kevin stepped forward again. "I believe that Dr. Skorski has included my translations of the conversations I had with the then-village-chief on that, but you'll probably be more interested in the US Army survey done the following year. Traces of highly carbonized and possibly meteoric dust were found in the pine forest. There's no doubt about the sighting of a meteor, by the way. It was seen clearly as far away as Nagasaki. And, yes, Asura is downwind of Nagasaki. The Army couldn't determine if the debris was from the bomb or a meteor." Kevin stepped back, satisfied with his answer and reassured by the renewed shuffling of papers.

"The villagers say . . . Mrs. Massamo says . . . everyone but Mr. Toshita himself. What does *he* say about this bright light?" Dr. Sonja Radlow, senior member of the university's distaff faculty and past master of the art of getting her colleagues' attention, brought silence to the rest of the room.

Toshita himself stepped up, placing his hands on the lectern and revealing both his knowledge of English and his scarred, misshapen hands for the first time. "I have said nothing, except to those who ask—others may believe what they wish. For those who ask, for you, I reply that a year before a very terrible thing happened to Kyushō, to Nagasaki. There was death and sickness: sickness of spirit as well as body."

There was uneasy silence as Toshita composed his sentences and the gathering worried about what he might say. The Nuclear Specter loomed large.

". . . the bomb disrupted everything. It thrust its KI into everything: killing, sickening. There was much dying, much purging. There is still dying and purging as those who were there reassemble their KI. For one year I lived as a wild creature on the island of Kyushō. Purging myself, seeking my KI, I was somehow drawn to the pine groves above Asura. The bright light in the sky? A meteor, I suppose. I do not remember it. Perhaps merely coincidence. For myself, I think they found me too soon . . ." Toshita lifted his hands. On the left the three outer fingers were fused into a stiff malignant mass. The right thumb was a thin talon and the rest of that hand a swollen bruised-looking club that was pitted with open, half-healed sores. ". . . my purging was not complete. Soon I must empty myself again. The sickness gnaws at me still."

Those hands repelled the audience. They had repelled Kevin when he had first seen them. And, though the villagers denied it, it seemed likely that they too had been repelled at first. Toshita dissociated himself from the offending parts, giving them an independent, malignant influence of their own. Then, slowly, he exerted the force of his personality, his will, his KI into his hands again and they became pitiably human.

Many in the room were caught in the aura of those hands. Kevin could hear their own hands fumbling suddenly with the papers, covering inconsequential coughs, and drumming on the wooden chair-arms. The unlined ascetic hands of Albert Edward Davis were unaccustomedly concealed in the pockets of his suitcoat. Kevin's own hands were hidden at his sides. His fists unclenched only when Toshita allowed the long sleeves of his peasant-style kimono to fall down past his wrists.

"Ah, very well. Now, then . . ." Davis stepped between Toshita and the others, an instinctive exercise of the British privilege in ignoring the manifestly obvious. "Mr. Toshita has accepted our invitation to stay here at the University and participate in such interviews and tests as will be necessary to ascertain the truth of his claims and, incidentally, salvage Mr. O'Donnell's thesis. He is most eager to have Western acknowledgment of his principles and would, I fear, risk everything to convince us of his authenticity. Therefore, Dr. Skorski and myself shall be the judge of any extraordinary techniques."

The audience made no murmurings of protest or agreement. Kevin was fidgetting with anger. Skorski, even Davis, feared for the reputation of the department; feared the press and the civil rights fringes if they should get wind of the inquiry, but they had precious little fear or concern for the well-being of Sensei Toshita. Kevin fought the vision of his Sensei flayed open and strung with electrodes. He feared the unconscionable and could not convince himself that those same professors, academics, and researchers whose ranks he had always dreamed of joining shared his own conscience.

He was still battling with his fears when Toshita stepped to the lectern again and began to speak.

"I am honored and humbled to speak to so many educated people. Surely your knowledge of the things of the world is greater than mine, but what is your knowledge of the *way* of the world? Can you reach within yourself to find the spirit of your supreme center, the spirit we call KI and extend this KI as a dynamic force?

"Not possible? Not human? Do you think that the monkey searching for food in the trees uses a calculator to find the branches that will support him? No, he extends KI and brings himself to the branch. If a squalling monkey can do this, why have so many people lost their KI? With your KI extended, flowing, you must know where you are. With your KI extended you cannot be attacked or displaced by the weaker random forces swirling around you.

"KI is health, direction, but most important: harmony, a place in the unity, oneness with the resolution of opposites. It is within you now, as it has been since you were born. You use it blindly, blundering and hurting yourself and others. Now it is time to open eyes and use your KI; extend it!"

Toshita waited for the questions which came slowly, mundane and unimaginative, from the audience. The gathering of specialists had clearly determined that KI was magic, and magic was impossible. They sought only a secure confirmation of their beliefs. They ignored what Toshita had done to ask about what he had not. Could he bend nails with his mind? No,

KI was not to be exercised so foolishly. Could he read minds then? No, KI was not an aggressive explorer of private realities. Could he levitate his body? Could he tolerate garlic? Was he affected by the phases of the moon? And so on until the proceeding had taken the aspect of farce. Kevin stood poised to leap forward, screaming at their rude ignorance.

"Tell me, Mr. Toshita, is it not true that this KI you mention is nothing more or less than the same concentration that enables karate entertainers to put their heads through brick walls?"

Skorski was standing in the aisle straining his raspy voice to make himself heard. His inflections were sneering, but at least he had done his homework. Toshita accorded him his full attention.

"You have studied KI?" he asked.

"I know these demonstrations of will are the result of grooved boards and years of practice on harder walls."

"But you have studied Aki?" Toshita pronounced the word "eye-key" and brought a distinctly alien air to the room.

"I've heard of it," Skorski acknowledged harshly, dismissing it with his tone. "Mumbo-jumbo foolery dressed up with Zen and half-a-dozen other oriental philosophies."

"But you will demonstrate this 'foolery' with me? I would ask Kevin, but I do not think that you or your associates would trust him. You, yourself, I see, are above suspicion."

Toshita leaned over the edge of the raised dais offering to assist Skorski up. But the thin, nervous man vaulted the three-foot height without effort, revealing a fitness otherwise carefully concealed.

"Shall I throw a punch and have you throw me over your shoulder?" he challenged. "It's all simple physics: leverage, balance, angular velocities—no magic."

"True, no magic—but KI for drawing and directing the attack. But, I will not show you that." Toshita stamped his foot on the echoing wood floor of the dais. "You could fall through and the damage would be expensive to repair, would it not? So, instead, you just push me over."

Toshita spun down into a cross-legged Buddha-like pose,

hands hidden by the long sleeves of his jacket and an almost sly smile on his face. Skorski stood motionless, started forward a half-step and retreated. He stepped to one side and repeated the maneuver. Kevin could not see his advisor's face, but from the increasingly firm set to his shoulders guessed that Skorski was discovering how difficult it was to advance towards that calm smile. Perceptibly tense, Skorski finally advanced and gave Toshita a sharp rap on the shoulder, toppling the seated man onto his back.

"Not so hard, was it?" Toshita asked innocently. "Now I make it difficult for you. I will extend KI from myself to this wood, from the wood to the center of the Earth and all things. Now, you push me over."

Whatever Toshita had done to extend his KI to the Earth's center was not physically apparent. Skorski steeled himself and approached the seated man. He shoved Toshita's shoulder as he had done the previous time, to no result. He withdrew his hand and shot it forward in a karate-style punch. The impact resounded through the room. The more timid members of the audience could be heard gasping with surprise both at the obvious force of Skorski's punch and Toshita's complacently upright position. Skorski pressed both palms against Toshita's shoulder. He bent into his arms as though shoving a balky piano. Ridges stood out on his forehead, but Toshita remained immobile.

"You do not extend KI," Toshita explained, his voice unaffected by any indication of exertion. "Your force actually grows less."

Toshita pressed his own hand to Skorski's shoulder, then stood up, supporting Skorski's straining weight with one hand until that person staggered sideways and gasped for breath. The red pressure marks on Skorski's palms were visible across the room. Toshita bowed to the still-unimpressed Skorski.

Pandemonium erupted in the auditorium. Jolted, insulted by what they had seen, the audience came forward to join Skorski in staring at the nondescript, unchanged section of heavily varnished floorboards. They stared at Toshita himself and were emboldened to touch his jacket, his arms, but not his hands. Urged to perform the "trick" again, Toshita obliged, dismounting the dais altogether and seating himself on the cement floor of the basement room. At one point it seemed to Kevin that half the review board was pushing Toshita and each other while the remainder was on hands and knees looking for the presumed gimmick. Only he and Davis were excluded from this pursuit of knowledge.

"I'm not at all certain this is going to help your thesis," Davis remarked, leading Kevin back toward the elevator.

"That's what Skorski had in mind all along, isn't it?" The bitterness tinged Kevin's voice for the first time as he looked back at the amoeboid cluster of academics obscuring Toshita. "Make Sensei Toshita look ridiculous, like a stage magician. Keeps everyone from listening."

"They weren't doing such a good job of that before Skorski stood up, you know. But now, when they have to realize that he did defy common sense—I just don't know how they'll react. They aren't field men. Of course, the yogis can stop and start their hearts. The old bed-of-nails trick isn't so impressive— done it myself once. Walking on coals is a bit more so—I saw that done, back in 1924, in Malaysia, the monkey-men. Never considered it magic, just tremendous self-control. What Toshita does is simply an extension of that, tremendous discipline and self-control. But to resist the combined willful curiosity of that lot in there? I'm not so sure of my theories anymore."

"No, Dr. Davis. KI is more than discipline or self-control. It is a force, an energy, and no amount of curiosity could make a dent in it. Not even another Sensei could move Toshita-san once he extends his KI like that. It's a way of thinking more than anything else. Toshita-san uses that to demonstrate the power of KI, then he teaches his students how to extend KI themselves. If Skorski had been less resistant, Sensei would have taught him."

"Shall I infer, then, that you, too, have this KI? That you could root yourself to the floor as well?"

Kevin tensed. He had been taught the technique, and back in

Asura he would have been confident of his own center and extension. But here, in the castle, before Davis' sharply inquisitive eyes, he was much less certain.

"Ah, the magic only works sometimes and someplaces, eh?" Davis inquired, unperturbed by the admission of limitations. "Perhaps when we get up to my office conditions will be better?"

"If you don't mind, Dr. Davis, I'd rather stay down here until this is over at noon."

"It's half-past now. I don't think there's much cause to worry about your friend Mr. Toshita. I don't think he's the sort they'll push around."

Davis laughed at his own joke and led the way into the elevator.

His office was an expanse of dark wood panelling, stuffed bookshelves, and well-used leather chairs, and to Kevin's surprise it buoyed his confidence enough that he was willing to let Davis explore the beginnings of KI. The older man seemed more unwilling than unable to topple the younger and mostly eager to be taught the secret himself. Reluctantly Kevin agreed to the teaching and quickly found Davis exuberantly affixed to his office carpet.

It was fortunate, in a way, that Davis did not seem to tire of exercising his new-found knowledge, for Kevin found himself spending most of his time in that office. Despite Skorski's fears and precautions the student press got wind of the Toshita Project, as they dubbed it, and from there interest spread to the feature-hungry television news services. Kevin found himself in dignified, polite protective custody. He was kept separate from Toshita, who was sequestered in the University's Medical Center, and kept even more separate from the press which was, at any rate, less interested in his role in the affair than in getting an interview with, or at least a picture of, the modern-age magician. Kevin had been the catalyst—needed at the beginning and now unnecessary to the expanding reaction.

The skies turned a snow-belt leaden gray and winter descended in icy sheets that shortened everyone's temper and chilled enthusiasm. Davis' comfortable retreat became a dismal cell and, inspired perhaps by the runic scrawls still appearing in the building, Kevin plotted a daring escapade through the steam tunnels, rescuing Toshita from the psychologists then retreating back to the security of Asura.

His bold confidence was gone, corroded by boredom and ignorance. Surely someone had been convinced by what Toshita could show them, but so far no such excitement had penetrated to Davis' office. The paperwork flowed without excitement. No single test had overcome the scepticism, nor had any later analysis of a battery of tests. Only Davis still talked of KI with rising interest. He practiced breathing and sitting perfectly still. He would have done two-man exercises with Kevin as well, but the younger man steadfastly refused to try, knowing he would only reveal his own doubts and confusion. Return to Japan had become the only path for his thoughts: getting back to the place where he had found his own center before it was too late.

"You might try giving Hannah a hand," Davis suggested as the sleet drummed against the windows two weeks after the basement auditorium meeting and when Kevin's thoughts were completely in the pine groves above Asura. "We'll be getting the last of the reports in a few hours."

"Help her with what? She's got everything under control. She doesn't need to start a clerical nursury school at this late date."

For a moment Davis' face was as unpleasant as the weather. Kevin regretted immediately his sudden alienation of the one person who still acknowledged his importance to the Toshita Project. But before he had framed an apology in his thoughts, Davis was speaking again:

"She's got all the Project typing and collating in there. I've asked the review board for a decision over the Thanksgiving break, while the students are gone. Even at her renowned efficiency it's a major task. You're familiar with everything. You'd be the most logical candidate to read through the reports and make sure she hasn't missed anything."

Kevin caught the strands of opportunity and plunged into proofreading the transcripts and summations Hannah had already prepared.

The psychologists had supplied the bulk of the data. They had assaulted Toshita with a multitude of tests and concluded that by most measures Nakadei Toshita displayed only the "standard Oriental deviations" from the norm. Only the parapsychologists, measuring extrasensory perceptions, reported any interesting results. Kevin noted with a resurgence of hope that they eagerly demanded time for more tests and studies.

When matched against a machine, Toshita's predictive abilities were discouragingly normal. As a telepathic receiver, he read the thoughts of his human partners with results poor enough to be remarkable in a negative way. In the third group of tests, where others were the telepathic receivers and he the one transmitting a cartoon drawing to them, the results were "interesting." Without bearing notable resemblance to the target picture, each receiver had, however, produced a pattern similar to other receivers' attempts to reproduce Toshita's mind-images. The parapsychologists had included copies of the drawings, grouped by target image, with the notation that they considered the originals too valuable to send along.

Hannah did not mind when Kevin rummaged through her files and studied the copies.

"Of course there's a pattern," he announced, laying a handful of the sheets on Davis' cluttered desk, "that's Japanese!"

Davis looked at the scrawls. "Doesn't look like Japanese to me."

"Oh, it's like if you saw a kid writing all over a piece of paper—you might not be sure if there were words, but you'd know that there were letters. This is like a child's Japanese. Now, if they got some of the Japanese students here . . ."

"Which they didn't."

"But they could. They will after we tell them what's going on here."

"They won't. Pursue it yourself, if you want. I want this whole charade finished while the students are back home stuffing themselves with turkey. I want it forgotten by the First when they get back here. We're not going to tell the psych department how to conduct their tests any more than we'll question the hospital results when they get here."

Kevin's rebounding enthusiasm turned to quick anger. He snatched up the drawings and vowed to call the other departments. Davis, for his part, vowed dire consequences if Kevin moved an inch in that direction.

"The medical reports should be on their way over. With them everything will be finished. We'll make copies, distribute them, and by this time next week it will be over. Let this go for now, Kevin. Toshita's been in that village for twenty-five years and the world hasn't collapsed from ignorance. I suspect everything will survive until you can study it yourself."

"I suppose so . . . it's just that I've had a feeling all along that Sensei Toshita agreed to all this because he wanted things settled now. I keep thinking about what he said about his hands and the sickness that's still in them. He never talked about that back in the village. Maybe he knows something . . ."

"The medical people took extraordinary delight in the notion of examining a survivor of Nagasaki. Their report should be very complete. If Mr. Toshita is in medical danger from the aftereffects of the bomb or anything else, I'm certain that this will be an ideal place for him to be treated."

"He didn't receive treatment the last time."

"Maybe he never needed it," Skorski interrupted from the doorway where he had appeared unannounced and carrying a large Medical Center envelope. "From everything here, his long-term problem is lead poisoning, not radiation poisoning."

"How did you get the report?" Davis demanded, striding around his desk and taking position over that spot on the rug where he practiced extending his KI.

"You may be the chairman of the department, Al, but it's my student and my review board and my name on all the authorizations. I think you'll find the findings interesting." Skorski placed the unopened envelope in Davis' hands. "He may not be what he claims, but with the amount of lead he's got in him it is a miracle that he's alive at all."

"Lead's the final product of radioactive decay," Kevin replied, unwilling to accept Skorski's reluctant concessions and still contentious from his interrupted argument with Davis.

"I was of the opinion the half-lives were measured in thousands of years," Skorski replied.

"It's a probability curve, you know that. No one can predict when an individual atom will decay . . . but Sensei Toshita doesn't deal with probabilities."

"Do you expect me to believe that he extended his KI to each and every invading atom or molecule and forced it straight back to lead?"

"I did," Toshita said calmly from the doorway. "Though I've only just learned from your doctors the consequences of my misinformation about the poisons within me. I know now what I must do to rid myself of that day forever."

Faced now with Toshita, Davis, and Skorski, Kevin looked around the room for a location where he himself would feel the confidence necessary to disagree with any of them.

"Mr. Toshita, what are you doing here? I thought you were to stay at the Medical Center until after the board met?" Davis asked.

"I have been through the last of their tests now. There was no one waiting to lead me elsewhere so I followed Dr. Skorski back here to learn your opinion of the inquiries. Do you believe in KI now, Dr. Davis?"

"You've proven the existence of KI beyond any doubt, Mr. Toshita, but I'm afraid that we're no closer to knowing what KI is than when we started."

"You play a good game, Toshita," Skorski continued, "but magic? No, there are simple explanations for what you do. Just good, simple fundamental science that you've obscured with words. Maybe if you walk in here next year and the doctors find the lead is gone and the growths on your hands have healed, maybe then I'll consider magic."

"I shall be back."

"Yes, what was the report on your hands? Have they been able to find a treatment for them?" Davis asked with sincere concern.

"Their treatments were too drastic for my consent," Toshita replied.

"Tumors, wild things . . . they've got all the Latin in the report, but they told me there are differentiated cells there—nerve cells, liver cells, bone marrow. It's the sort of tumor a man can have all his life with no problems, then BANG! it goes up like a balloon. They want to amputate before it spreads any more," Skorski explained.

"But it won't spread," Kevin protested, "will it, Sensei? Your hands are the same now as they were when you entered Asura."

"Medically impossible, not from the state they're in now. It can't have started more than a few months ago—these things just don't take that long, Kevin." Skorski's voice softened as he continued: "Why don't you admit it now, all this KI business started after you got to the village. You invented the stories to bring your friend back to the States for medical treatment. I understand that—we can make allowances. His case is interesting in a medical sense."

"I am not a liar, Dr. Skorski. If it took me a few months to report about the Sensei it was because I was skeptical too, but I wasn't so pigheaded as to assume everyone else was a liar when my theories couldn't hold the facts." Kevin had reached back for his convictions and found them still strong despite neglect.

"Kevin!" David interjected.

"I'm tired of being treated like the prodigal son around here. Sensei Toshita's convinced me that there's magic in the world and in everyone living on it. Good simple fundamental principles—just like you said, Skorski—but magic, the ability to defy probability in a consistent and observable way. Sure, you'll always be able to find some other explanation—but we'll go after the probabilities until even you can't hide behind explanations and coincidence. I'll prove it. I've just shown Dr. Davis some things the parapsychologists missed—things that defy probability."

"Kevin, that's enough! You were provoked, I can understand your reaction, but let it be. Go back to Japan and finish your study of the village. Forget about magic. Let it be."

"You surprise me, Al. I'd about given up. I figure the board'll give him the license to complete and publish his damn thesis on magic. I figured you were a believer from the start."

The lights began to flicker as Skorski spoke. Heightened winds drove the sleet against the windows. The exterior lights of the campus buildings tried to come on, flickered, and plunged the entire area into darkness. It was only late afternoon, but the men in Davis' office were blind to the walls and each other. Unconsciously they moved closer together and spoke in hushed tones. Sirens could be heard racing down the campus roads.

"Believer?" Davis answered Skorski's pre-darkness question. "Of course. Kevin's shown me how to use KI. It's a force, just like they say it is—a simple, effective way of thinking, devilishly easy to do when you put your mind to it. I've lived in the bush with men and women who believed utterly and successfully in magic, but they were never able to translate their faith into modern society. Toshita's got the potential ability to do just that.

"Oh, I've always known magic worked in the bush, but I thought it would stay isolated, wild, beyond domestication as it were. Toshita could teach this magic to anyone. Some could pick it up from a how-to-do-it book, if we let the mass of people know it was possible. I've been hoping for some nicely inconclusive studies, enough evidence to salve O'Donnell's pride but nothing compelling. But I'm afraid the stuff *is* compelling, and I'm not sure just where our responsibility lies.

"Kevin, think about it yourself, listen to what you're saying—you too, Mr. Toshita. Do you really want the cynics investigating KI? Look at the circus that's sprung up around here: reporters, cameras. . . . Hannah says someone's been taking our trash each night and examining it piece by piece. Is this the sort of thing you want? Voyeurs now, worse later?"

Hannah heard her name and entered the office. She had lit a candle for herself and, hearing the conversation going on in semidarkness, set it on the desk beside Davis. She left the room without a sound.

"I want people to believe in KI—in Sensei Toshita. The world needs to hear what he has to say."

"Does it? Do you intend to make a media prophet out of him? A new Christ or Buddha? Is our world ready for Toshita's KI?"

"Sensei Toshita's not a maniac."

"He doesn't have to be. Our world is too fragile to withstand the forces you propose to tap." The candle flickered to Davis' emphatic words.

"You'll try to override the review board, Al?" Skorski asked, the malice gone from his voice and replaced by genuine astonishment. "I've talked with them—they're going to let it go—the old spirit of inquiry. The challenge is there, you gave it to them. We can't close our eyes to it anymore. It's us or them, you know."

"I'll stop it, or resign in disgrace."

"I will withdraw myself from the investigations." Toshita spoke into the shadow of Davis' bleak statement. "I was wrong. I heard only you, Dr. Skorski, and those like you. Your perceptions exceed your wisdom, and I thought I could guide your wisdom. Now I hear Dr. Davis and my own ignorance."

"But Sensei, you said it was time. You said you felt it within you." Kevin stepped forward, isolating Toshita from the others and meeting his stare without flinching. "There's so much to be done! You can't let someone say 'the world's not ready for this knowledge yet,' and walk off the stage!"

"I felt the sickness in my bones, not my wisdom," Toshita shrugged. "Even the wisest monkey falls out of the tree sometimes. It is not the time for me. Dr. Davis is correct, the world is too fragile for magic."

Kevin turned around to stare into the bookcases. He made a fist and smashed it into the dark, varnished wood. Pain shot up his arm and released the tears that had been trapped in his eyes and mind. The lights flickered again, then rose to accustomed brilliance. Kevin blew the candle out.

CAMPUS DAILY

(December 1) The Anthropology Department announced, over the Thanksgiving break, the results of the academic inquiry into the Toshita Project. Mr. O'Donnell's thesis, substantially revised, has been accepted. Mr. O'Donnell will remain here continuing his investigation into effective nonrational thought. Mr. Toshita has returned to his village.

In a related announcement, the retirement of Dr. Albert Edward Davis as chairman of the department was made public. Dr. Davis had been chairman for fifteen years. In his letter of resignation he stated that there were still many things he wanted to do which could not be done from the 'castle.' He could not be reached for comment. It was believed, however, that he had already departed for an undisclosed location, possibly in the Orient.

Dr. Ralph Skorski has been named interim department head. In a statement issued to the press, Dr. Skorski expressed admiration for his predecessor and, speaking specifically of the Toshita Project, said the department had an obligation to bring the darker side of man into the light of day.

BARRY B. LONGYEAR
MISENCOUNTER

Fura's particles whirled high above the canyon floor, seeking out the nourishment in the storm. A red-yellow cloud separated from the others and followed the currents to gather around Fura. *"Now, Fura, why do you not eat?"*

"I am, Mother." the child rippled with a greenish glow. *"See?"*

The cloud gathered tightly around Fura. *"You are still unhappy about the trick Pago played on you."*

Fura struggled against the envelope of his mother. *"You treat me as a child!"* Fura stopped struggling and sulked. *"Pago won't get away with it! You'll see!"*

"You mustn't think that way, my child. Pago is your friend."

"Not any longer, Pago isn't."

The large cloud sagged, then opened. *"You must go play for a short while, Fura, but be back in time for the rest."*

"Yes, Mother." Fura seeped through the opening, then bent a wind current to his will, taking the child along the length of the canyon, away from the others. Pago was always playing tricks on Fura. The others laughed when Fura told them that Pago had sealed him into a cave. He had missed a rest trying to get out, and had been very frightened, but the others had only laughed. And, even more, Pago wouldn't let Fura play with the wonderful toys he made. Pago would tell Fura to go away and make his own. Fura's particles gathered, became dense and dark red. *"Just you wait, Pago. I'll get you."*

Fura sensed two figures far below on the canyon floor standing next to a larger object. They were white and moved about on two tiny lower appendages. The object was cylindrical and stood up off the canyon floor supported by four thin braces. Fura almost forgot his anger as he admired the three things. Pago did make the most wonderful toys. Fura swept toward the things, then whirled in place as he thought of an idea. *"Just you wait, Pago. Just you wait."* Fura turned abruptly and streaked toward a large arroyo cut into the canyon wall.

Stebbins wiped the dust from his faceplate, studied the instrument in his hand a final time, then turned to his companion. Baker was wiping his own faceplate and staring down the length of the canyon. "Nick, it looks like Mills was right."

Baker turned his clumsily protected body until it faced Stebbins. "What?"

"The glow discharges in the clouds eating up the organics on Mars. I've been getting excellent readings on those clouds at the end of the canyon. See any?"

"No. It's too light." Baker turned again and looked down the canyon. "Jerry, did you see that one dust cloud?"

Stebbins attached his instrument to his utility belt. "What dust cloud?"

"It separated from the storm at the end of the canyon, came toward us, then veered off into that gulch over there."

"No. Why?"

"I don't know. Seemed kind of queer, that's all."

Stebbins lifted his arm and checked the chronometer attached to the arm of his pressure suit. "We better get settled in. Launch is in forty-eight minutes." He looked back at his companion. "Come on, Nick. We knew from the Viking landers that life on Mars was virtually impossible. Now we know why."

Baker turned toward the MEM Lander, *Eagle VII*, and keyed the transceiver mounted on his wrist. "Mike, we're getting ready to go upstairs."

His headset crackled with static generated by the distant

dust storm. "I read you, Nick . . ."—a wave of static wiped out the transmission from the orbiter—". . . if you could turn the tv camera toward *Eagle* before liftoff."

"Will do." Baker turned and followed the cable out to the tripod mounted with the remote control camera that had jammed with dust. "Jerry, do you think anyone's watching this show?"

"I doubt it. The last Lunar mission was beaten in the ratings by 'Mary Tyler Moore' reruns. Anyway, how much of a picture can they be getting with all this interference?"

Baker adjusted the camera, then keyed his tranceiver. "Okay, Mike. Is it go on the launch being controlled from the orbiter?"

" . . . ffirmative."

"Okay. We're entering the *Eagle* . . . "

Stebbins looked over at Baker to see why he had trailed off in his transmission. "Nick, what's wrong?"

Baker lifted an arm and pointed down the canyon. "What in the ever-loving hell is *that*?"

"What's . . . oing on?" crackled Mike from the orbiter.

Stebbins turned and caught his breath as he saw a giant figure lurch out of an arroyo in the wall of the canyon. With twin glowing coals for eyes, a chestful of multi-colored lights, and great swinging arms and legs, the figure was advancing toward the *Eagle* at a rapid pace. "A robot? Is that a robot?"

"Jer . . . is it? Point the cam . . . "

Stebbins swallowed. "Nick, aim the camera at it, then let's get into the *Eagle* pronto!"

Baker twisted the head of the camera around, then keyed his transceiver. "Mike, are you getting this?"

"Holy . . . sus!"

Stebbins reached the ladder first, climbed up, and entered the door. Close behind, Baker swung around for a last look. Coming out of the arroyo behind the robot, three white saucer-shaped ships streaked toward the *Eagle*. Baker turned back, ran the remaining steps, and flung himself through the door. "Jerry! They've got ships! We've got to get outta here!"

Stebbins looked up from strapping himself in. "But the window—"

"To hell with the window!" Baker fell into his couch and strapped himself in as the door closed. "We'll sort it out once we get outta here!" He took a quick look out of the triangular window set next to his headrest. The robot was only a hundred meters away. "Mike, do you copy that stuff?"

" . . . ready whenever you are." A pause. "What in the hell . . . ships are over your position!"

Baker flicked banks of switches in a blur of fingers. "Now, Mike, give me ignition!"

"Nick . . . those ships . . . over your position!"

"Dammit, next to that pile of junk outside, I'll take the chance of a collision! *Push the button!*"

The burst of the ascent engines slammed the two astronauts into their couches, and in a few seconds they were above the yellow-red dust storm. Baker let out his breath, checked the cabin pressure, then cracked and removed his helmet. After Stebbins had removed his own helmet, Baker smiled. "Well, I guess that answers the question about life on Mars."

Stebbins shook his head. "That was a robot, not life. I'll bet those ships were robot ships as well."

"But—"

"Nick, Mars can't support higher order lifeforms, and did you see that robot? A head, arms, and legs? That robot was modeled after the form of a humanoid species. You see anything down there with a head, arms, and legs?"

Baker wiped the perspiration from his forehead, then lowered his arm and wiped his hand dry on his leg. "No. I guess not."

Stebbins pursed his lips. "It's probably an advance force from outside the solar system, checking out the planet. Maybe Earth is next."

Baker frowned, then pointed at a bank of indicators. "Let's start sorting this out, Jerry. If we don't make it back, the aliens may strike without warning."

Fura uncompacted his particles, and the ships and robot again became a cloud. He whirled in glee as he sensed Pago's toys flying away. *"There, Pago. You'll never find them!"* Fura sensed something remaining and he streaked down and surrounded a pan-shaped thing supported by the braces he recognized from before. As he approached it, he could sense food covering many parts of the thing, and thick wads of food stuck here and there, and covering thin metal strands. Fura felt his particles drawn toward the feast, as though they had wills of their own.

"Fura, my child, it is time for the rest."
"Mother, I don't feel so good."
The large cloud enclosed the child. *"Fura, you have been eating! Where did you get it? Pago?"*
"Yes, Mother. He, he tricked me!"
"Humph! It is time for the rest. We shall meet about this later, Fura!

Fura felt the wind leave his particles, but as he settled toward the surface, he swore. *"One of these days I'll get you, Pago! Just you wait and see!"*

JAYGE CARR
THE WONDROUS WORKS
OF HIS HANDS

Mixed termpairings are seldom successful;
mixed crews are invariably disastrous.
—*very* unofficial Service proverb

Zondra was deeply immersed in analyzing an amusing substitute for mitochondria when she abruptly realized that her body was signalling *URGENT!* Sighing mentally, she withdrew her consciousness from the Analysis, reintegrated body and mind, de-Linked both from the complex, and raised the privacy hood to find out what the Great Mother had gotten through the supposedly impervious helmet, the body-mind separation, the complex Linkage, *and* her concentration.

"—mushbrain," her normally phlegmatic male-dupe Huw was actually shouting. "What the Great Whirling Wheel possessed you? Vegan slimemolds have more sense! You—"

Zondra darted between the two men, gently urged them apart with a firm hand on each chest. "Kelvin it, Huw," she soothed, trying to Link directly, and failing because of the roil of his emotions. "Easy, easy, bud, what's the matter?"

But Huw, thrown off the rhythm of his unaccustomed tirade by her intervention, could only sputter and glare.

Zondra turned to Faisal, who only hiked his chin a little higher—so that the neatly pointed Van Dyke seemed directly at her—and said, with awful precision, "I am an engineer, not a crech attendant, nor an instructor of preformers, nor the dictator of this vessel."

Which told her exactly nothing, except that behind the rigid falcon's face—blazing attractive for a Natch was her private opinion—was a fury matching Huw's.

"You," Huw spoke with finality, "are an idiot."

Zondra winced. The long months jammed together in the small scout could lead to sheer murder—don't think about the proverb about mixed crews—but what had set Huw off like that, without warning? She tried to Link again, and failed again. If he were deliberately shutting *her* out . . .

Huw whirled, stomped away toward the storage lockers.

"Faisal," she couldn't Link with a Natch—or anyone not a dupe off her line—outside the complex, so she was thrown back onto words. "Please, what is all this?"

Faisal shrugged, the pale green eyes narrowed to arrow-slits. Huw was grimly clipping on an induction suit. "Huw!" The problem with Faisal would have to wait. (Anti-Construct prejudice? After all these years as a team? Ridiculous! Now if it had been . . .) "Wait'll I get mine on, Huw. You know you mustn't go outside alone."

"I won't be alone." He headed for the deconn lock, to the soup this world they were exploring called atmosphere. "Flower's already outside, has been for hours. And he *knew*, and didn't bother to say a mumblin' *word!*"

"What can happen?" Faisal defended himself. "She's protected by an induction suit, fully equipped. I checked her out myself."

Huw turned. "What can happen?" he repeated. *"Anything*, that's what! She's green, Faisal, green, a rookie, raw as a new-canted 'bryo. And you let her go out—alone."

Faisal's rather narrow shoulders drooped. "You're right, Huw, she's green. That's why I didn't even try to stop her. And if you go out and bring her in, like a matron collaring a runaway preformer, she'll never forgive you—and her next prank will be something even more outrageous!"

Huw was an atom-for-atom dupe, "born" adult, but he had edited memories of his Constructed original and several cloned intermediates. He understood Faisal; all three of the veteran crew members had winced at Flower's fiery response to the merest hint of criticism—or help. "Rookie!" He made it a curse.

"But—we can't just leave her out there, and us in here worrying."

"What do you think I've been doing," Faisal's voice was dry.

"Worrying," Zondra supplied. "Don't fret, boys. You've no excuse for going outside, but I do. I want some more specimens. And I'll keep a neuron or two on our too-eager Rookie with a Personnel locator while I'm out."

"That'll just give us *two* to worry about," Huw objected. He finally Linked, and she felt his concern.

She winked, and sent him a warm ##thank you don't worry##. He was physically older, but she had been duped off a later (and, of course, female) version of their mutual original. She had more "generations" of memories. Sometimes—but only sometimes—it made her feel quite maternal toward him. "But since I mentioned I was going out, didn't you decide to check one of your geo sites, Huw? And if Faisal just happened to be Linked into central because he's controlling a team of mechs—checking out something on the hull, Faisal?— then . . ."

"Neat," Huw nodded, "put on your suit." With a quick grateful glance at Zondra, Faisal seated himself at the main panel and Linked in.

At which point the alarms went off.

Huw triggered his induction suit and dived into the deconn lock; Zondra was frantically adjusting hers. Faisal Linked, ordering central to flood the area around the scout with light and half-a-dozen other frequencies and demanding scanning input in the same thought, while physically yelling into the comm, "Flower, acknowledge! Flower, acknowledge!"

"Stay out of this lock!" Flower's excited voice came through central and the suitcomms. *"Is it still out there!"*

"Cargo lock!" Faisal cursed. "Is *what* still out *where*, Flower?" Huw was muttering the deconn countdown out loud, Zondra silently cursing that she'd followed him into the personnel lock, restarting the inexorable countdown which now trapped them both. "What's in the lock with you?" Faisal choked.

"Not *now*," Flower answered. "Is that *thing* still hanging around outside?"

"What thing?" Faisal was at the end of his patience.

"I don't know, it's horrible," Flower babbled. "Like a giant twenty-meter-long slug, all shapeless and slimy and—ugh! It was chasing us!"

"Don't anthropomorphize," Faisal automatically repeated the slogan of the Service. "For all you know, that slug has an R.Q. of 1000 and a saintly disposition."

"All I *know* is, it has the appetite of a Thuban four-mouth!"

"Who's 'us'?" Zondra asked the all-important question.

"I've found an aborigine!"

"Now, Flower!" It was an incredulous chorus. Part of Flower's problem had been too little to do. Her share of duties was the "mind" sciences, and for four worlds straight they'd found no traces of intelligence. And no signs on this one, either.

"I'm going to call him Elvar, after the first nonhuman to learn a human language," Flower asserted.

"Elvar doesn't sound like a Cygnian name," Zondra said. The deconn was over, but she Linked with Huw, and after a quick Linked discussion, they re-entered the main area, offed their suit-fields, and Linked into central with Faisal. There was no more unforgivable insult than overriding a specialist's decision in his own field. Faisal was trying to adjust the lock viewers to get a better look at whatever was cowering beside the girl.

"Not Cygni," Flower was impatient with anybody who didn't know *everything* about somebody else's specialty. "Elvar was the earth-dolphin taught to speak by the legendary genius, Lilly Darwin. Besides, he looks like an Elvar."

"He?" asked Huw.

A giggle. "Most definitely a he. He's not one to hide himself under a kiloliter basket."

"Well," said Faisal, "I'm scanning, and whatever was chasing you seems to have left. Why don't you try luring him into the prepared-for-live sector of the hold. Meanwhile the rest of us'll suit up for a firsthand look at your find."

Elvar was the most human-appearing nonhuman any of them had ever seen or heard of. The similarities were so overwhelming it took considerable time to notice and appreciate the differences. He was an erect biped—the top of his head just below Flower's shoulders. And he was, as Flower had said, most definitely male.

Huw and Zondra Linked. *##i see what flower meant about not hiding his light under a basket—jealous huw##*

##stunned is the word—it must weigh a quarter of what he does##

##imagine what it'll be like when he's grown##

##you mean he isn't##

##my educated pre-testing guess is early adolescence assuming i'm not anthropomorphizing too much and his species isn't neotonic—species retaining immature characteristics past puberty that is##

Delighted. *##you are jealous##*

Without the threat of the giant slug, Flower couldn't keep Elvar in the lock, much less lure him into the hold. But he wasn't straying away from the safety of the ship either. They set up a shelter for him protected by the harsh outside lights but in the shadow of a strut. In the bright light he glowed richly crimson; in the shadow, dull maroon. He was "clothed" in a coat of hair-fine cilia that waved gently in the high-pressure, fluid atmosphere of the giant planet.

For the rest, he had huge, owlly round eyes, fully half the area of his face. Below was a three-cornered mouth, like an upside down T, the upper segment ridged into a vaguely nose-like effect. His "hands" were really the base for eight radially sited, mutually opposed, cartilege-stiffened tentacles, roughly the length of a man's finger and palm: more versatile than human fingers, but less powerful. And there were other differences, internal and external, that promised Zondra many fascinating hours.

The third time Zondra emerged from the ship for more of her careful tests—made despite Flower's protests and sullen kibitzing—Elvar immediately bounded away into the surrounding murk.

Hurling accusations at Zondra for frightening "her" Elvar,

Flower struggled through the ooze after him. Zondra followed, but her light showed only Flower and the rough, miry surface.

Flower was hysterical. "You lost him! You made him run away! I hate—"

Zondra picked out depressions in the goo that might—or might not—be Elvar's tracks. "That must be his trail," she asserted over the wails. "He can't have gone too far. Come on. We'll follow his tracks and bring him back."

"He's probably still running," Flower sniffed. But she fell in behind Zondra.

He wasn't.

He was hiding in a depression just beyond the outer lights. He waited until the two women were almost on top of him, then he leapt out.

Startled, Zondra jerked back and cannoned into the equally startled Flower. They went down together into the slimy muck in a tangle of arms and legs, sending up geysers of fine, slow-settling mud. Elvar landed on top of the heap but was off again almost immediately, having knocked them further into the sludge.

Being half buried in treacherous goo was a claustrophobic experience. But Zondra thought she detected a more personal revulsion in the desperate way the younger girl heaved her away. And had Flower really hissed, "Get off me, you *thing*!"? Zondra was too busy trying to regain some semblance of equilibrium to be sure.

When the two women finally struggled into half-erect positions, Elvar was dancing around them triumphantly, waving Zondra's specimen sacks—all empty.

If Flower had been worrying about having given her feelings away, she forgot her worry in a sudden burst of laughter, as she realized the significance of the empty sacks. "Oh, Elvar, you little *sneak*! He ate the specimens. He didn't want to wait to be rewarded this time, he—he—he—" She laughed so hard she slipped back into the ooze.

"Well," Zondra could laugh at herself, too, "it solves one question. He can eat everything I meant to try him on. And—"

she rose and shook herself, so that the goo sticking to the outside of her field flew off in all directions, "one of them was a synthesized *fake*, so we don't have to worry about feeding him any more either." She watched, without extending the helping hand she would have offered a few minutes earlier, as the other girl struggled to her feet. "Let's go. We've work to do. We haven't gotten started good yet."

However poorly he did in Flower's other tests, Elvar was a mechanical genius. His slender tentacles could slide into the most complicated puzzle and have it apart in separate pieces in times that Flower flatly declared were impossible. Universal records—until Zondra suggested hiding Elvar's favorite eats in the centers of the puzzles; then he beat his own times with ease.

Flower recorded everything he did. Besides eating, he liked to stack the "blocks" they'd given him—odd scraps that Faisal had turned out from the machine shop—into piles and knock them down again.

While Flower was recording more data than she could evaluate, Zondra was running into difficulties. Either because of the lights, or the continued lurking presense of the giant slug, most of the local fauna regarded the ship as an unhealthy locality. So Zondra and Faisal were away on a specimen-hunting expedition when the giant gooseberry wandered into the camp.

Huw spotted it on a scanner and commed to warn Flower.

"I see it, worry-wart," she commed back. "It's big, but it doesn't have any weapons. It doesn't even seem to have a mouth. Looks just like a big ball. I think I'll corral it for Zondra. She doesn't have anything even resembling it; besides, it's the prettiest scarlet color I ever saw."

Flower picked up a large specimen bag and circled the gooseberry cautiously, afraid of frightening it away.

With one of his scanners, Huw spotted Elvar making his top speed—away. "Don't get too close to that thing, Flower! Elvar's afraid—"

At which point they found out exactly what Elvar was afraid of.

A long, whip-thin tentacle uncoiled from beneath the gooseberry, zoomed out, and wrapped around Flower. She screamed, jerked back, and lost her balance; her captor started dragging her away. The field of her suit gave it little purchase, but by wrapping several coils around limbs and torso, the gooseberry maintained its precarious hold. The tip of the tentacle beat frantically against the field, leaving a milky splotch wherever it hit.

The struggle sent up a fog of muck. Huw, cursing, switched the scanners from visual frequencies to microwave, jammed a slave repeater into his cybsocket, and dived for a suit and the lock. Once in the lock, he was helpless until the deconn was through its cycle. He shut his eyes and "watched" through the repeater what was going on outside.

Flower and the gooseberry had reached a Mexican standoff. It couldn't hurt her inside the suit; but, slowly and persistently, it was dragging her away from the ship. Her heels tried to dig into the ground; all she accomplished was to send up more gushes of scum.

"Flower, there's a rifle by the lock!"

"I know—I can't reach it!"

"I'm cycling out now—just don't let it pull you in. I can't use the rifle if you're in range!"

If Huw could have shortened the cycle, he would have; he couldn't have cared less if the ship's air contaminated a whole world. But the ship's designers, in their wisdom, had anticipated that reaction. There was nothing he could do but wait— and watch—and curse.

The gooseberry shot up suddenly. Both of Flower's feet dangled futilely, and the gooseberry sailed off, Flower trailing behind him like the tail of a kite.

At least, that was the program. Huw spilled out of the lock just in time to see the gooseberry's flight develop a hitch.

Or rather, a hitch-hiker. Elvar leaped for the tentacle stretched between the gooseberry and Flower. His arms and legs wrapped around it; all his tentacles gripped the thrashing limb. His mouth opened—

Huw gasped. He had never seen Elvar eat anything *big*.

Zondra could have told him that the three segments of Elvar's jaw were only connected by his equivalents of ligaments, that what looked like wrinkles were actually deep, deep folds in his neck and shoulders. All Huw knew was that he saw Elvar's mouth open—and open—and *open*, until the open mouth was bigger than Elvar's entire head.

The gooseberry tried to defend itself, but it had to untangle its whip from Flower to attack Elvar. Seeing that her protégé was threatened, Flower grabbed the lashing tip and held on grimly.

Elvar bit. He had rows of hardened epidermal cell growths instead of teeth, but they were equally as effective. Elvar bit, and bit—and bit through.

In the seconds it took Huw to skim from the lock to the battlefield, Elvar—though keeping a wary eye on the whip which Flower was unwinding from around herself—had happily begun to dine on gooseberry. A disappointing meal, for all its size, Elvar was to discover, since internally the gooseberry was mainly gas.

In the aftermath of relief, Huw was furious. He gave Flower a tongue-lashing that the gooseberry would have envied. She pouted and shrugged, sullenly muttering under her breath such remarks as, "My suit protected me," and "Worry-wart, nothing happened, did it?"

Huw broke off his harangue to salvage some samples of gooseberry for Zondra. With what Flower claimed was a justifiably accusing glare at Huw, Elvar grabbed and ate the whip—all but the last half meter. Huw had never seen him pass up a possible eat before, so he gingerly slid a sample bag around it and sealed it in, stamping "Caution" all over the outside.

As the watches passed, Flower still had only Elvar's off-the-scale mechanical abilities to encourage her, but Zondra soon had a fair knowledge of his physiology.

"Well, he can eat *almost* anything," she reported with a chuckle. "What looks like it might be a nose is just part of that amazing mouth of his. But he can smell, nonetheless. Those dimple-like pits in his cheeks are heat detectors. Around them is a ring of skin stuffed with sensors that react to the various chemicals in the atmosphere around him."

"So—he smells through his skin." Faisal, like them all, had seen weirder.

"And breathes completely through his mouth," added Huw. "And what a mouth!" He shivered, his bland, intelligent face worried. Early Constructs had been inhumanly beautiful, but that had caused too much resentment. Now they were simply humanity improved: flaws edited out, streamlined, superbly intelligent and efficient—and looking, some claimed, as though they had been designed by a sculptor of undoubted talent but without a spark of imagination or creativity. "I'll bet he could eat something as big as he is, without chewing."

"That's necessary," said Zondra. "This world has its or-ganics, formed by space radiation and drifting down, or by planetary heat, especially near the volcanic areas. Call them the "plants," species that can use energy to convert dead material into living matter. But they're all microscopic in size, not enough concentrations of energy to support larger. So most of the "grazers," the species that live directly off the plants, are microscopic, too, or at best filter feeders a few centimeters long. And then there are the animals that feed on the grazers, and the animals that feed on them, and so on. At each stage, there's only about a ten percent efficiency. Each gram of Elvar may mean ten thousand grams of plants at the bottom of the chain. There's lots of organics, but they're spread thin; he's got to be able to take advantage of anything and everything he can get—as long as it doesn't eat him first."

"Does the new vibrator work?" Faisal asked Flower, chang-ing the subject.

"Oh, yes. I'm sure he'll respond, as soon as he realizes I'm trying to communicate."

But after Flower had headed outside, Faisal asked Zondra, "can he really hear with no external ears?"

"Yes, through bone conduction. He can hear. Only—"

"Only what?"

"Flower hasn't made any true contact yet, for all her efforts, and we all agree she knows her specialty." Zondra had finished re-programming her holo-adornment, and she pirouetted, showing herself off to the men, encased in a fantasy all pale blue and cool lemon and silver glitter.

##you look like the inside of a diamond##

##ice and fire—you would wear orange slashed with scarlet bud##

"Well, that atmosphere is a problem." Faisal was thinking that the two had always holo-adorned alike—until Flower had come aboard, a last-minute replacement. "Elvar's sensory equipment is so very different." He remembered his own initial reaction to Constructs, fresh from his provincial, conservative world: sleek as seals, and as unhuman. But it was hard to believe that a Service-bred, Natural or not, could still cling to the attitude he'd long ago outgrown.

"Except for his eyes." Huw had returned his attention to the business at hand. "Why eyes in this darkness, Zondra?"

"Because so many of the animals here are bioluminescent—they generate their own light. And in this darkness, even in this soup of an atmosphere, that light travels."

"That doesn't make sense, either," Huw frowned. "If predator pressure is as bad as you say, why advertise?"

"I can answer that one," Faisal grinned. As long as Flower wasn't overt about her prejudice, there was little he could do. "Because the one instinct stronger than individual survival is race survival. They're 'advertising,' as you so delicately put it, for a mate, hoping to find Mr. Right before Mr. Wrong finds them."

"On the button, you pragmatic engineer, you. I may make a behaviorist out of you yet!"

"Allah forfend!"

"But there may be a better reason why Flower hasn't been able to make contact yet. If that head of his is big only because he's having to interpret a flood of low-level sensory data, if there's nothing there to communicate with . . . It's happened before—a race that looks intelligent, but isn't."

"Hard Luck!" and "Shoonagrin's Planet!" the two men said together.

"I hate to discourage Flower, but I'm afraid that's what she has—"

"I have not!" The indignant voice made the other three turn. Her face was so flushed that the freckles she refused to camouflage disappeared for once.

##that red face against that green hair##

##bud if you say ONE WORD##

"I came in because that *thing* is lurking out there again, and I wanted to try that adapted sonic you were working on, Faisal. And after that," Flower divided her glare impartially among the three veterans, "I want you all to take a little walk with me. You're too shipbound. You depend on those holoandroids too much."

That started an argument which continued outside. None of the veterans wanted to leave the ship unguarded. But they finally gave in to Flower's repeated, "I want to show you, all of you, where I found Elvar. He *is* intelligent. He is, he is."

##i wonder why that thing keeps hanging around## Huw Linked to Zondra, as they trudged along behind Flower and Elvar, whose preferred method of progress was a series of bounding glides that carried him along faster than the humans could manage. The scout did have vehicles, but as Faisal pointed out, they were close to their design limits here. Anywhere they could walk to from the ship, they could walk back.

##probably senses the waste organics we've been dumping and thinks there's a big meal somewhere around##

##if we aren't careful it'll make do with a littler meal—elvar or one of us##

"I thought you had that thing, Faisal," Zondra spoke aloud. "That sonic rifle you came up with is a work of genius."

"Who would have believed a thing that size could move so *fast*!"

"Well, the next time it shows its ugly face—"

##hey zondra how do you know which end is its face anyhow##

##the end that's coming at you of course bonebrain##
##(censored)## "Well, the next time it—what's *that*!"

"It—it looks like a witch's castle," said Zondra slowly.

"The Amethyst City instead of the Emerald City," said Faisal, who had a sneaking fondness for novels about early space exploration.

"That," Flower's voice rang out triumphantly, "is Elvar's *home*."

The entrance was a groined archway, over eight meters high and about six wide. Other openings at higher levels were in exquisite proportion. A gentle rise led into the dark archway.

Huw, atom-for-atom duplicate of a genetic Construct, felt atavistic prickles at the base of his spine. He dug in his heels. "*I'm* not going in there," he announced loudly.

"It's empty," Flower's voice was sad. "Elvar's the last one left."

"Oh, come on," Huw snapped, angry because he was afraid without knowing why. "Don't tell me a shrimpo like Elvar built this!" ##and you're not going in there either zondra##

"Men not much bigger than Elvar built the pyramids on Old Earth," Flower retorted. "And the entrances to the oval ziggurats on Cynthia are less than a meter high."

"They crawled in," Zondra said, interrupting her Linked argument with Huw. Her specialty had enough overlap with Flower's so that she was familiar with some of the more baffling mysteries.

"Nonsense," Flower sneered. "Did they crawl through those thousands of meters of passageways, too?"

"Under the influence of religious fanaticism—"

"Enough," Faisal interrupted calmly. "Argue back at the scout, where we don't have to worry about someone's inductor going out. For now," he tilted his head back, vainly trying to see to the top of the immense structure, "I have to agree with Huw. No telling what's hidden in that thing."

"Our fields protect us," said Flower, tone implying, "You cowards!"

"My dear Flower," Faisal smiled. "We are now touching my

specialty. Our inductors are designed to protect us in a variety
of environments, but they're dangerously close to their limits
here. The pressures alone— Add another factor, something big
enough to swallow you whole and carry you off. A rock,
even . . . "

"Nonsense. I've already been inside a dozen times. Nobody's
left, I tell you."

"Even if Elvar's tribe is gone," Zondra eyed the immense
structure suspiciously, "no telling what else may have decided
to move in and set up housekeeping."

"Looks like the other way round to me," said Huw. "Somebody else—somebody big—lived here and moved out, and
Elvar moved in. And I for one don't want to meet the original
somebody, if he decides to take up residence again."

"If you'll *just* come inside for five minutes," Flower pleaded.
"You'll see. Elvar's people *did* build this, they lived here once,
and they were intelligent. But poor Elvar, all alone, he's gone
feral. And they're all dead, all those lost geniuses. Oh—you—
you—come and see for yourselves!"

Flower suddenly "ran" inside at the top speed the atmosphere and miry surface allowed. Faisal, with a wry shrug at
the other two, followed.

"No use all four of us risking ourselves," his voice came
through the comms.

Huw and Zondra gloomed at each other, then Huw drifted
over to examine one of the columns curiously, while Zondra
sifted through the ever-present ooze.

A few minutes later Faisal appeared in the entrance, saying,
in an odd voice, "You two better come in and see this for
yourselves."

They entered a huge open room. Their lights wouldn't reach
the ceiling. "By the Cosmic Egg," Huw swore.

"Big, eh?" agreed Faisal. "I'd have to use a computer to work
out how to support vaulting this high in this gravity."

"Instinct?" asked Zondra doubtfully.

"Did instinct do this?" Flower was over by a wall. As she

spoke, her light illuminated a statue on a carved plinth. The others gathered around it.

"Wow!" was Huw's verdict.

"A fossil," said Zondra. "A once-living being converted to stone."

"That was my original reaction," said Faisal. "But there are hundreds of the things here, all sizes, from a few centimeters to so tall that all I can see are the legs."

"It's so beautiful," Zondra said softly. The figure was an athlete caught in motion, like the finest Greek statues. Knees bent, weight on balls of feet, arms pumping for balance. Elvar by Praxiteles. The only oddity was that the huge lemuroid eyes were shut.

"They all are," said Faisal. "Look at this one." He held it in his hands, a miniature kneeling Elvar, caught in the act of stuffing something in his mouth, twisting around to see what had disturbed him. The pose was so child-caught-with-his-hand-in-cookie-jar that Huw and Zondra laughed loudly.

"That's adorable!" said Zondra.

"There's more of these, all over," said Faisal. "We're going to have to recommend a full Anthropo survey of this world. Even the walls are relief-carved."

"No paintings, though," mused Huw.

"Without light," Flower snorted. "How would you like to carve in the dark, by touch alone?"

"Could they have had some sort of natural sonar, too?" Zondra wondered.

"What's important is, Elvar's race is *dying!*" Flower flung it at them. "So far we've only found one, Elvar himself."

"Will you look at this one!" Huw's light had caught a kneeling statue, frankly erotic.

"They'll never dare show *that* on New Victoria," Zondra was amused.

"Aren't you listening to me?" Flower's voice cracked. "So far we've only found one."

"Doesn't mean a thing, moon-face," Faisal reassured her.

"We've only scratched the surface of a tiny fraction of this world."

"There may be an entire tribe, only a few kilometers away," Zondra added.

"Or maybe they only come here every so often, for a religious festival or something, and Elvar's just an early bird," finished Huw.

"And maybe there's only one more left, wandering around somewhere, and if we don't find her for Elvar—"

"Suppose," Huw couldn't resist, "we find her and *she* turns out to be a *he?*"

"Ohhhhhh," Flower ran sobbing out. Faisal started after her, but Huw caught his arm.

"Let her grow up a little, Faisal. You can't play baby-sitter the whole cruise."

Faisal hesitated, then nodded.

"Let's take some holos of these," Zondra suggested. "Give her a chance to calm down."

They wandered through immense columned passages, taking an occasional holo, regretting it immediately when they spotted a superior specimen. Faisal was about to suggest collecting Flower and returning to their ship, when her scream echoed in their comms.

They raced with nightmare slowness through labyrinthine passages, cursing.

Flower and Elvar were in the huge entrance room, dodging the giant animal.

"Flower," Zondra screamed, "keep something between it and you. It feeds by sucking its prey in!"

Faisal still had the rifle. He triggered it—and something screeched, a high-pitched keening that vibrated their skulls and made their teeth ache.

Faisal fired again. The animal swooped out through the open arch.

"We'd better stay inside until—" Huw started.

"Elvar!" Flower screamed.

The small biped had bounded out after the giant. Without stopping to think, Flower charged out after him, the other three on her heels, futilely shouting at her to stop.

Outside the slug hung motionless, despite its vast bulk floating about half a meter above the ooze. Now that it was still, they could see more details. A ring of short tentacles or barbels surrounded a triangular maw that had to be a mouth; but if there were eyes, they were hidden in the pendulous rolls of flesh. Elvar bounded toward the thing in great leaps.

"Elvar, *stop*," Flower sobbed.

Elvar jumped straight up into the "air"; at the height of his leap, he exuded a luminous cloud that slowly expanded around where he had been. The animal lunged, the huge "head" passing through the cloud. The three veterans caught up with Flower, forced her back against a wall.

"Assume he knows what he's doing, moon-face," said Faisal.

"You've been saying all along how intelligent he is," panted Huw.

"Shoot it, shoot it, shoot it," moaned Flower, struggling against three-to-one odds.

Again the leap, the cloud, the lunge. Again Elvar was not where the huge head passed.

"Fascinating," murmured Zondra. "I wonder if that defense is instinctive, or has to be taught . . . "

"Ghouls," Flower raged, sobbing and struggling, "he's defending *us*, and you wonder whether or not it's instinctive."

"I don't think you need to worry about Elvar, Flower," Zondra was positive. "I just wish I could get a sample of that gas."

"I—I think you're right," Flower snuffled loudly, her struggles subsiding. "That—that thing's slowing down."

It was. Its movements became slower and slower, until it lay quiescent, the outer folds of flesh pulsing rhythmically.

"It's giving off something, too," Huw gasped. "Look, around it, the fluid's starting to *glow*."

Elvar was bounding around his fallen (or, at least, quiet)

victim like a demented dervish. ##zondra what are you do-ing## She was walking calmly down the ramp, her feet sinking in the ooze.

"Don't worry, I'll be careful. I want to try for a sample of this.

"That thing may not be—" Faisal objected.

"The rest of you keep back. At the first sign of life, yell, and I'll come a-runnin'."

"But Elvar—" Flower whimpered.

"Cheer up, Flower," Zondra was brisk. "For all you know, this is some sort of puberty rite, and now he'll be able to form a harem of female Elvars—"

##LOOK OUT##

Elvar had leaped, knocking Zondra away. She rolled and came to a stop amidst spurts of ooze that floated up and slowly sank. They all watched, frozen in horror, as Elvar, his mouth distended to its fullest, clamped himself onto the giant animal. His hands, tentacles spread wide, sank into the soft flesh; his legs, too, held tight to a ridge of flesh forced up between them.

"Pull him off!" Flower implored.

"No," Zondra was grim. "Wait."

"Please!"

"Wait—and watch."

Elvar's head was rotating, actually burrowing into the trans-lucent flesh, the mouth urged deeper and deeper. His hands were tearing, forcing, excavating . . . .

"Look," said Zondra. *Those pulsations are helping him.*

"Allah protect us," Faisal was awed. "They are!"

"Ohhhhh," from Flower. Her mouth opened and closed; knowledge saddened her eyes. "*Zon*dra," she wailed.

"Yes, dear," Zondra nodded, putting an arm around the younger woman's shoulder. "I'm sorry." Neither of them real-ized it was the first time one of them had voluntarily touched the other.

"Can't we *please*—"

"No." *Very* firm. Her arm tightened around the thin shoul-ders: I offer you comfort, a shoulder to cry on.

Flower drooped under the alien arm, biting her trembling lip, eyes fixed on the grotesque scene.

"Faisal," Zondra said tiredly, "take Flower back to the ship. I want to see the end of this. Don't worry, Huw can stay with me, though I don't think our—ahhhh—large friend will be feeling any too frisky for a while."

"I should think not," Huw gulped as he watched Elvar's head disappear completely within the pallid, doughy flesh. ##she's right—ghoul##

"No, I'll stay." Flower's voice trembled, but she stood proudly erect. As Zondra's hand started to drop away, Flower's hand covered it and pressed fiercely, before dropping hurriedly away, as though embarrassed. "I must. I owe him that, at least."

"Good girl," Zondra patted her shoulder absent-mindedly again, her eyes still fixed on the two aliens.

Elvar's legs let go and he hung limp, his head, shoulders, and arms vaguely visible through the translucent body of the monster. The animal shuddered once and sank to the ground, to lie pulsing very, very slowly.

"You're not just going to leave him like that?" Huw was shocked. "Surely if we all pull together—"

"It would be the worst possible thing we could do," stated Zondra. "I called it a puberty rite—talk about sad truth spoken in jest!"

Flower nodded slowly, her face glistening with tears.

"What do you mean?" Huw was getting angry.

"It's simple, really. I—no, let's get back to the ship and relax. Then I can explain—"

"Explain what? Plasma you to ions, Zondra. *Tell* me!"

"At the ship, when we've all had some nutri and kaffen. I think we'd better leave our—friends alone, for now. Let me just place a Tag—" The specimen collectors, jars, nets, Tag-gun were all attached after the inductor field was activated and so were outside it. Zondra moved close to the large animal and injected a glowing Tag into it with practiced skill.

"I still say we ought to haul him *off*," Huw growled.

"Don't compute until you have all the necessary data, dear."
And for the first time, to his dismay, she shut him out.

All the way back to the ship, and during the programming
and even the consuming of a simple meal, she remained closed
to him. The women only picked at their food, but Faisal (to
Huw's fury and grudging admiration) not only made a hearty
meal but also managed to sip his kaffen even more slowly than
Zondra.

"Now," said Huw. "Explain!"

Flower ran her finger around the rim of the cup of kaffen
she'd poured for herself and then left undrunk until it had
cooled. "The ironic thing," she said, "was that I *wanted* it to be a
walkabout. I wanted—and it was. Oh, it *was!*"

"I'm going to program your computer to give nothing but
Gilbert and Sullivan mixed with *Beowulf*," growled Huw. "Jargon, jargon, jargon. What's a walkabout, why did you want it
to be a walkabout, and why are you so so upset because it was?"

"A walkabout," Flower explained, staring down at her
fingers nervously twisting together, "is common in primitive
tribes, in various versions. The immature—usually, but not
always, only the male—has to prove himself by surviving on
his own for some fixed period."

"I see. That would explain why Elvar was alone."

"Right. Sometimes the candidate spends his time meditat-
ing, waiting for a vision to show him his totem animal. Sometimes he has to kill his clan animal, to prove his manhood.
Afterwards, he becomes a full member of the tribe, or at least is
considered adult, and he can get m—m—married." Flower
covered her face with her hands.

Zondra gathered her in, and Flower wept against the no-
longer-alien shoulders. "Easy, dear, easy. It was his destiny, all
along."

"What," Huw's voice was dangerously calm, "was his destiny all along?"

##zondra (censored!!)##

"To get married."

"You mean, if he survives that whatever-it-is out there, he can get married?"

"He's married now."

Flower looked up, with a weak smile. "You'd better say it, Zondra. The men are about ready to strangle you."

"All right. He *is* married, *because what we've been calling the slug is the female of Elvar's race.*"

Huw bit down on his mug so hard he actually dented it, and Faisal's mouth dropped open. Luckily, he caught the crystal mouthpiece of the hookah he'd been smoking before it shattered on the floor.

Faisal recovered first. "Evidence, Zondra."

"Intuition, mostly. Educated guess. I couldn't get close enough for a total Scan, but what I did get of her internal organs was similar to Elvar's. I can name you a hundred species where the larval form bears no similarity, inside or out, to the adult. The only way to know for sure is to raise the animal, and watch it, to see if it changes as it grows."

"You mean," Huw was almost stunned speechless, "Elvar is going to grow up to look like that—that *thing?*"

"Don't anthropomorphize. I think—I think he's as big as he's going to get."

"Allah preserve us!"

"You've got it. Sexual dimorphism isn't that uncommon, especially where there's a reason, like scarcity of food. The female is useful to the species, as long as she keeps producing eggs. And the more she can produce, the better the chances for race survival. The male, on the other hand. . . . I liked Elvar, too. But at least this is better than being eaten afterwards. With some species, the female only needs to be fertilized once, after which the male becomes . . . superfluous. Elvar's species have taken another route. They live scattered because food is hard to come by. But when the female's fertile, there he is, the male, ready to fertilize her—because he's part of her. As long as they both do live."

"That's—incredible."

"No more than burning a widow on her husband's funeral pyre, I'd say. Elvar's life expectancy, as a parasite on his wife, is probably a lot better than his chances on his own. And he's helping to perpetuate his species, to boot."

"You're—sure?" From Faisal.

Zondra shrugged. "Pretty sure. Nature repeats herself, after all. I've seen that pattern before. I just took a while to recognize it. Elvar did seem—well—human, to me."

"Don't anthropomorphize," said Flower dryly.

"But who," Faisal had decided the hookah wasn't damaged, after all, "carved the statues?"

"Elvar's wife, I imagine, and her ancestors. That's *her* home we were in, not his. Though she'd probably spread enough sex pheromones—organic chemicals—around so that he was attracted."

"That's why he was there, waiting for her to come back," said Flower.

"Fair's fair. She waited long enough for him, didn't she? And while she waited, she—amused herself, by carving those statues. How, I don't know. But—they were all male." ##oh bud can you imagine—the loneliness##

##i'm here—i'm always here##

##i know—but all the poor onlies in the universe##

As though she had somehow caught the Linkage, Flower shivered. "She—she's so alien. Do you think we'll ever be truly able to contact such an alien mind?"

"That, Flower, is up to you."

"Oh!" Almost visibly, Flower gathered herself together. "I— I'll *try*." Her back straightened. "I'll do my best—with—" she looked around at the others, and her hand slid into Zondra's, "—your help."

Behind her back, Huw, smiling broadly, shook both hands over his head in jubilant triumph. Faisal nodded, grinning. The crew of the scout had finally shaken down and was ready to tackle its newest problem.

GEORGE FLORANCE GUTHRIDGE
TAKEN ON FAITH

The Thiosans came out of the desert city, hurrying toward us by the hundreds. Their shoulders were hunched, heads down, faces dark within the hoods of their gray robes. Some fell in the ankle-deep dust, were quickly helped to their feet. Carsen and I stood on the shuttlecraft's gangway. His face was pale but hard. My heart pounded. Our laser-rifle squad, crouching in shallow pits hastily dug on each side of the gangway, shifted nervously.

The horde crested the rise and kept coming. A terrible odor, a smell like rancid meat, reached us. Carsen frowned down at me—like many people of Oriental ancestry I am rather short—then, grimacing against the stench, he again faced the natives.

Despite the stench, they were possibly hominids; perhaps human. Or so data from our unmanned probes had suggested. Their civilization was agrarian, a single inhabited valley on a planet ninety-nine percent cold desert. Their city sprawled beneath barren, protective peaks; the serpentine rows of earthen huts along the sides of the valley reminded me of unaligned molars. Slanting dustdrifts lined the streets. Such was the world to which we had come to establish diplomatic relations—at any cost.

Thirty meters from the shuttle the Thiosans formed a ragged semicircle. The tallest were just over two meters. All had blocky shoulders, gangly arms. Their faces—what I could see of their faces—looked angular, chiseled. Their gray robes billowed in the wind. Somewhere in the crowd a baby began to squall, a strange, gasping cry. Carsen and I moved to the end of the ribbed gangway. An ex-Army officer turned diplomat, he was tall and broad-shouldered, and had one of those charismatic smiles that makes you want to listen.

He pulled himself up to his full height and let his gaze roam the crowd. The Thiosans hushed. Some jockeyed for a better view. He opened a narrow box. Within its silk lining gleamed a medallion inscribed with a tiny relief-map of Earth. The only thing I held was my heart, in my throat. But I was now more excited than frightened. It was for this I had given up a lucrative Midwestern healing practice. Like the rest of the delegation and crew, I had had my left lung replaced with a combined subsystem breather and air purifier, and a vocalizer had been installed in my larynx. The second thoughts that had plagued me, the pain I had suffered from the operations—all suddenly seemed worth the effort.

Eight Thiosans pushed through the crowd—two men and six women, if size were indicative of sex, or if gender was even a consideration. They huddled. Their murmuring was slow-voiced, words seemingly chosen with care. I hoped the shuttle's computer-mic, turned up full, was picking up the whispers. The sooner we deciphered the language, the sooner the information could be fed into our vocalizers.

One of the larger individuals stepped apart from the crowd. Sunlight crossed his face. A dark, piercing eye surveyed us. The nose seemed sculpted from granite. Moving his head instead of just his eyes, he gazed the length of the shuttle. Something knotted in the hollow of my stomach.

The left side of his face was a purplish ooze.

Then he pointed toward the sky. His hand, composed of a thumb and two stubby fingers, was matted with black hair. The others looked up. I opened my mouth to speak, but Carsen gripped my arm, his smile never wavering. We were to allow the Thiosans the first move.

The Thiosan's arm dropped. His shoulders slumped. He

mumbled to his comrades. More pointing. Then he turned and trudged away, the crowd parting. He was wearing some sort of clogs; they slapped his feet as he walked. He moved off down the rise, toward the city, his head bowed. The other seven plodded after him. Then the crowd left too. Few looked back.

The wind was cold against my cheek. Old pains in my chest and throat suddenly returned.

Morning came cruelly. I awoke with a headache; I never could sleep well sitting up. Dust drummed against the shuttle. I staggered outside, tired and ill-tempered. I still felt sluggish from the months of suspended animation, and I was frustrated over the Thiosans' reaction. All we could do was wait, and watch. And hope the Thiosans would return.

Carsen and some of the crew members were standing close to the craft. Dust swirled off the mountains like brown snow-mists. The sun, a red giant, was a hazy bulge beyond the peaks. Shielding my eyes with my arm, I squinted into the storm. The city looked empty.

I remembered other cities: sleek aircars, sumptuous hotels, elegant women and midnight dinners, lovely desserts served in oval beds. Such amenities had been commonplace during my years as a healer, but gradually they had become no more important than colorful dying leaves scattering before a Kansas wind. I was making money, but effecting few cures. It had become an empty life. My return to school had meant my leaving the secure, respectable healings of the Midwest, with its easy money and easy living. Audiences had been astute, interested, respectful—and, for all practical purposes, incapable of being cured. Having come to accept healing as a natural phenomenon involving a sudden transference of energy, they had lost their faith-produced receptivity. I was a well-paid anachronism.

Now I wondered if my decision to become a xenologist had just been chic romanticism. I felt drained and depressed.

Goggled, Carsen came over. "I tell you, Jonathan-Lin, it's damn frustrating the way this diplomacy business keeps my hands tied. I think we should march into that city and intro-duce ourselves a little more forcefully." He had to shout in my ear to be heard above the wind. "What do you think?"

"I'm supposed to assess people, remember? Not situations."

"What?" He cupped his hand behind his ear.

I waved him off and started up the gangway. I was just entering when the sky glimmered with silver. We watched two more shuttles land, and I breathed a little easier, knowing I'd be busy and a possible confrontation with the Thiosans would be delayed.

We spent the afternoon unloading the housing floaters, huge dirigible-like trailers. Tying and securing these down in the wind was a major operation, but the prospect of a semiperma-nent home, away from the cramped quarters of the shuttle, lifted our spirits, and we worked diligently.

I was just raising a mallet above a stake, while Carsen, supervising, had walked back to check on the progress of the other crews, when suddenly he sprang forward as though knocked down by an explosion. Dazed, he lay looking over his shoulder, dust spraying upward in a cape of dirt where he had been standing. The crew member who had been holding the stake for me looked up, white-faced. I rose, stunned, gazing at Carsen.

The cape whirled into a dust devil two meters high. Carsen's arms were raised to protect himself against the spinning dirt. Then he saw me and started yelling, his face contorted. The wind swept away his words. He staggered toward me, more crawling than running. I went to help, the dust beating against my hands and face. Carsen gripped my shoulders. His face and goggles were a brown mask. "Something . . . under my feet!" he screamed.

I squinted into the dust devil. Then suddenly, as though collapsing from within, the swirl ceased. Dirt downdrifted. The wind died so abruptly that the labor of my breathing sounded thunderous. Then my breath caught in my throat.

In the dirt was a tiny head.

A statuette, I realized. The features were squarish, roughly carved. Its eyes opened. They were globular and blind, like those of fish in a cave, as if the world offered nothing worth observing. My blood chilled.

"Oh, my god," I heard a crew-woman say. We stood in stunned silence. The eyes shut. The wind came up again.

I looked at Carsen. His face was drawn, creased with dirt. He put an arm across my shoulders. We watched as the wind gradually exposed the enigmatic figure.

That night, Carsen Montgomery Brusso—Northamerica's ambassador to the Global Council—made an emergency flight to Mother. With him, encased in an antiseptic, bomb-proof box, went the first artifact humankind had removed from the planet Thios.

A week passed uneventfully. Carsen remained aboard Mother. The rest of us continued setting up the base, watching the Thiosian city through scanners and scopes. A feeling of equilibrium seemed to have returned to Thios: the people neither excited by our presence nor attempting to remain unseen. Sometimes we watched Thiosans shovel dust from the streets; they used back pouches to haul it to the edge of the city, where huge dust piles reigned. Usually they simply dug paths.

The crew welcomed the repose. Terran receptor ships had so far encountered two alien species besides the Thiosans, and the crew was relieved not to be faced with situations similar to those of the two other expeditions—either pressed to observe the billion details of protocol demanded by the lizard-like Belanese; or pressed into a fight, as with the Demurai, those cluster-eyed halfmen who inhabited asteroid ships. The Demurai threat was why our mission on Thios was so important. A base here could be militarily significant, and the Thiosian culture might be a link to a more extensive civilization.

It was an anxious week for me. I was eager to begin my anthropological studies, and the stretch of desert between our base and the city seemed wider each day.

Carsen finally arrived back one afternoon. There seemed a new purposefulness to his stride, a look of urgency in his eyes, as he moved about the base, peering toward the Thiosian city and taking notes. "Dinner tonight in my floater, then we'll talk business," he told me, scarcely looking up from the clipboard he was holding. "Twenty-one hundred hours. Be on time."

That night we had soysteak and an alcoholic drink made of fermented milk and tasting slightly peptic. "It's called *sumash*," Carsen said. "The Thiosans brew it."

My pulse jumped. "But how . . .?"

"The laser squad was ordered to gather information."

"That's my department," I said coldly.

Carsen leaned over the table, his eyes tight and hard. "If you think that on this mission you're going to play the dispassionate observer, you are sadly mistaken. You will be in the midst of things sooner than you realize. And deeper than you ever expected."

"So fill me in."

He released a slow breath. "The statuette we found—that found us, to be more precise—was not simply a piece of artwork. It's known as a *Riomina*—a Thiosian bible, you might say. The one we've got was apparently some sort of sentry. Our presence triggered it. Its message, if you can call it that—verses that seem to be some kind of prayer—is emitted as vibrations. The vibrations caused the dust devil we saw. Anyway, we hooked up the thing to Mother's computer and spent several days getting what information we could out of it.

"The planet seems to have been settled about three thousand years ago by eight families who were either colonists, or exiles, or simply voyagers who crash-landed—we couldn't tell which," he went on. "Life was pretty grim—this place obviously isn't a paradise—but over the centuries the Thiosans did develop a certain degree of sophisticated technology, and the population began to increase. Then, about a millenium ago, two events coincided that changed their history. A messiah named Dahka appeared, and about that same time a plague started ravaging the populace."

He gazed at me steadily. "It's a dreadful disease, and it hasn't stopped. Think of it, Jonathan-Lin! A thousand years! They call it *Benziis*. Usually only the very young and the very old are afflicted. But the majority suffer it sometime, and few survive." He was silent for a moment. "I see," I said softly.

"No. You don't—yet." He sat back, clasped his hands. "Most of them die horribly, racked with pain, sweating and freezing with fever. Hideous purplish splotches decay their flesh—we saw it that first day, remember?" He paused. "According to Mother's analysis, the Thiosans are physiologically different enough from us that we can't contract the disease. And those computers better be right; so far our antibiotics appear ineffectual against it."

I banged down my glass. "No statuette's verses could have supplied data about physiology!"

"There were details we had to find out. The laser squad was told to gather information. No one delineated how. They found a volunteer."

"I am *not* going to condone that kind of savagery!" I went into the mainroom, stood looking out the floater's window toward the city. "And don't give me some bull about the ends justifying the means because of the Demurai."

For a long time he didn't answer. Then, "The Thiosans used to pray to this Dahka to eradicate the disease. Now they pray only for the pain to lessen. They believe he caused it somehow, and that someday he'll arise from the dead to take it away. That's apparently why they were so passive after we landed . . . and why they don't seem to make any great effort to keep the dust removed from their streets. Our ships came from the sky—but not from their heaven. Their heaven's in the dust, where Dahka's buried. Dahka, God of Dust."

His voice took on an oddly hollow sound. "Command wants you to try healing the Thiosans," he said finally.

I turned to face him, thunderstruck. "*What?* You're crazy!"

"Perhaps."

"Even if I could cure some of them, I wouldn't attempt it. Maybe you've forgotten—I'm trained not to interfere. Besides, when I returned to school I swore to myself that my career as a healer was over and done with."

"You're damned naive to think you were chosen for this flight only because of your Ph.D. in xenology. That's not exactly an unpopular field, you know."

"I'm well aware," I said angrily. But I was lying. It had been obvious that Command had chosen me because of the totality of my background, yet I now realized I had never accepted the ramifications of that fact. "I am a delegate, not a member of the crew. I do not have to obey Command's orders."

There was a silence. Then he crossed toward me, stopped suddenly, and with a sigh sat down on the sofa. "If you could have seen the Thiosan the laser squad brought in . . . ."

"So their methods got to you?"

Carsen's face flushed. "Yes, there was pain—but not torture. I watched the whole thing on the video. I agree it isn't pleasant having a couple of electrodes inserted in your skull. But that is very little compared to the pain that man had obviously been experiencing all his life." He broke off. "You think I'm an opportunist, a manipulator, but you're wrong. It's true, when I learned of the disease, that I wanted the cure merely because of what that could accomplish for our mission. But it was a horrifying thing to see the terror that man has been living with all these years. Now . . . now I also want to see an end to that kind of pain."

I was beginning to feel the weight of an overwhelming burden. "But—the population of an entire planet!"

"You've got to try," he said.

The next day I became the first Terran to live outside the base perimeter. Carsen believed that the fewer associations I had with other humans, the better my chances were of being accepted by the Thiosans. We hauled my small floater to the far side of the city, within the shadow of the tallest peak, and for the following week I rested and meditated and memorized, gathering my strength and presence of mind for the task ahead. But whenever I gazed across the valley at those stark, random houses hunkering beneath the vast sky, I felt like weeping. The odds against success were impossibly high. To heal a few

Thiosans might be possible—but to save an entire world! So when Carsen brought down his hopper one evening, dust spewing and the floater straining against the force, I met him with a growing feeling of diffidence and despair.

"We've found a woman who's agreed to see you," he yelled, without cutting the engine. "The disease is in its final stages." Carsen was shouting at the top of his lungs. "She could last another year or so, maybe."

Hunched against the wind, hands in pockets, I frowned at his callousness. "She's not too far gone, is she?"

His face strained in his effort to hear. "Oh. No. Hell, I don't know. You take a look."

I waved in acknowledgment, went inside the floater and changed into a thermalsuit. The winds were growing colder each day, and though I disliked the suit, Carsen's hopper was one of the XM-p models Command had hurriedly developed during the early stages of the Demurai war. No heating system. Soldiers, apparently, are supposed to have skin like walruses.

The sun shone reddish-gold on the hopper's finlike wings as we flew toward Traage. Beyond the city and the base, the wastelands were a spiritless, endless expanse of desert festered with balebrush.

Traage, one of the Thiosian city's eight districts, was almost a city in itself. Though a single, twisting street might separate one Thiosian district from another, the members of each district generally considered themselves distinct—or so the continuing biological and psychological investigations of the laser squad's "volunteer" had informed us. Each district's members were thus similar to a large, extended family. The situation naturally created economic problems: although farming had been evenly divided among the socialistic Thiosans, the quality of that land hadn't been. Traage had fared the worst.

Which was probably why Carsen had chosen it. Matters might go badly if I were unsuccessful in my efforts, but maybe slightly less so than if I failed in one of the the "wealthier" districts.

We decelerated. The hopper hovered, then came down onto

one of the broader streets. Dust clouded the windshield. Bare-foot children, the hoods of their robes thrown back, watched us climb from the machine. Barely curious, their eyes looked vapid, death-conscious.

We stopped by a door in a windowless alley wall. Carsen knocked. No answer. The icy wind slapped our faces, took our breath away. He knocked again, then doubled his fist and pounded. I waited nervously, trying to put from my mind that Carsen and Mother's computers could be wrong and, touching a plague victim, I might end up as a victim myself. Back on Earth I had handled patients with a variety of illnesses, but never, as I could recall, someone whose disease might be both contagious and deadly. I now knew how physicians must have felt who had battled yellow fever or smallpox before cures had been developed. Occupational hazard. I gritted my teeth and stared toward the door.

A latch clicked, the door was pulled open a few inches. A drawn, haggard face appeared. The woman seemed middle-aged, straight auburn hair hanging down the sides of her face, within her hood. "Oh. It's you. And you brought the man you told my mother about." Her words, translated in my mind by the vocalizer, seemed out of synch with her lips. Her eyes slit toward me. "Come in."

We squeezed through the doorspace she allowed us, and were instantly blinded by sooty darkness. There was a grating sound, like metal rasping against stone. A guttering flame came alive in a bowl of yellow liquid on a table. In the dimness the woman's face seemed even more angular than before.

"This is Tas," Carsen said to me. I nodded hello, but she ignored me.

"You know where to find her," she told Carsen. She plopped down on a hardwood bench, lit a Terran cigarette in the flame, and handed the candle-bowl to Carsen. Watching her, I felt ashamed, suddenly, as though we were exploiting her.

Then Carsen and I turned and groped our way down a floorless, dust-filled hall past several arched wooden doors. "Yes?" a thin voice asked. We came back one door, entered. Dim sunlight was slanting through a half-closed window; Carsen snuffed the candle. A woman was lying on a pallet in the corner. The air reeked of plague. Just beyond her stood a meter-high statue, a figure similar to the one we had found and taken aboard Mother, except the eyes were not slit horizontally. I sensed they would not open.

I knelt beside the woman, taking her hands in mine. Her eyes registered fear, but she did not resist. "Please, trust me," I said. Her hair hung in loose white strands; her mouth was stained with coughed-up blood. "I am the servant of Dahka," I told her, carefully articulating each word, my voice tinny as the vocalizer made its instant translations. "He has sent me to help you." Her tongue worked spastically; her breathing was irregular. Her eyes were glassy and sunken, as though screwed down into her skull, and the flesh beneath them was loose and blackish.

I hesitated, then touched her throat. Her Adam's apple bobbed. She began breathing in short harsh puffs, and though she did not jerk back, she watched me fearfully, her eyes rolled down unnaturally. At last the eyes closed, and I could sense her trying to steady herself. Her face relaxed, then her hands lifted, fell back, again lifted. Fingers as thin as a skeleton's curled in hope around my wrists. A feeling of sureness impinged upon my unease.

"Dahka says you are to be healed and to live," I whispered. Slowly she nodded. My hands went to her temples; power rose within me. I prayed, "Dahka come into me. Dahka help me." My blood began to warm. My muscles tightened. I pressed the woman's temples gently, and began moaning the first canto of the *Riomina*.

> "*Keep me, O Dahka,*
> *in your spirit sense until I*
> *return to your dust. For if I*
> *stand alone on the freezing desert,*
> *I shall be no taller than myself,*
> *and the winds will frost my soul.*"

I felt my power alive within me for the first time in years. I half-closed my eyes, exulting in the single-mindedness and pleasure the sense of rising power always brought. It was that bodily power, more than the curing, certainly more than the money, that had given me the most satisfaction back on Earth—and also the most frustration, for there I had experienced my power without being able to put it to effective use.

The woman became a blur, and though aware of her breathing and of the rancid-melon stench of her diseased flesh, I concentrated only on the poetry. I had known the verses less than a week, yet felt a reverence toward them. The long hallucinatory hours I had spent practicing cantos in front of the mirror in my floater had been more inspiring than exhausting.

The verses gripped me as they had then. I was forced out of the impersonal monotone I knew I should maintain and into tonal interpretation. I hoped the woman would not be offended. But if she did respond to my slightly altered delivery, it might ease the transference of her receptiveness from the cantos to myself.

I lost my fear and repulsion of the disease. I gave myself over to the verses, reveling in the words until the room seemed apulse with language. Suddenly, more than anything I had ever wanted—more than the money I had consoled myself with during my healing years, more than the xenology degree I had thought would vault me into higher ideals—I wanted to cure this old woman. Not for her or for Carsen or for the mission did I want it. For myself.

As I was nearing the end of the eighth and last canto, the woman's receptivity seemed strong—but not intense. I would need more time, greater power! My concentration tightened. I *willed* forth my power. The muscles constricted in my throat, and my heart pounded. I felt as though I were trying to will an orgasm.

At last, at last, I felt my body tide over into power. My hands were hot. My blood surged. Too late? The last verse slipped through my lips. Desperately I pressed the woman's temples very, very hard. Commanding the disease to quit her flesh, I suddenly released her.

Her eyes snapped open. She weakly smiled. Then she grimaced, stiffening. Her hands dropped to her sides. Her breathing became little choking sounds and suddenly stopped altogether. Carsen, eyes wide with fright, stooped beside her, ready to administer mouth-to-mouth.

I stopped him. I would wait a moment more. Just one more instant before giving up hope. I held my breath, my pulse racing.

Her body spasmed. She moved onto her side, toward the window. She coughed.

"The sun is up today," she said, turning back to me.

I sighed with relief and smiled. "Yes."

The disease had parched her lips into deep bleeding cuts, yet her face was radiant. Her gaze darted toward the door. Tas was clutching the doorframe, her eyes cold. Trembling, the old woman reached out. Tas's eyes widened in disbelief; her mouth opened; her chin began to quiver.

I helped the old woman to a sitting position. She tried to speak to Tas, but was overcome with emotion. Tas swallowed back tears. Arms extended, she moved as though entranced across the room. "Mother?" she said, her voice quaking. She knelt, touched her mother's lips.

"Do you remember," the old woman whispered, "how before I was stricken you and I used to drive the wymeres in from the fields? We shall do it again, my daughter. Soon."

Tas secured a rag and toweled the old woman's skin, then we examined her. Her fine, thick body hair was sticky and bristly, but pus no longer oozed from the sores. I concentrated, reading her emotions as I worked. Her lack of pain was not a delusion. She truly had been freed from *Benziis*. In time, her skin would once again be dry and healthy.

Seated beside us, Tas watched closely. With her hands in her lap and her knees tucked under her, she seemed more like a teenaged girl than the hardened woman of an hour ago.

The old woman muttered something about "candles," and closing wrinkled eyelids, fell asleep. Tas looked at Carsen and me with quiet, expressive eyes. She took Carsen's hands and pressed her forehead to his fingertips. Then, taking my hand, she rose and began to guide me toward the door. I glanced at Carsen. He shrugged—and smiled. "Custom," he said, adding, "There is no harm."

Tas led me to the door at the end of the hall. Hinges squeaked, and I gazed into a room filled with statues set into shallow hillocks of dust. These statutes were also slender and meter-high, the arms to the sides and the eyes emptily fish-like, but the figures were of children.

"My brothers and sisters," Tas explained. "Only I lived past adolescence." A network of paths crisscrossed between the graves.

Tas walked to the far wall and drew back a tapestry depicting the Thiosian wastelands—the unyielding desert beneath the reddish sun. Set waist-high into the wall was a bedchamber, an alcove with a row of unlit candles at the head of the pallet.

"This was Mother's bed until she became ill," Tas said. "She wanted to die in the same room where Father is buried." Then she said matter-of-factly, "We'll sleep together here."

I stared, incredulous, as she calmly pulled her robe off over her head. She was wearing only a thin gray waistskirt. She shook her hair. I gazed upon her Thiosian body, then looked away. The physical differences were too great for me. She had turned and was climbing into the bedchamber when I left the room.

The interior of the duraplastic tent Carsen had had erected was hazy with dust. My eyes stung. My throat was raw. Gripping the pulpit of stacked shipping crates, I had been chanting for nearly an hour, without success. A week had passed since I had healed the old woman. How I had let Carsen talk me into a group session, I didn't know. It was a hostile group. Arms folded, the Thiosans huddled on the makeshift benches below me, their heads darkly cowled. Carsen had pledged Tas to secrecy about our triumph. Then, working through her, he had promised to return the *Riomina* statuette if the Thiosans came to the tent. Over a hundred showed.

Struggling not to miss a verse, I left the pulpit at last and moved to the front of the platform. The Thiosans still did not

look up. Yet I had to get through to them! They had to respond
to the verses! For if I failed to raise their energy levels, I could
not begin to cure them.

I started down the platform's three shallow stairs. The night
wind was whistling outside the tent, and the top of the tent was
sucking in and out with such force I could hardly hear myself.
The draft from the side doors pierced me. Though shivering in
my gray robe from cold and frustration, I remained as rigid as
possible while I chanted, my fingers and forearms out-
stretched, my elbows tight against my sides. Inwardly I swore
that Carsen would either get some heat in here, or next time I'd
climb into that cumbersome thermalsuit. If there was a next
time.

I stepped down the last stair and into the dirt. Dust flurried.
A large Thiosan in the front row nodded solemnly, not in quiet
derision but in reverent appreciation. Others followed his example.

Suddenly I understood. Of course! How stupid of me.

Dahka. God of Dust.

I could have kicked myself. I was alien enough to them—but
to be preaching the holy verses without demonstrating a basic
understanding of the words' meanings!

I knelt to scoop up fistfuls of dust. Then, arms fully extended, dust trickling from my hands, I moved down the aisle
and toward the Thiosans. Faces began to emerge from hoods.
The cheekbones were stark; the lips, deep brown and full, were
badly chapped. The eyes—only moments earlier dull and in-
sensate—gleamed with anticipation.

A slight response, but enough. I moved to the front row and
knelt before a girl I had spotted earlier in the service. Large and
heavy-boned by Thiosian standards, she nevertheless possessed a certain fragility; even within the formless robe she
appeared vulnerable.

Startled, lips parting, she jerked back.

I scooped up more dust and raised my fists to just below her
chin. Her eyelashes beat and settled. For a long, agonized
moment we remained in that tableau: me, kneeling, quietly
chanting the *Riomina*, arms extended and becoming heavy; she,

immobile but not rigid, statuesque but not stonelike. Then her face softened, her lips quivered. Looking at me with damp eyes, she began to recite after me, her voice low and hoarse:

"Along the road without end,
through the pain we all share,
your icon will touch me, O Dahka,
and I shall be reborn into dust."

Deeply I stared into her eyes, opening my mind to her, opening my mind to the poetry. I now recognized what earlier I had only intuited. Repressed yet glowing in her dark sunken eyes was an innocence struggling to live, a receptiveness such as I had never encountered on Earth.

My emotions quickened, caught fire. The verses seemed to ignite into flames. Slowly at first, then with increasing intensity, finally in a thoughtless abandon I couldn't control even if I had wanted to, I felt myself being released from selfhood. Energy surged through me. My flesh seemed afire. Suddenly the girl and the words became one. The audience and the tent fell away from me, blazing into a pinwheel of spinning color, as I found myself sliding down the rainbow of verses and into her soul.

She reached out. Her hands, thick and matted with silken auburn hair, appeared strangely beautiful. The dust poured from my fists as of its own accord. "Dahka," she whispered, eyes shining with tears. Her head tilted slowly down. She stared at her hands. "Dahka."

The last bit of verse issued through my lips.

"On the final day of wind,
when the dawn learns that Thios
has returned to dust, no one
need record the passing of Time."

My mouth was open. Consciously I closed it. I became aware of the dust in my throat, of the stiff ache in my knees, of the

Thiosans leaning forward on the benches, heads cocked, their faces gleaming and dark.

I touched the girl's shoulders. She continued staring at her hands, her breathing raspy. Her shoulders felt taut, muscular. The stench of her disease invaded my nostrils; I was repulsed by the smell, but my heart went out to her, and my hands eased along the serge robe, up her neck. Her muscles tightened. I gripped the hood; she shivered and looked up, her eyes darting from side to side. No longer were there sacred verses to bind Thiosan to Terran. If only she would remain receptive long enough for me to touch her temples.

I pulled back the hood.

"*No!*"

Lurching away, she covered her head with her hands. Her hair was a mass of oozing, purplish-black oil.

I swallowed thickly to keep from retching. Again I reached for her, my heart slamming against my chest. Suddenly a second hand—large, powerful—settled and tightened on the girl's shoulder. I peered up. The man next to her was scowling, eyes puckered, lips tight. His hair, cut in bangs, made him appear both boyish and ferocious.

My head was pounding, pounding. I lowered my hands and looked down the aisle at the shadows sweeping across the back wall. Then I was conscious of the girl's sobbing. The man, apparently her father, tucked his arm around her shoulders and put his cheek against her hair. His face hovered above me like a dark cloud.

Anxiously I again peered toward the back, but there were only the shadows. Uncertain what to do, I bowed my head to the dust, feigning prayer. Carsen was with the hopper, hidden nearly three hundred meters away. The only other human help was the crew, at a distance of several kilometers.

Then a stooped, tottering old woman came shuffling up the aisle. She would take two or three faltering steps, catch herself on someone's shoulder, again stagger forward. She thus moved from row to row, her bandaged feet leaving broad tracks in the dust.

Without rising I took hold of her wrists. She struggled to her knees, her back to the audience. We faced one another. Her breathing, harsh and heavy, made her face wrinkle and ease.

I glanced away momentarily at the girl, who watched me intently. Her eyes were full of tenderness, full of humiliation; the Thiosans, as with people in most cultures, seemed shamed by disease. The girl's father settled back, his face bland. He watched the old woman with that abstract curiosity I had witnessed and loathed in the audiences back home.

"Help me," the old woman said, bringing my gaze back to her. The words sounded mechanical. Her back rose and fell as she struggled for breath. "Help me."

Then she smiled, toothlessly, the crows' feet accenting her wrinkling eyes. I returned her smile with a cold look, and the smile vanished. I lifted back her hood. She put her hands and her forehead into the dust, apparently intensely praying. I cupped her chin, lifted her head. Her eyes were closed, and it occurred to me she really was praying. The old woman's piety made me self-conscious.

My fingers found her temples. Her hair, a filthy gray snarl pulled back across squarish ears, felt coarse, gritty.

No power ached in my fingers. I felt unclean, touching her, hypocritical and ashamed.

Not that it mattered. My face was furrowed with pretended emotion; the muscles bulged in my forearms. I pressed the side of her head.

She blinked up piteously and seemed to look at me from the very fronts of her eyes. I was hurting her. I tried not to, but she angered me.

I pressed again, then released her. Her shoulders, rigid before, sagged. Her eyes rolled back; for a moment only the whites showed. She fell forward, catching herself with her hands. She remained that way, in a half-faint on her hands and knees, and I felt my heart stop. No telling what the Thiosans might do if she passed out.

Say it, I thought, the words raging in my mind. *Get up, woman. Don't spoil things now. Don't let your people down!*

She lifted her weary head, then sat back, finally managed to get up on one knee. She wavered, and for an instant I thought she would again topple into the dust. But somehow she remained in imbalance, as though leaning against a wall of solid air. Then, pulling up her robe, she began to unwrap the dirty bandages from her feet and legs. "Take the rags off," she mumbled, her skinny, hairy fingers working furiously. "Take them off."

She tossed the first bandage aside, shifted position, and began fumbling with the other. The crowd's murmuring became a noisy buzz. Stooped, she smiled through chapped lips while she finished the second bandage. Then she rose and, lifting the bandage at arm's length like a snake, made her way back and forth before the amazed audience, her purplish legs no longer painful. The Thiosans rose, their flat auburn heads nodding and bobbing.

"His hands speak," she said, "for Dahka." Though her voice was huskily straining, to me the words sounded terribly hollow.

The girl's father was frowning. He took the bandage from the old woman and turned it over carefully. His eyes were darkly expansive, unreadable. Holding my breath, I imagined myself having to sprint through the dust out to Carsen's hopper, the Thiosans clutching the hopper's runners as the machine struggled to lift off toward the Terran base. Where I would be safe. Where I could forget.

I hated using the old woman, hated giving into Carsen's idea about having a standby, "just in case." But then, I *had* cured the old woman once.

Finally the Thiosan handed back the bandage. He lowered himself to the bench, his brows thoughtfully knit. Apparently he was satisfied the purplish gel I had smeared on the bandages was the real thing.

The old woman bowed before me, took hold of my wrists, touched my fingertips with her forehead. Her eyes were closed. Her murmured, "Thank you," was sincere. As she walked toward the door, I understood why she had consented to the deception. It was not merely repayment for my having cured her. She believed it was protocol.

I felt an odd mixture of sentiment and shame as she pushed the door open with her shoulder. The tent heaved and bulged from the inrushing wind. I was suddenly aware of my shirt beneath the robe being wetly plastered against my skin. I rose, shivering.

A hand motioned. I started. The hand motioned again. The Thiosan was pointing to his daughter. Nuzzled against him, she appeared terribly alone, peering up at me with large, awe-stricken eyes. I went to her. Trembling, she cupped her hands over her knees, sphinx-like. My eyes locked with hers. I leaned closer, focusing my mind, silently commanding her.

I concentrated, staring intently. Then slowly, slowly, slowly her hands raised. She lifted back the hood of her robe, her face a soft and pliant landscape. When I lightly touched her throat, she swallowed but did not look away. Warmth suffused me. My fingers slid up her lightly furred, throbbing neck and under her hair; the outer edges were not affected by the disease. I touched her earlobes, her hairy ears, her temples. The world around me trembled and was lost in quavering illusion.

Pus oozed across my hands, but I felt no nausea—only a phantasmal lightness, only the sweet taste of union. She shut her eyes, lashes settling on sallow cheeks, lips slightly engorged. Holding her head between my hands, I felt as though we were moving in a graceful dance across the star-dazzled universe.

I brought her away from the bench, my hands encouraging her. We knelt together in the cold dust. Her breathing beat in time with my heart, and I felt myself drawn to her, drawn into her, drawn beyond the emotional limits usually involved in healing. I knew I should not resist the emotion; I did not resist it.

My fingers tightened. Flames curled through my arms. I realized she was unconsciously becoming nearly as much instrument as I. No longer merely possessing her, I was being pulled into her vibrant energies. I ceased to think. My hands were seared with pain. I was aflame, my selfhood crumpling like a bit of burning tissue, and I was spiraling down my arms, building into my fingertips. The pain intensified. I wanted to cry out. I wanted to let go. My face contorted and my eyes slit in agony.

Suddenly—a flood of lava. My energy poured into her with an intensity I had never before experienced. It was as though I were making physical love to her—but it went beyond that.

The pain dissipated, my hands fell to my sides. I huddled on my knees, eyes closed, head down, hands tucked against my sides. Consciousness wavered. Pain returned to my hands and ebbed and again returned.

Finally I raised my head. The girl's eyes were glazed. Her father, bending over her, was massaging her shoulders, his huge hands working with surprising dexterity. Several other Thiosans—eyes wide, mouths open—were leaning close to him.

Then the girl turned and put her head against her father's chest. Tears rolling down dust-caked cheeks, she tried to speak to him. Her mouth worked, but no words came. She smiled, weakly at first, then in glowing joy, and he returned the smile. She looked toward me, her lips forming barely audible words that struck my mind like unending echoes. "Dahka bless you."

I stood, giddy with exhaustion, but exultant. Other Thiosans were already filing from the rows, their robes lifted so as not to catch on the benches. With trembling hands, and aching with rapture, I beckoned forward the sick and the dying.

I lay in bed that night, ecstatic with happiness. The gentle rocking of the floater lulled me. I remembered the faces of the Thiosans in the tent. Strange how their features had momentarily become etched with anguish, as though something ineffably precious were being taken from them, when I had lifted from them the terror of *Benziis*. Then their anguish had translated to joy, their faces beaming, their receptive minds free, filled with the spirit of Dahka. After the session had ended, they knelt in a line before me, pressing their foreheads to my fingertips time and again as I trudged through the holy dust to Carsen's hopper.

Yet none of the Thiosans had seemed so receptive as the girl. The flux and flow of her energy still seemed alive within me. I rolled over, lost in thought. The room pulsated with shadows . . . with memories. I remembered my family's pride: my great-grandfather, a devout Catholic who had fled China two centuries ago, only friends and luck and a fast train saving him from the advancing communists. And my father, tears in his eyes when I graduated from seminary (a necessary prelude for a healer), and me, in cap and gown, embarrassed not by his emotionalism but by his obvious belief. Embarrassed because I too believed, but not in his god, no matter how much I would have liked to. For me, divinity lay in the power—healing power—invested in me. Invested in all of us. Except I could control that power, use it for good, and that made me different from other people. Whether better than they I didn't know, and I'm not sure I ever wanted to know. Just *different*. Closer, perhaps, to immortality.

The door buzzer sounded.

I switched on the video. Wearing a white, hoodless robe, the girl from the session was standing before the door. Her head was tilted. She seemed interested in how the floater was hooked to the groundpins, and the effect of her tilted, curious head made me smile. Then she looked up, combed her hair back with her fingers, her cheeks golden bronze in the floater's light. Again the buzzer sounded.

"Come in." I met her in the mainroom. She looked at me silently, her lashes thick and long, her hair a shining cascade. She appeared vibrant.

I felt drawn to her. And yet I wasn't. The physician-patient relationship exists even in healing. Besides, physical attraction and the emotionalism of healing are not necessarily connected—in fact, rarely are connected. Perhaps I was drawn to her out of pride. And in her own way she was beautiful. But she was also Thiosan.

She introduced herself; her name was Valiq. I started to offer her a drink, when she spoke.

"You are my one and only Lord."

Her sincerity startled me. Her blasphemy startled me. "I am but the messenger of Dahka," I said.

Her eyes smiled in answer. She stepped closer and, wordlessly kneeling, brought my fingertips to her warm, throbbing forehead. Her body's odors rose to me: the aroma of ceremonial *pergo* soaped into her hair, the scent of new sandals, the smell of body heat. She lowered my hands to her lips and ran her tongue across one of my palms. Her robe was tied at the neck with a small bow. I reached to undo it.

And stopped. The vision of Tas a week before in that headstone-filled antechamber suddenly returned: her chest veiled in furry hair, her eight dog-like nipples rippling with light as she pulled off the robe. I had not been shocked, but shamed. Shame held me now.

"Get up," I said huskily.

She blinked.

"Please, get up."

She rose, frowning, puzzled. "I wish to sleep with you only to thank you," she said.

"I know."

"Yet you still refuse me?"

"Yes."

She turned without speaking, crossed the room to the door, then turned back again. "I suppose it was foolish to think a man like you would accept my gratitude," she said, opening the door.

I was angry at myself for having offended her. "There *is* something you can do," I replied. "I need help with the healing sessions."

She thought for a moment. Then she nodded without looking at me. "I will help," she said, her voice somber. "But I think it would be better if you failed. Or if you left us."

"Why?"

"Because if you cure my people, they will think you a god."

"You mean prophet."

"To us they are the same thing. Both bring promises . . . and pain."

The tent was uncomfortably warm for the next healing session—Carsen having had a heating system installed—and packed with tense, watchful Thiosans. Except for one woman in the front row, the Thiosans were standing, eager. She sat alone, legs crossed, one sandal dangling from the toes of a slim, golden foot. Her gray, velvety robe was embroidered across the bodice with a flowery pattern. She was clearly one of the city elders, perhaps one of the eight who had come forward that first day.

She glanced up as I passed. Her hair was coiffured in neat white curls beneath her hood, and her facial features were less angular than those of most Thiosans. She possessed unusual grace and poise. But her right eye was purplish and swollen shut. A lump of flesh drooped from the lower eyelid.

Still, the woman obviously belonged to one of the city's wealthier districts. She enjoyed power and opportunities unavailable to her fellow Thiosans. I feared her. But if I could cure her, I could reach anyone on the planet.

I mounted the first of the platform stairs with apprehension. The Thiosans hushed, began sitting. Slowly, the words issuing from deep within my heart, I began to chant the *Riomina*. The wind beat against the tent; I scarcely noticed it. I raised my arms and, in a whisper rising to a crescendo, the Thiosans took up the poetry. Their eyes kindled. The words rang out clear and resonant.

By degrees the light dimmed, and dust began to mist through the tent. Now the interior was in semidarkness; the Thiosans were amorphous chanting figures. I pointed to the rear wall; a curtain swished aside and, haloed by a spotlight, Valiq stood blinking into the haze. She was dressed in a flowing, shoulderless Terran gown, her hair combed across her shoulders, the hair on her arms and neck shining and healthy, her face powdered to catch the light. The audience gasped, and I stifled a smile. Carsen and Valiq had worked for hours on that look.

The chanting wavered at my distraction, but strengthened when I stepped down into the dust and motioned the Thiosans forward. A line formed quickly, then suddenly parted as a Thiosan couple passed through, carrying a boy about ten years old. They laid him carefully at my feet, in the dust. His hands were fisted, his arms stiff against his sides. His head tossed from side to side in delirium.

Perhaps he was just naturally receptive. Or perhaps his parents had told him of the miraculous Terran healer before the boy had lapsed into coma. Whatever it was, when I pressed his temples tightly and commanded that he be healed, I could feel instantaneous receptivity quaking within him. I set my teeth against the sudden pain in my hands, and he blinked once, twice, then opened his eyes fully. "Nai-wa. Nai-wa!" His mother swept him up in her arms. The chanting became raucous joy.

Then, as abruptly as it had begun, the uproar quieted. I wheeled around. The woman from the front row was kneeling by the stairs, lips atremble. She lifted great handfuls of dust in offering, then bowed, pressing her hands against her face. The dust clung to the oily right eye. When she looked up again, taut with emotion, her face had an eerie, half-monstrous appearance.

As I approached, she pulled back her hood, her throat uptilted. Her eyes were filled with fear and yearning. She had the look of a woman who was about to submit to an abusive lover's every insane desire, and who would do so willingly. She removed a small comb-beret from her hair, then lowered her head into the dust, her hairdo tumbling forward. She was softly crying. Crying from fear—and from hope.

I knelt beside her. The other Thiosans began to chant again, almost singing the poetry, the verses no longer the monotonous drone of traditional Thiosian rituals. I shuffled my hands through the dust, stirring it up. The dust entered my nose, stung my eyes. I concentrated. My mind rankled with hypocrisy. I realized I cared little for this woman. I wanted to cure her not for her sake but for mine. And for her people. Through her I could bring the Thiosans out of their groveling, fever-ridden disorder and into the twenty-second century. For that I would be revered, perhaps even deified. In this part of the galaxy the name Jonathan-Lin Chang would be famous forever. And worshipped? Who could criticize me for healing a woman for all the wrong reasons? Who dares malign a Schweitzer or a Gandhi, a Pasteur or a Jain-tan? Results speak for themselves, motives are insignificant. Here, at this moment, I could be at the threshold of divinity, capable of becoming the religious leader of an entire planet. It was a necessary hypocrisy.

I touched the woman's pulsing eye, and she shuddered. I sensed she was holding back from me. Her will was a sheet of metal in deepest space, closing me off from immortality. I brought all my mental powers to bear, spiraling toward her through the infinite void. The barrier warped and shred apart.

It was almost too easy. I passed through her will and into her soul, without effort. My hands briefly burned as I lowered them from her face. The flesh around her eye was still swollen. But the eye was clear and open.

Her lashes fluttered, eyes brimming. She bit her lip in happy relief. Her smile became wry and wistful, and gradually she regained her self-composure. Having given herself over body and soul to an alien in front of a hundred witnesses, she acknowledged her debt to me with a mere nod. Then she rose, bowed slightly, and moved to the door.

I stood, stunned by her rude disregard. The chanting continued; the Thiosans seemed to accept her attitude as perfectly natural. Suddenly the woman turned and began to walk back to me. As we came face to face once more, I was amazed at her glowing countenance. She kneeled grandly to me, and the chanting died. For several minutes there was a profound silence. Finally she rose and quickly left the tent. My heart felt strangely leaden. A troubling weight seemed to descend upon me. I had succeeded, yet felt as if I'd somehow miserably failed. Back home, unable to substantially help people, I had thought a series of healings would stir me to great joy. It had, the first session. Not this time.

I extended my arms, motioning the Thiosans to come forward. Like a crushing wave, they surged toward me.

A month passed, and during the next two healing sessions the crowds became harder and harder to control. The years of passivity were over; no longer huddled on the benches, their faces sullen and downcast, the Thiosans were now a constantly pushing, jabbering mob, reaching out to me, crying out to me for help. The sessions became scenes of mass hysteria. Microphone in hand, I had to conduct the healings from the platform.

Images hung nightmarishly before me: infants with bloated, discolored skin, a pregnant woman with her robe pulled up and hands clasped over a belly covered with purplish scar-tissue, an old man silently crying, loose flesh beneath his chin drooping over pus-slimed neckhair. Carsen finally agreed we'd have to let things cool off for a while. We used Terran guards to let only a few Thiosans at a time into the tent.

"You can't exactly blame the Thiosans, you know," Carsen said. Listening to his glib explanation, I sat slumped in the lounge chair of my floater, eyes closed and fingers steepled. I was terribly weary. "You should have anticipated this. Remember, their ancestors were dying from *Benziis* when ours were fighting one another with swords and coats of mail." He seemed as excited as a schoolboy at a circus. "By the way," he went on, "the microbiologists aboard Mother have intensified their study of the disease, and—here's the irony of it all—they've discovered the *Benziis*-producing spores are carried in the dust." Allowing that to sink in, he frowned at me. "Well, I suppose we've all suspected that the whole time."

After a long silence, he opened the door. "Come on, snap out of it. I know you're exhausted, but you're winning. Command thinks you're on to something here. Your influence over the Thiosans is beginning to be greater than any of us expected. The city elders have opened negotiations with us for a base. And Jonathan-Lin, we've found another of those sentry-bibles. It's more complete than the other one—contains references to a homeworld, within the Chanti cluster. It seems our dear god

Dahka was also from that world. Came here, and apparently died here. We're not sure why he arrived; maybe he dropped in to see how the folks were doing who a couple milleniums before had been kicked off-planet, or something. Who knows?"

"Don't mock," I told him.

He frowned, then, shrugging, left. He and Valiq were going to spend the night exploring the city and each other.

I felt numb. I tried to close my mind, tried not to think about the power that was coming within my grasp. Pride and its associated illnesses, omnipotence and self-deceit, are the bane and crucibles of prophets . . . of any leader. Happenstance and my own desire had placed me on a pedestal. My vision of myself, open-armed, helping a world at my feet, had given way to the nightmare of a diseased throng clutching at me wildly, desperately. Salvation, salvation, sal— I was just falling asleep when the phone hummed.

It was the base. "Had a woman come to the guard post just now—a Thiosan woman," a man on the screen said, his voice nasal. "Seemed to be in some kind of shock. Said you'd cured her mother of that plague they all have, but that her mother was sick again. 'Sick unto death,' she kept saying. Her name's Tas, or Tac—something like that. We had a hell of a time getting that much out of her. The Captain's with her now."

"I'll be right over."

The man swiveled, relaying this information to someone off-screen. Then he turned back. "The Captain says to meet her outside the front gate. He's rather concerned. This has never happened before—having a Thiosan come here unescorted, I mean."

"All right, I'll be right there," I answered, scowling. I went into the bathroom and washed my face with cold water. My mind was darkly churning. A relapse was almost unheard of in healing. Incomplete cures, certainly. Outright failures, of course. But I was positive I had completely cured the old woman. And I *had*. The disease had been eradicated. True, her energy level had been rather low during the healing, but still . . .

I had my own hopper now, but I wished Carsen was along for company as I flew toward the base. The flight was tedious. Finally the lighted rows of floaters flickered into view.

The base perimeter had been extended. I set the hopper down just to the left of the main gate, next to a scraggly tree. A white-helmeted guard approached, laser rifle at the ready. He jumped onto the hopper's wing, poked his head inside the cockpit and nodded, then helped Tas climb in. She moved in a daze and sat down without a word, staring straight ahead at her reflection on the inside of the hopper's windshield.

"Good luck," the guard shouted, shutting the door.

We flew toward Traage. Tas was wearing a robe decorated on the front with a series of colorful chevrons. Her lips were soft and full. Her features appeared gaunt but beautiful; yet her gaze was rigid, staring at her staring reflection. My hand was sweaty on the controlstick. I wanted to comfort her, reassure her. I tried to speak, but the words rasped in my throat, and I swallowed them.

The darkness yielded before our running lights. And finally, Traage. I came in low over the houses, searching for a landing site. In the darkness the streets were a mishmash.

Then Tas pointed downward, and I eased the hopper to a bumpy landing. Except for that one motion, Tas remained expressionless. Her hands were loosely cupped over her knees, her head stiffly immobile. I reached across her to open the door. She did not move. I frowned, climbed out, and went around the hopper. I tugged her arm lightly. Almost mechanically she stepped onto the wing; I jumped down and took hold of her waist.

She gazed at me as I helped her down. Her eyes were devoid of emotion. Then she started slogging down the alley, walking like a zombie, the cold wind billowing the dust. I caught up, tried pulling her by the arm to hurry her. She jerked away.

The door to her house was stuck but not locked. I put a shoulder against it, pushed, and went pitching headlong into the mainroom. Candles flickered throughout the house.

Tas continued to stand in the doorway. I could hear mur-

murings behind her; apparently other Thiosans were coming to
see what the commotion was all about. "Mother is leaving me,"
Tas said in a slow, hypnotic voice. She was not speaking to the
other Thiosans. Nor to me. "She is going away."

I went alone to the old woman.

She lay in the same room as before, her breathing shallow.
Then she doubled over, coughing. A bubble of blood formed at
her lips, popped, and trickled down her chin. She gurgled,
then her normal breathing-pattern returned.

She was staring past me, toward the statue in the corner. A
second statue—that of a woman—stood beside it. "Mendoe?"
she rasped, "is that you?" I said nothing. Continuing to gaze at
the statue of the man, she would not have understood me
anyway. Her cheeks were gnawed and slimy, and now I could
see her lips had been completely eaten away. Deep cuts lined
the outside of her mouth.

Starting to concentrate, I gripped her hands. The skin felt
loose and slick. I had the feeling that if I took my hands away,
her skin would peel off. Her robe was pulled up slightly, and
her legs were slimed with dark-purplish goo. Nausea swept
over me, yet I forced myself to concentrate.

Quickened by fear, my energies mounted. I shut my eyes
and brought my mind to bear against the disease. With a new
effort, I hastily whispered the verses from the *Riomina*. Kindled, my energies glowed within me. I squeezed the old
woman's hands, but got no response. I squeezed tighter, my
mind channeling, struggling, streaming into her like liquid fire,
searching for her receptivity. Pain sliced through my guts. Pain
distorted my features and clawed my brain; I wanted to cry
out, but could not. In a final, agonized straining, I expended
my last measure of energy. My hands fell away. Drained even
of tears, I hunched forward, panting from the effort, racked by
pain and the realization of futility. My chest seemed a hollow
cavity the wind might whistle through forever; my heart had
shriveled and blown away.

I could not cure the old woman. I knew now I could not cure
anyone of *Benziis*—not for good. Though I might dry up the

disease in someone for days, even weeks, it would only return with greater fury. All those I had treated would die—would probably die sooner, in fact, than if I had never set foot on Thios, but had let the disease run its slow though inevitable course.

"Forgive me," I whispered. My eyes shut for an instant; I swallowed thickly. "Forgive me."

"Mendoe?" the woman asked again, incoherently calling her husband. Shadows seemed to move in a slow circle along the edge of the candlelight. She continued to stare toward the statue, toward the dream-laden darkness. She was now beyond pain, beyond the harsh Thiosian world. A lustrous film was slowly coating her eyes. She tried to speak again; her lipless mouth opened, closed. Then her fingers stiffened, the bones showing through along the knuckles and upper joints. In horror I glanced down to discover my hands covered with scaly flecks of skin. Her eyelids lowered, but she did not succeed in closing them; the glaze across her eyes became complete.

I sat benumbed. Suddenly there was a shuffling, and I looked up to see a gleam of stone poised in the air. Tas had entered the room. I watched helplessly, unable to move as she took a final step toward me, the statue held menacingly. I did not have time to dodge. The statue came down, whistling past my ear.

And she smashed the back of her mother's skull.

I jumped up, attempting to pin Tas's arms. We grappled as though in slow motion, but her arm was already in midair and, twisting at the waist, she again brought the statue down. The base thudded dully against the old woman's skull. Blood and bits of grayish matter splattered the wall.

Tas cocked her arm a third time. The edge of the statue was a dripping reddish ooze. I grabbed her wrist, she blinked, then her gaze leaped to her mother. Her fingers opened; the statue fell.

"Mother?"

Hands clasped over her mouth, eyes closed in pain, Tas slowly sank to her knees. Sobbing, she put her head down in the dust. The small of her back trembled, and her breathing was spasmodic. "I should not have waited," I heard her say, her voice filled with self-hatred. The trembling grew more pronounced, and her hands were balled into fists. "Oh, Dahka!"

At last she raised her head and combed back her hair with her fingers. Fighting for self-control, she lifted a small water-filled bowl from the shadows. Dipping her fingers into the bowl, she began rapidly dribbling water into her mother's blood-spattered eyes. Finally she emptied the remainder of the water onto the old woman's face. Scooping up fistfuls of dust, Tas poured them into the wet, half-closed eyes. And kissed each eye in turn.

Then she looked at me, lips mud-stained. I retched. She gazed at me for a long time, her eyes glistening. She started to speak, but tears came. She bit her lip. Gazing downward now, her arms held rigidly at her sides, she wept in silence.

"I remember my fourteenth summer," she said finally, softly, not looking up. "The summer most of my brother and sisters died." Then, her voice cracking, "The summer my father died. It was a very bad time. Many people died. The wind smelled of grief. Mother made me promise that, should she be stricken, I would not let her die in misery. Dahka says we are to ease the pain. I was young, but there was no one else to do it. Mother even carved her own icon. Now, when she needed me—now, when I'm old enough to understand—I failed her."

Tas stared at me. "I thought you could help. So I left her in pain and went to find you. I trusted you. But now I know you killed her before her time. *Benziis* is slow—very slow. But the disease came back and swept her away. . . . I trusted you."

There was silence.

"Get out."

Outside, a crowd was waiting. Half-blind with angry frustration, squinting into the dusty wind and dawnlight, I stumbled into the mob.

"He's here!" someone shouted. A roar went up; the crowd surged forward. Gray hoods thrown back, their faces came bobbing toward me. For an instant I thought of going back into the house; a woman fell on her knees before me, blocking my way. She lifted an infant. Squalling, eyes screwed down tightly, it twisted against her hold, its flesh swollen, scabby. The woman's eyes implored me. I backed away, staying close to the building but moving in an awkward, lurching fashion toward the hopper.

The crowd roiled around me. The stench of their flesh was sickening. I continued to move toward the hopper, but I suddenly seemed to be toiling up a steep hill. The dust seemed alive, seemed to swirl around my ankles, impeding me. Thiosans were falling to their knees, gripping my hands, kissing my palms.

"Get back!" I shouted. But now the people in the rear were pushing forward. I was wedged against the wall by jostling, shoving bodies. The Thiosans' mingled receptivity, pulsing and pounding, rocked my senses. A sea of hands clutched at me.

"Let go!"

"I've been true in my worship," someone pleaded.

"Lord Dahka's Messenger, I only ask you . . ."

Thrusting the woman aside, I managed to squeeze through the clot of shoulders. Ahead lay the hopper. And another beside it. Carsen's! I started to cry for help when suddenly a thin, wiry youth leaped toward me, scrambling across the backs of some of those who were kneeling.

"Save me! Save me, Lord!" He grabbed my wrists, frantically pressing my hands to his temples. I struggled to free myself, but he clung on with unbelievable strength.

His efforts produced a chain-reaction. The crowd went wild. Arms ringed my neck—some Thiosans tried to pull the youth away from me, others sought to hold onto me. Hands clawed my shoulders, my face. As I stumbled forward I glimpsed Carsen's face at the edge of my vision. I took another step, then fell, flailing helplessly. Even as I fell the youth clung on, landing beneath me with a startled gasp.

Dust filled my eyes and mouth. Choking, I tried to regain my feet. A knee slammed my ribs. A sandal thudded into my jaw. I tried to scream, but couldn't. The world became dust and darkness.

Something was dabbing my eye. I winced. Someone familiar but unrecognizable was squatting before me. Slowly I focused. It was Carsen, handkerchief in one hand, a flaregun in the other. The dawn was cloudy with reddish smoke. Through the haze I could see some Thiosans at the far end of the alley, peering back quietly.

Then I saw Valiq. She was kneeling beside Carsen, one hand against his back to steady herself, her eyes darkly anxious. Suddenly I wished Carsen had let the crowd trample me to death. I sensed the disease was within her once again. There were no outward signs of it, but soon, I knew, *Benziis* would ravage her flesh at a savage rate. Who would release her from that pain? In the end, when her flesh was purplish and charred and she would be praying only for death, who would have the strength to lift that statue and carry out Dahka's command?

Her father? Carsen?

I pushed away Carsen's hand, walked silently toward my hopper. I ducked under the wing, climbed into the cockpit. So Valiq would die. The wealthy older woman would die. All those I had cured would die, and the negotiations over our base would come to a standstill—for the time being at least, until gradually the furor I had caused would wither. New children would grow up to fill the vacancies left by the others' passing, and the name Jonathan-Lin Chang would be forgotten.

But perhaps, I thought as I looked toward Carsen and Valiq standing in the dawnlight, arms around one another, just perhaps I would have left something else behind. Not my name. Rather, the Thiosans' remembrance of happiness, however brief.

It was consolation, but not great consolation, and as I jammed the controlstick forward, I knew I was rationalizing. Valiq's words came back to me—*gods bring promises, and pain*—and suddenly I understood why I'd felt I was taking something precious from the Thiosans whenever I was effecting a cure.

Eradicating *Benziis*, I was destroying an ancient, terrifying joy. Whether Dahka had introduced the disease, or if its outbreak had merely coincided with his arrival, was unimportant. It had become linked with him—and therefore linked to a homeworld the Thiosans had lost but could not forget. *Benziis* was not just a disease. It was cultural memory . . . and the very basis of Thiosian civilization, although, caught within its terrors, the Thiosans probably failed to recognize that fact. *Benziis* was what kept the Thiosans—people capable of producing children by the litter—from quickly overpopulating a planet with such a tenuous ecosystem. That was why the dust was considered holy. The Thiosans worshipped the disease; only secondarily did they worship Dahka.

I flew across the city, lost in thought. But finally I was forced into decision. I could turn left, toward the wastelands—fly until the hopper ran out of power and martyr-like I ended up as wreckage among balebrush. Or I could turn right, toward the base, the next flight to Mother—to do what I could in another capacity.

Not as healer; or as xenologist. Perhaps something between savior and student. As an aide to the microbiologists working on a cure? Or better: as apprentice to the botanists involved in terraforming, so that the desert and its vast mineral wealth could someday become useful? The Thiosans could break from their valley and . . . perhaps eventually, with our help, seek a homeworld among the Chanti cluster.

Command wouldn't like my refusing to work on-planet.

To hell with Command.

I turned right.

RON MONTANA
LOOSELY TRANSLATED

ipped at a slight angle and still tinged with the bronze afterglow of entry, the small diplomatic courser descended silently into the fog-whipped depths. It came in almost slowly over horizon point—if one could call the bister scar where gray atmosphere met misty moor, horizon point—dipping leisurely, with no evidence of external thrust or the internal sensing devices that were furiously searching for Landing Site One, the site the pilot had managed to overshoot in a fit of anxiety and gross inexperience.

Inexperienced, yes, to the finely tuned and highly volatile manipulations of planet-fall in a fleet scout ship. But was Federation Ambassador Detrich worried? No. Not the least bit. Not so you would notice anyway, from the strained expression on his flushed jowls as he shot a pudgy hand across the board in front of his jutting stomach and frantically palmed the automatic over-ride that would let the on-boards take over and possibly put the ship down with a minimum loss of life.

The good ambassador, as is wont with most diplomats, had ignored the bank of red lights that had been flickering for the past two minutes and, at the last second, finally realizing he had botched it again (that being the singular quality that stood Detrich head and rounded shoulders above the rank and file, his ability to admit he had botched it), allowed himself to relinquish command of his tiny vessel and let science take over.

Science did, and the scout righted itself with a wink of flame starboard as it settled nicely into a midcourse correction that brought it back to the proper trajectory. The engines retro'd with such ferocity that the ambassador lost consciousness, probably the ship's way of protecting itself for the remainder of the landing.

And such a landing it was! The kind the tri-vid boys would have described as a silver demon screaming into the wind as a lance of violet incandescence pierced the slate mist to lick hungeringly at the tundra below. For an instant the ship hovered on tips of fire, like a conquering Khan over a prostrate maiden, then came down in a blaze of glory and a perfect three-point landing . . .

In the mud.

Looking at it technically, the landing was more a plop than a splash, but on any given planet you're bound to find a group that will argue semantics, so in keeping with the diplomatic nature of the mission—the ship *splopped*.

The good ambassador came to in time to watch the ship sink to the level of its outboard pods and promptly began to curse the ship, the Service in general, and the Contact Corps in particular. An Earth type planet, eh? Sure it was Earth type! Here was the worst London fog topping what closely resembled the Florida Everglades!

His heated soliloquy was interrupted by the main screen beeper. He thumbed the control and gazed upon the face of the Contact Corpsman who had been first to touch down on this nameless ball of crud some sixty E days ago and said, in the artful manner he had of addressing subordinates, "Goddammit, Hemsley! What the hell's this place supposed to be, anyway? Okefenokee East?"

Hemsley's eyes widened and his youthful features braced to attention. "Ah, sir . . . your Ambassadorship, sir . . . the primary field reports gave a complete breakdown of the topography and atmospherics, did you not—"

Detrich interrupted to avoid being put in a position of admitting he had not scanned the field reports, thereby losing some stature in the eyes of the child that confronted him. "How old are you, boy? Never mind. When you've been around longer, you'll realize that the first thing an Ambassador does is to fully acquaint himself with the lay of the land . . . so to speak. But this? . . . is this . . . habitable?

"Yes, sir! Reptile bipeds, about Class Three in development—"

"Class Three!" Detrich's usually florid features gave way to purple as he shouted into the screen. "How in the hell are we going to communicate?"

"Oh, they have a language, sir, admittedly very fundamental, actually just a series of rasps and clicks, but I've been working on it for the past two months and I can make myself understood pretty well." Hemsley was smiling now, bright rows of even white teeth, and shining confidence.

"I hope so, young man, for your sake. I don't plan to spend any more time in this, this . . . place . . . than absolutely necessary."

"Running Late, sir."

"What?"

"That's what I dubbed that planet, sir. You see, I was a little behind schedule when I touched down, so . . ."

That figures, thought Detrich.

Hemsley met Detrich at the lock which was now even with the goo that lapped at the sides of the ship. His slight figure was overburdened with an extra rainsuit and a cumbersome pair of large mud shoes. He was short of breath, and the faceplate of his suit was fighting to dissolve the dew that hung in the air over Landing Site One like a planetary mask. Nevertheless, he was still smiling. "Let me help you with your gear, sir. The natives will be gathering at the site in a few minutes and it wouldn't do to be tardy."

Detrich wrenched the equipment out of the smaller man's grasp. "I can dress myself, youngster, and I dare say the lizzard-people can wait a bit for the Earth Ambassador-at-large."

With this he proceeded to don his rainsuit and to fumble with the bindings of the mud shoes. Now, Running Late's gravity was about two-thirds that of Earth. Add that to the fact that Detrich had been under zero gee for some time, that he knew absolutely nothing about mud shoes, that he had the grace of a pig on ice . . .

Hemsley helped the ambassador out of the ooze and scraped the slime from his faceplate so he could breathe and so that the flow of obscenities flowing from the heavy man as he righted himself could be understood.

They were. After the tirade had subsided, Detrich managed to calm himself and said very, very softly, "Contact Corpsman Hemsley, and I use that term of address in the present tense only, I have come over a hundred and fifty light years at great expense to the Federation, not to mention my irreplaceable time, to go through the motions of declaring this planet exploit-able and to advise whatever semisentient life that exists here that they are now under the kindly protective mantle of the Federation. I am fast becoming convinced, Hemsley, that the semisentient life here is limited to the pathetic figure that now stands before me. No, don't interrupt. Let's just get over to the site and meet the high mucky-muck, or whatever the local shaman prefers to call himself, so I can deliver the Federation's message of peace and mutual trust and then get the hell out of here before my usual good nature disappears and I start to get irritated with you! Okay, now move out."

"Aye, aye, sir!"

Aye, aye? Christ!

After thirty minutes of hard sloughing, the two men reached the landing site base camp, a one-man bubble erected in the trough left by the departure of the ship that had deposited Hemsley and his equipment to make the first contact with the locals and then await the official arrival of His Excellency, the Ambassador. His Excellency, the Ambassador, whose perspi-ration level had, ten meters back, reached and surpassed that of the surrounding mist, gazed for the first time upon the beings he was to establish diplomatic relations with. He swore.

There were ten of them standing—if one could call balancing on leathery tails with splayed feet spread wide apart and webbed toes dug into the slime that surrounded them, stand-ing—in a rough half circle in front of the bubble and glaring at the two Earthmen with expressions on their jagged-toothed snouts that could at best be called hostile; at worst, carnivo-rous.

"They look kind of mean to me, Hemsley. Are you sure we're safe?" Detrich asked, his face paling behind his damp faceplate.

"Perfectly safe, sir. They seemed to be a bit aggressive when I first contacted them, but when I managed to make it clear that a representative of the Federation would come to welcome them into their rightful place in the scheme of things, they seemed to understand and have waited patiently for your ar-rival while I learned as much of their language as I could. Here, let me show you." With this Hemsley leaned forward as far as he could stretch his slight frame without falling over, hunched his back, placed the middle finger of his right hand alongside his nose, and waved his left arm in a large circle.

The leader, a short, fat croc, acknowledged the greeting by placing one taloned hand on his crotch and scratching furi-ously.

"There, sir, you see? That's the official recognitioning sign, equal to equal. They're ready to talk."

"That isn't what it looks like, but if you say so, Hemsley."

The conversation that followed is, of course, loosely trans-lated.

"Okay, Hemsley, tell him we come in peace, we come from far space."

"The skinny one says: we come in peace, we come from our space."

"Their space, huh? Tell him I am the First One and if he speaks wrongly I shall eat of his flesh."

"I think he said: first come, first served, sir."

"Good! That's the right attitude. Tell him there is much to be gained by a meeting of our two races and that I am honored that one so exalted as himself would treat with us."

"He says there is not much to be gained by meeting with us and that we should treat him with honor."

"Tell him I will honor him by letting my mate eat his eyes!"

"Now we're getting somewhere, sir—he wants you to take a look at his wife!"

"That's all I need, Hemsley. They probably have the same customs as Earth Eskimos!"

"I don't think so, sir, I haven't been offered any—"

Detrich placed his forefinger in front of his pursed lips and whispered, "Shhh."

"*Your lordship! He says—*"

"*I'm not blind, fool. Tell him I demand satisfaction! Tell the fat one that his actions have made me small in the eyes of the gods and that if he wishes to live he must leave this holy place.*"

"Something about being satisfied with your actions, sir, and may God bless you, for staying."

"Exemplary, Hemsley. Tell him we wouldn't think of leaving, that we're going to test our mettle here!"

"*He says: they will never leave, they are here to steal.*"

"*ENOUGH! Seize them! Prepare the cook fires, we will eat them before the next storm!*"

"Sir, we've made a major breakthrough! I think they're inviting us to dinner."

JEFF DUNTEMANN
MARLOWE

They found her through what was left of the Chicago Public School system: a dirty seventeen-year-old, dressed raggedly, with unshaved legs and hair chopped off close to the head. Her pale blue eyes would not follow lessons in the discolored books longer than a few minutes, and her bone-thin fingers would not move a pencil through anything but intricate doodles. By then her teachers no longer cared. Maria came to school because it was an empty, quiet place, away from the violence of the streets.

One day the teachers handed a test to all the older students in the public schools. On many pages of a little booklet were intricate drawings. Immediately beneath the drawings were questions about the details in the pictures. Maria liked to look at pictures, so she took the test. She obediently answered all the questions and did not wonder what the test was for. A few weeks after she took the test, some men spoke to Maria's mother and took Maria away with them in a big shiny white car.

Maria was singled out because she could *see*.

The hospital was a monstrous place of blinding, dazzling white. Maria had to squint to see in the big room where they had been teaching her. There were no windows anywhere, but people dressed in white were always bustling around pushing intricate machinery or people in wheelchairs. There was a great deal to look at.

"Surely you can talk, child," the fat droopy man said to her.
"I can talk."
"Then why won't you talk to us?"
"Nothing to talk about."
The fat man was bending over the small school desk they had given her. His leather belt was glossy and black, but from its lower edge it had begun to crumble into tiny shreds. Maria had little choice but to stare at his paunch, which stretched his crisp white shirt drum-tight where it nudged his open lab coat aside. Little wrinkles appeared and disappeared in the shirt as he breathed. The lab coat, like everything else, was blinding white and very clean, except around his neck, where Maria could see the damp gray ring of sweat-grime. His trousers, made of a stiff raspy gray cloth, bulged slightly at the crotch. There were lumpy things in his pockets. Maria, glancing down to escape his small prying eyes, noticed two coins caught in his left trouser cuff. He was a sloppy eater for there were faint food stains on the front of his trousers.

Maria hated him.

"Well, we've been talking to you for nearly two weeks now, but you haven't said very much. We're going to pay you a lot of money for this, a lot more than most girls your age ever get. Do you remember everything we've taught you?"

He stood up straight again. One lower seam of the lab coat had begun to fray slightly.

"I remember."

"Are you going to do what we taught you, Maria?"

"I'll do it."

He kept following her eyes with his eyes, cruelly demanding that she meet his gaze. "It may hurt a little bit, but you're a big girl now."

Maria shifted on the desk seat. "I'm getting hungry. Could I eat now, Dr. Fitch?"

The fat man released a noxious, garlicky sigh. His teeth were white only at their edges; close to the gums they were a dirty yellow. His fingers clutched and unclutched at nothing, just as the fingers of the street-boys clutched and clawed at the weapons they held in their back-alley attacks. Fitch was a street-boy who ate regularly, that was all. Maria wanted him to go away.

Dr. Fitch turned from Maria and pulled a phone from a wall console. "Fitch here. Send a tray up to Classroom D. Now. Might as well be lunch." He roughly set the phone back in its cradle and left with one of the round-faced men who followed him everywhere. Maria heard their voices echoing down the dazzling white hall.

". . . raped only six months ago, Dr. Fitch. I'm surprised she isn't completely autistic!"

"Nobody's going to rape her here," echoed Fitch's loud voice.

Maria's lip curled as she waited to be fed. Tomorrow was surgery, whatever that was.

When Maria broke through the eggshell-colored mist and assembled her world around her again, she ran slender fingers over the hard transparent plastic collar which completely encircled her neck. Its inner surface had a layer of soft foam which held it in place against her skin. Behind her neck her fingertips could barely reach the little flared rectangle which guarded a dozen tiny metal pins. They were sharp and cold and felt like teeth. This was the Interface. Maria had heard the words in the classroom—"electrodes" and "neuropulsors" and "cerebral resonances"—all of which she had taken care to remember, but she understood nothing. It itched under the skin where she couldn't get at it, and there was a dull pain when she moved.

The anesthetic took a long time to wear off completely. All that day she flashed to memories that rose brilliant as a street-lamp and knife-blade cold. Moaning, she pushed them away and wished for sleep, but memories flowed and distorted and became terrible dreams:

Fitch, a hovering balloon dripping slime. "You are going to meet a stranger, Maria. He will seem to be inside your head. He won't hurt you. His name is Marlowe. He is two feet tall and has green teeth. Do exactly what he tells you."

Maria, in chains, a rope tight around her neck, was led down endless hallways. The rope gnawed at her neck with its own teeth. Fitch threw her into a dungeon made of polished sugar cubes, so white and gleaming that she could see nothing (white . . . like the doctor lamps, white like the nurse-cap, white like the haze that fell and threw its arms around her). The creature leaning against a streetlamp held a knife. His crotch was bulging.

"*Hi. I'm Marlowe. Nice ass, Babe.*"

Fitch did not see her for several days. Younger, skinnier men came into her white little room, poking and prodding her with machines that rattled jagged red lines onto long curling worms of paper. There were no sweat stains under their arms, nor neck grime around their collars, nor food spots on the fronts of their trousers. Their breath was always pleasant and damp, like flowers crushed between fingers. They handled her gently, but they always smiled insipidly at her.

They treated her like one of their machines, Maria thought. They seemed to hum as they went about their work. She grew bored with them.

Finally Dr. Fitch came back, and several of the skinny non-men followed behind. They lifted her carefully from her bed onto a cot with braces and motors beneath it. Fitch crossed a wide, cold plastic strap over her stomach and pulled it slightly too tight.

Marlowe was coming. Knife-sharp memories lurked behind her eyes, ready to be flashed upon:

Hi, Babe . . .

"Marlowe has no eyes," Fat-Fitch kept saying. The room was bare and spotless, with nothing for her gaze to fix upon. She ended up staring at the crown of his head, where little brown spots speckled the scalp beneath his thinning hair. "You're going to be his eyes. You're a very perceptive little girl. Your teachers all said very nice things about you."

Maria doubted it.

They rolled her out of her featureless white room into the blinding white hall. Maria lay quietly staring as the hexagonal light-panels flowed by above her. They hurt her eyes, but she was on her back, and the memories pressed too close for her to close her eyes.

Pregnant? That means a trip to the Hospital, three free meals, and a ten-buck abortion bonus. We're doin' you a favor, Babe!

Finally two huge white doors whisked aside, and the cot stopped rolling in a huge, high-ceilinged room filled with machines. The nonmen plugged cables into the machines and began to push buttons. The cot throbbed and became distorted, shifting her gently in its grasp until it seemed the shape of an easy chair. Fitch hovered over her.

"Marlowe knows just what to do. Do exactly what he tells you."

Just do what we say, Babe, and you won't get hurt.

Panicked, Maria sought to fix her eyes on something to drive the memory away. Across the room, on a large cot bristling with tubes, wires, and machines, lay a woman in a hospital gown. Her head had been shaved, and her eyes were wide and empty. Tubes went up into her nose, and wires were taped to her bald head. The hospital gown was cut open around her bulging belly. Some kind of metal plate seemed to be embedded in her abdomen just below the navel. Glossy black cables drooped from the plate and fell into the machine-jungle. Her chest slowly rose and fell. A string of saliva was running from one corner of her thick-lipped mouth, and a nurse dabbed it away as Maria watched.

A horrible taste began to rise in Maria's mouth. Those empty eyes . . .

Fitch saw Maria staring and turned the cot away from the woman and the hideous machinery. Maria was silently grateful.

"This is important. Do exactly what Marlowe tells you."

"I want to go home." Her voice was hoarse.

"Think of all that money, Maria!"

"No, I just want to go home!"

"Your mother signed the papers."

Mother. Cold hands and endless questions. Maria shivered

and shook her head. One of the skinny men drew up beside
Fitch and took her hand. "Don't be afraid. No one will hurt you
here. Your mouth sounds dry. Drink this." He smiled, handing
her a conical paper cup. The little mouthful of fluid tasted of
mint and warmed her stomach. Maria felt herself relaxing.
Drugs, as usual. Maria looked away from the smiling nonman
and returned her gaze to Fitch once more. Every time she
looked she saw another discolored vein, another tiny scar,
another food spot on his bulging trousers.

"Hook her up. We're losing time."

The little foam pillow behind her head had a hole cut
through it to the cot beneath. Maria felt the nonmen touching
the back of the collar, meshing the snake-like cables to the
collar's teeth.

At once: White like the doctor lamps . . .

It became a hot buzzing in her head.

Marlowe is coming.

Hi!

What was there to do in this world except look?

Maria sat on the windowsill, her small frame half-draped by
the dirty blue curtains, her young body pale in the night. Inch
by inch, her gaze slowly crept down the casement, following
each lump and crack and smudge in the faded green many-lay-
ered paint. To her eyes each crack was an ocean trench, narrow
and deep, with a bottom full of splintery secrets. Each scab of
flaking paint was a moth-wing straining to break free.

The window faced north, and the sun never shone directly
through the ancient, slightly crazed glass. At night the cold
blue glow from the streetlamps transformed the cracks and the
flecks of paint and made the casement a wonderland of shapes
and shadows. The streetlamps, unlike the sun, never moved.
Their shadows stayed always the same. Maria knew them
better than she knew the sight of her own face in a mirror. She
imagined each shadow to be etched into the wood from decades
of marking the same places.

As she watched, on the street below, scuffing through the
scattered garbage, came two street-boys. They were young,

younger than she, but they saw her in the window and made obscene gestures with upraised hands. Their other hands were fists, each holding a knife ready to zip from its sheath at the touch of a button.

She remembered cold steel against her throat.

Spread, Babe.

The child-woman recoiled from the window, wriggling back until she felt the chill of the iron radiator behind her. Cold steel, cold iron, cold air, all around her. She could imagine her mother's cold face watching her from the doorway of the darkened bedroom. In Maria's eyes the room was coated with frost, from the scarred formica of the ancient kitchen table, to the bent and grimy sheet-metal kitchen cabinets, to every crevice and flaw the three rooms had collected in more than a century.

Suddenly there was a starlike flicker of yellow warmth.

"Maria."

She put her hands behind her. clutching the cold wall. Her intricate vision of the casement, the street, and the cold apartment began to dissolve.

The voice came again, a gentle fire. "Maria, this memory has *life*. I want to see more!"

She clamped her dream-eyes shut, but the star remained, just inside her trembling eyelids. Slowly she relaxed, but she kept her eyes shut, to keep the world a swirling abstraction. Hesitantly, in her old habit, she began to concentrate on the star. But what could she see in a star?

There had been a rainstorm once, late in July. Hot winds had swept the streets free of filth, and the rain had come shroudlike from the skies, to flow in torrents through the alleys and black gangways. It continued into the night, and very late the electricity had gone out. Maria had sat on her windowsill and had looked out through the night over the crumbling city. The only light came from the sky, where lightning still coursed through some of the breaking clouds. Overhead the clouds had scattered, and through their roistering frame had shone a single brilliant blue star. It was high and clean. It took away her fear of the lightning and the wind.

"Marlowe . . . ?"

"Yes, I am Marlowe. Let me look out at the world through your eyes."

The star moved forward from inside her eyelids, permeating her retinae in minute explosions of multicolored light. At once she was warm, with the star's light filling her mind. Years ago, when her hair was long and the streets weren't so filthy, a big man had touched her that warm way. She had hugged him. He was warm. Mother was cold. He had gone after a while.

Now there was Marlowe.

"You need my eyes?"

"Open them. Let me look out."

Maria fought back a dizzy sensation and forced her eyes to open. The huge white-walled room filled with chomping machines tilted one way and then another, shifting in and out of sharpness. Her stomach tightened, but there was nothing there to send upward. She looked straight ahead and stared at the first object she could focus on. It was one of the machines, and Maria traced every angle of its squarish housing and the smallest detail of its flashing panel and shining switches.

"The thinking machines. You see them so well. It was only a blur when I tried to look out through *their* eyes."

His words flowed like poetry, taking the stiffness from her neck. The warm feeling in her head grew warmer, a gentle crowning presence that let no fear trouble her. Maria continued to trace the machines with her eyes, taking note of every minute detail. After scanning every machine she could see, she moved to the people in the room: the nonmen, two puzzled nurses standing ready, and Fitch. Fat-Fitch was standing over one of the machines, watching as rows of numbers and symbols came rattling out onto a long roll of paper.

"It's working. He's describing the core memory unit—calling it a resolution factor of nine point nine nine. He's getting it *all*."

The nonmen shuffled around the room while Fitch mumbled and pushed buttons. Maria methodically went from object to object to person to object in the room, scanning everything with her clear blue eyes. No detail went unnoticed. A pile of paper grew on the floor beside Fitch. He was getting excited.

"Okay. It'll do the job. He's describing *me* now! Kellogg, bring over the drawings. Votero, get the infranertial core. Let's put them to work."

FLASH—*Come on, Babe, go to work. This blade's for real.*

Panic flooded Maria. The room began to blur before the onslaught of the memory. The numbers stopped rattling out of the machines.

"She's getting upset about something. What a bundle of nerve ends! Try electrosedation. We can't stop now!"

Somewhere someone pushed a new button. A heavy cold oiliness pressed down on Maria's thoughts. The memory slipped away. "Marlowe . . ."

He was still there. "Close your eyes, let yourself fall into grayness. I have so much to tell you, Maria."

It was strange not to see anything. There was no detail anywhere. Maria had nothing upon which to fix her searching eyes. The world was a pastel swirl endlessly blurring and flowing around her with no trace of ground or sky or horizon.

She felt Marlowe's warmth rising around her. Suddenly he stepped out of nothingness into her presence, at once sharp, vivid, and corporeal. For this time Marlowe had a body.

At first something about him reminded Maria of the non-men: slender, unpretentious, self-contained. He wore a suit of baggy clothes, open at the neck and cut from cloth which was coarse but colored a deep blue. His face—she scanned it, remembering every curve, every soft curl of brown hair shot with gray. His large eyes were gentle, hazel flecked with grays and greens. Something about him came in on a memory, and she tracked it down relentlessly but easily in her mind. So seldom in her life had faces contained just that same concerned kindness. She thought of her father, lost across years that blurred any details beyond usefulness.

Now that soft face was reborn in Marlowe.

"Maria." He smiled. "Are they treating you poorly?"

"They keep saying they'll give me lots of money."

"Endure. It won't last. Nothing ever does. You can set yourself free, here, now, with me."

She believed him. Her fear was gone before the awesome gentleness of his face, leaving only a heavy drugged weariness behind. "I . . . know. It's all so weird. Where am I? What am I really doing?"

"Where are you? You're inside a vision. I created it from images remembered out of your life. You're inside your head, Maria. The only place that counts, in the final analysis."

"But *why*?"

"You're helping me answer some questions for them." The kind face frowned. "They are afraid. They're running. To what, or from what, I don't know. I understand very little about their world. They impress their urgency upon me. That's all. In any case, to solve certain fundamental problems they needed a new kind of mind: one absolutely at ease with abstraction. So they made me."

"Made you! But you're *real*." She hesitantly reached out and touched his shoulder. The cloth was rough, but the flesh beneath it was warm and alive. "You're no machine. I've seen enough machines."

He took her small hand and held it in both of his. "Cause and effect, cause and effect. Your parents made *you*, and you're no machine. Neither am I. I am . . . different, that's all."

"Have you answered their questions?"

"On paper, so to speak. The answers were complete a long time ago. They are dealing with problems that people with senses cannot envision. I have no senses. Nor do I have the limitations of senses. They asked me what 'space' is. I thought about it, and told them. They asked me what 'time' is. I thought further, and framed an answer. All within the language of logic and mathematics, of course. And then, Maria, they needed you."

She felt a real human pulse beating next to her palm. "What can *I* do?"

"You have senses. You *see*, and see with *quality*. You search your world for detail, for shape, for color, for all the subtle relationships that careless people overlook. You perceive more about your world than anyone else they found, and further-more, you do it objectively. You make no judgments, you create no illusions for yourself. What you see is what is there. You can look at objects they place before you and see every detail about those objects. You ask no questions of yourself as to what those objects are or what they do. All you must do is perceive every detail, and make it available to me.

"Until now I dealt with pure abstractions, and they worked with the real world. I told them how to deal with space and time, and now they are building machines to manipulate space and time for them in a particular way. But they are working in the dark, the dark their senses confine them to. While their machines take form, I must guide them. They will show you drawings. I will tell them where their errors lie. They will show you machines. I will tell them where the devices will fail."

"And I just . . . look."

"Yes. My pure abstraction and their crippled reality have to merge. You are the bridge."

"A bridge."

"Yes."

To be walked on. She did not reply. Maria was looking down at her body. Her arms were no longer matchsticks. They had a fullness they had never possessed before. Her hair was long and lustrous, longer and more lustrous than it had ever been. Her legs, like her arms, were smooth and gently curved in a way they had never been. In the past Maria had spent hours examining a forearm, or a single finger; she knew what sort of body time had given her.

"This isn't real. None of it. I'm not real. You're not real. It's all drugs." She looked down at her bare feet, smooth, white, uncallused.

Marlowe sighed. "Maria, this is the core of the problem. Look, here." The strange man released her hand. He cupped his hands together. Slowly he closed them against one another, and then slowly he opened them again. In the cup of his hands was a pool of *something*.

Maria looked very hard at the space between his fingers. She thought of feathers, she thought of the pages of some transparent book flipping and flowing, she thought of waves of silk churning in some obscure but definite pattern. She tried to single out an individual sheet within the mass, but the moment she fastened on one, it disappeared into the throng. In a few moments she shook her head and turned away her eyes. "*Time*, Maria. This is what time looks like."

"It's drugs. They're torturing me."

He shook his graying head and smiled with infinite tenderness. "No. Please don't turn away."

She looked back to his face and concentrated on seeing the detail in his eyes. His hands still held the pool of surging transparency.

"Time and space are not the same for me as they are for you. Here, now, I took this little handful of time and lifted it out of its sequence. I've turned its direction against that of our continuum. Now I'll put it back, but I've left it turned against the direction the rest of time takes. Watch."

Marlowe closed his hands, rubbed them together, made some difficult-to-follow motions with his fingers, and opened his hands again. Flashing through all colors of the rainbow, a fountain of turbulence leapt a few inches from his palm and froze. The opalescent shaft rising from his palm had no definite edges, remained no particular color. When looked at directly, it defied the eye to perceive anything at all about it. From the corner of Maria's eye it seemed a frozen flame slowly drifting through every color she knew. Maria was entranced.

"Is this real, Maria?"

"All I have are my eyes."

"Yes, yes, as do all human beings. But your mind deceives you. *Here* you have no eyes. What you 'see' are only fragments of memory stolen from your past. What I have are two moments of time turned against one another in eternal stalemate. It is a frozen sliver of forever. It cannot change. The space it occupies can hold no life, no energy, nothing but *now*. It is a perfect abstraction. It is the only real thing you are aware of right now."

Maria began to tremble. What was real, save what she could see? How real, she had often wondered, could the world be to the blind? *When all senses vanish, what remains?* Time: duration. Space: extension. Maria raised illusory arms to cover her illusory face.

Marlowe raised the sliver of forever in his hand and brought it down on his illusory body. The body splintered into fragments and fell into the nothingness all around. But Marlowe himself remained, the warm yellow star. Maria whimpered behind her arms.

"What you see is not real. Not any of it. Take off your body, Maria. You don't need it here. Throw it away."

"No. Please, no. It's all I have . . ."

"Nonsense!" came the thunder from all around her, and Maria found herself spinning in a vortex of illusory body fragments, an arm flying away to one side, a leg to another, a shower of fingers scattering into nothingness beneath her. Then all was gone, and there was nothing. She had no eyes to see with, but there was nothing to see. There was nothing but time and space . . . and Marlowe and Maria.

"There you have it! Inside you is some essential quality, some substance which goes beyond all sensory illusion, a thinking spirit to which only time and space are essential, and to which all else is mere detail. Is it real, Maria?"

"No . . ."

"But you experience it!"

"Yes, but then what . . ."

"Accept it!"

"Please help me."

"You don't need help. Accept it, Maria! Let all else be blown away. This is what matters. Accept it!"

Her body gone, her senses dissolved in abstract nothingness, Maria still found herself aware of a strange somethingness permeating her thoughts, of a distance between one end of a notion and another as it passed before her mind. Could that be space? How odd to think of it as something other than the inside of an empty box. It was a *feeling*. And with that feeling came a rush of moments past her, and an awareness that one thought is not as *new* as another. How simple it was to note the passage of time without the clutter of reality to distract her. Curious . . . But somehow very real. "I do. Yes. I accept it, Marlowe."

A feeling of wide peace washed over her.

"Now. Now we can begin. Open your eyes!"

Real eyes snapped open. Maria's mind grappled again with light and shape and motion. The machine room was still there. Fitch and the nonmen clustered around her. Two new objects had been set up in front of her cot.

"Look here, Maria. Look where I'm pointing." Fitch's flabby hand indicated a square screen perhaps a yard wide. On the screen was a complicated drawing of some object, seen in three perpendicular views. Maria took it in briefly at first, then glanced to one side. Supported on a motorized stand was the object the drawing depicted, now made real in burnished metal. It was roughly cylindrical, with holes and notches and strange curves interrupting its form. Maria looked back to the screen.

"Examine this drawing, child. Go over every line. Observe every junction. Let nothing get by you. Immediately afterward do the same for this." He pointed to the cylinder. "Scan this object. Observe every detail. And do just what Marlowe tells you. That's a good girl."

Maria swallowed hard, squirming from remembered terrors. Every time she looked at Fitch the memory started coming back . . . . Finally he left to examine the stream of symbols Marlowe was sending him. Maria began at the top of the screen and forced her eyes along the incomprehensible green lines, noting every turn and change in the outlines and cutaways. She felt the warmth of Marlowe deep inside her, humming his dialog with the machines. She finished the first perpendicular view, scanned the second, and the third. Without stopping, afraid Fitch would turn his attentions to her again, she pounced on the metal object and began to scan it furiously. If she concentrated totally on seeing, she could forget her discomfort and fear. Nothing mattered anymore but getting away from there, away from Fitch, away from the blinding white weight of the hospital on her soul. If she did a good job, she would get home with the money all the sooner.

After what seemed like hours later, Maria's eyes began to blur and lose the ability to focus. The numbers on Marlowe's printouts thinned and stopped.

"She's getting tired." Fitch pushed a few buttons. Maria's head buzzed in different hoarse tones. "She's getting numb from the electrosedation. Might as well shut down until tomorrow."

Maria closed her tired eyes.

"Marlowe."

"Yes, Maria."

It was pleasant not to have to use her eyes for a change. Maria relaxed and thought for a moment of the flowing somethingness cradled in Marlowe's illusory hands. Imagine holding time like that . . . It made her fingertips tingle. She shook out of her reverie and concentrated on the warm yellow star glowing somewhere within her.

"This was all very real today, wasn't it, Marlowe? These machines, my eyes, you . . . Even your touching time and space."

"Within our private reality, beyond the limitations of your senses, yes, it was all real."

"I know, I know. But I *do* have senses, and there is a real world somewhere out there. And somewhere out there is you. Where are you . . . in *my* reality?"

There was a long pause during which Maria could only sense the tall, gentle presence through all her pain and fears. The nonmen were fumbling with the connection behind her neck. "Within your reality, Maria, does it matter?"

His warm star-fire died in an explosion of electronic loneliness. Disconnected and disappointed, Maria was wheeled back to her little white room. Sleep was deep and dreamless that night.

Marlowe was her morning and, humming behind her eyes,

Marlowe filled her day. Each day began with the jarring snap of the cables making the connection to the Interface, and he was waiting for her. Each time he held some new wonder for her, some revelation of space and time to make her tingle and tremble. He bent scraps of space upon themselves until they vanished. He poured tiny angular time-streams in patterns all around her. All this she knew without eyes, and without hands he led her through strange spacial convolutions like a dance begun and completed without stepping out of place. In time such antics no longer terrified her. Marlowe hummed knowingly while she followed him through each impossible act.

He comforted her through the long days, and even in the middle of scanning at times the symbols would stop, and Fitch would turn red and press buttons. Marlowe would not begin again until he had spun a rainbow for her and told her to endure. In the deep, solitary nights alone she wished he had some physical form, so that she could put her very real arms around him.

Maria was beginning to forget the hatred and hunger of the streets. At the hospital they fed her well, and although they sometimes seemed to ignore her, they never mistreated her. A sparkly eyed nun with a gruesome crucifix pinned to her breast gave Maria pencils and paper to draw with. Maria repeatedly sketched her own face from a mirror propped up against her knees, and she watched over the weeks as the face on the paper grew fuller and rosier. She had begun to draw herself smiling, when before she had only drawn uncommitted pouts. She drew her eyes happy and blue.

Her hair, which she had always kept chopped and straggled to make her less attractive to the street-boys, was beginning to grow out. She decided to let it grow.

One day when the usual nonman (who over the weeks had begun to look more and more human and likeable) came to roll her into the machine room, Maria asked him if he could explain the strange objects which she was examining for Marlowe.

He leaned against the white wall and grinned. "Maybe I'm not supposed to say, but . . . the government is building a starship. The devices we are showing you are parts for a machine to drive it faster than light."

"Oh." She thought of the single brilliant blue star, and how bright and clean and hopeful it had looked over the dirty tenements of Chicago. She smiled. "I didn't hear a word of that, you know?"

He laughed quietly. "Good. I didn't either."

Two seconds of final communion, in Marlowe's strange inner world:

"Marlowe, we're doing a job, they all keep telling me. The job will be finished someday, I quess. I'll have to go home. What am I going to do then?"

"Just what you've always done: Live."

"But I've never really been living. Just . . . looking."

"What strange counsel you ask me for! I'm afraid I can't tell you how to deal with your world, Maria. Unless . . . Perhaps you mean that in your past life you have been passive, letting the world push you along, never asserting your own will against it. You must learn to make your own decisions, and to stand by them. You have been an object, to be acted upon by the world. You must decide what you think of your world, and then guide your life by those judgments. *Act*, Maria, or be acted upon!"

Don't like it, Babe? Whatcha gonna do about it?

Old hurts and terrors made the echoing electronic snap a cold clamp on her soul.

One of the nurses had given Maria a new hairbrush, and Maria brushed her hair faithfully every morning after breakfast. She ignored the stinging pain from the back of her neck when she raised her arms too high above her head. She wanted very badly to attain a quality she had thought about, sometimes craving it, sometimes fearing it, all the short years of her adolescence: to be pretty. But to look . . . desirable. To be pretty was to attract the attention of the street-boys and all the horrors that leapt at her from dark corners.

Nice ass, Babe.

The face in the mirror by her knees made her cry. The picture there was of a person soft and clean and well-groomed. It terrified her.

She had long lost count of the days spent with the machines and Marlowe. A cold dripping winter had faded into a gray spring, then into the beginnings of a struggling summer. Every day now she walked through the halls with the young oriental nurse, or sat in the sun on the roof of the hospital, high above most of the gritty air smothering the city. Her legs felt free again. They no longer had to run. She kept telling herself: good, too good. They'll want me. They'll have me.

"Marlowe, what will I do?"

"Act, or be acted upon. Make that decision. The rest is detail."

Far into one cold night, Maria awoke abruptly from a night-mare of street-boys and endless black alleys. Her eyes burned. She forced them closed, pressing her face into the coolness of the pillow. She dreaded to sleep, because of the fears that always waited beneath her conscious mind. The low busy hum of the hospital was everywhere in the darkness, but it was futile to take comfort in that. The world of her nightmares was the real world. It would have to be faced when the "job" was finished. She would have no place to find shelter.

So Maria, hungering for Marlowe's unreachable comfort, fled inside herself. She threw away the body that reminded her of pain and bulging crotches at the point of cold steel. Abstrac-tion swirled around her, and she was free. Without hands she dipped into the velvet time-stream flowing everywhere around her and drew away a tiny moment endlessly turning its silken leaves. *Time.* How real it seemed as an entity alone, when before it had always been an ill-perceived stage upon which reality played its gritty course. Without hands she squeezed it and watched the misty sheets flow more quickly. She pressed harder, and the tiny moment turned furiously, caught in her grasp as a vortex with neither beginning nor end. Without eyes she watched the moment of time she held turn past centuries, and only slowly did she realize that what Marlowe could do, she could also do. Time and space were no longer mysteries.

Maria shivered all through a body which wasn't there, and she set the tiny moment back into its place in the stream of time. That morning when she awoke she found a small circle, yellow and crumbling as though with extreme age, on the bedsheet where her hands might have lain.

"Marlowe, what have you done to me?"

He tasted the memory which she presented to him, and he sounded pleased. "I've taught you to deal with abstraction as I do."

"But why?"

"Because I must."

"They told you to. Fitch told you to."

"No." She felt his smile, gentle and reassuring. "You will have children, Maria. You will teach them the things you have learned, and they will live a better life for your experience. Through that experience you will live long beyond your years. I will have no children. How else can my experience live on after me?"

She found herself growing flustered. "It won't do me any good."

"It will, it will. I can explain to the men what you can do, and they will pay you to work for them."

"No!" The thought chilled her. "They'll hurt me."

"Are they hurting you, Maria?"

She thought of the dispassionate look in the nonmen's eyes, of the hollow feeling of being connected to a clattering box, of the need at times to scream out against the smothering whiteness of her prison. Details.

"You aren't about to understand. Go away."

The hairbrush paused in mid-stroke one morning not long after, when Maria heard the nonmen coming down the hall toward her room. They were talking loudly.

". . . but eleven months! How long does Fitch think he can

push it before the hormones take over?"

"He'll push it as long as he can. It was hell on Earth to make the damned thing start growing to begin with, and then communicating with it . . . . He doesn't want to have to do it again. They're pumping the poor woman so full of stuff it makes me sick."

"Thank God she doesn't have a brain to feel with. Oh, here we are."

Maria hid from the day under a conscious pall of looking and seeing. Then, those last seconds:

"Marlowe, I know what they're doing. You've got to stop them." The coldness in her inner voice shocked her.

"Stop them? Maria, I don't understand."

"Of course you don't understand. To you it's just details. Our whole world is just details. Those details are everything to *them*. They know you're not going to last, and they wanted you to teach me how to play with space and time so that they won't have to make another one of you when . . . when . . . it's horrible, horrible! Don't you know what you're doing?"

The soft voice, for once, was hesitant, unsure. "I am pursuing a goal I understand."

She wanted to cry out with frustration. "A goal they fed you through a tube along with everything else. You're a tool. I'm a tool. We're just clicking machines to them, and they're using us!"

Marlowe stood within her for a long time, silent and troubled, before the nonmen broke the connection between them.

The six-inch cube hung within a metal frame scarcely a foot in front of her. Maria scanned it from top to bottom. When the numbers stopped clattering onto the printout, one of the nonmen rotated the cube about an axis, and they began again.

She had not spoken to Marlowe for almost a week. He refused to understand, and to hear him placidly deny her fears hurt too badly.

The scanning had gone on for an eternity that day. When she finished the outside of the cube they unfolded it, moved it nearly beneath her nose, and she scanned its intricate inner surface through an illuminated magnifier. She wished for those first days, when he had always been close to her, whispering encouragements. The emptiness he left behind was heavy. Head aching, Maria went on.

Unexpectedly, motion: the idiot-woman turned her head, and moaned.

Chaos.

"Good God, we've got another month of work yet!" Fitch turned from his controls and began shouting. "Get the surgical team! Brandt! Bring up pressure inside the incubator and sterilize the lock. Somebody hit her with something to slow her down. Try thioptemisol. Time! We need time!"

Fitch pushed through the confusion of machines and scurrying technicians to the cot on which the woman lay. Her protrusive belly began to jerk convulsively.

At once Marlowe's warm omnipresence broke through Maria's inner barriers. It was flushed with pain.

"Marlowe!" Maria screamed it aloud, wrenching her head back. She felt the spasms as though they were her own. "Marlowe, what's happening?"

Two nurses in surgical dress rushed into the machine room.

"The end of my long moment in time. What a strange and versatile abstraction this thing life is!"

"Don't talk nonsense. Tell me what's happening!"

"Ask yourself, Maria. You knew all along."

The idiot-woman jerked on her cot. Maria felt a hot knife jab through her pelvic area. Yes, she had known, but it had been too much of a nightmare to come true.

Fitch had donned a mask and sterile gloves. He was positioning the idiot-woman's legs.

"It's a good world," Maria found herself whimpering. "You'll like it here. I promise."

"I have my doubts." His warm star wavered, cooled a little. "You were right, in a way, Maria. A creature who cannot see that he is being used cannot be saved. Try to make some good of what I've taught you, and go your own way. You're free. I told them that I had failed, that no sensate human being could perceive space and time as I do. I told them that you were growing more distant from me, and that you could never again do what you are doing now. I have never lied before, Maria."

"Thank you." She reached for words which made no sense beyond her and Marlowe's private abstract world. "That makes all the difference, all the difference in the world . . ."

Maria felt something give, and Marlowe's strange inner orientation within her mind twisted some impossible way. He was slipping away from her.

"No!" She screamed aloud. The pains were hot and intense. "No!"

The final pain was the popping in her mind as one of the nonmen pulled the cable from the Interface behind her neck. Marlowe's twisting presence vanished from her head. Maria began to sob uncontrollably.

"Get her out of here," Fitch ordered. "Jesus!"

Two of the nonmen pushed the cot out into the hall. Maria kept craning her neck to see the sluggish movements of the idiot-woman in response to automatic pains.

Maria's tears had soaked the soft cloth covering the cot's padding. They lifted her from the cot and tucked her gently into her narrow bed. She forced herself to withdraw her sobs and lie quietly. Every time she lost control of herself they had some drug or button to crush her into unnatural sleep. Not this time.

Maria waited several minutes after the nonmen left. She had never given them any reason to lock her in her room. The door stood slightly ajar. It was not difficult for her to squirm into her old clothes and to brush her new-grown hair a different way. She walked confidently into the hall and strolled quietly but nonchalantly back the way she had come. Some of the scurrying nurses and nonmen looked at her strangely, but none broke stride in her direction.

No one noticed her until she had already triggered the twin doors to the machine room and stepped boldly inside.

Moments later, Marlowe was born.

Maria screamed. Fitch's hand held a bulbous monstrosity, pink and streaked with fresh blood. Its head was massive and misshapen. An intricate network of purple veins covered skin so thin that white bone showed through from the cranium beneath. The rest was a shapeless sac bearing no resemblance to the human form. It had no limbs, no face, nor anything but the drooping purple cord connecting it to the idiot-woman's body, and the blood-slick black cable buried in the base of its skull.

"Act, dammit," she sobbed. Two nonmen who had seen her enter the machine room burst through the twin doors. They took her by the arms and, always gently, began dragging her back to her room.

Let them run to the stars.

They had pulled the wires from her brain and cut away the collar which had encircled her neck for so long. They had written Maria a very large check, made out to her personally and not to her mother. The big shiny white car had driven her home, but before facing that again Maria ran several blocks to the commercial strip along Halsted Street. She had seen something there once, and she had to know . . .

There it was, in the dirty window of a storefront that had TRAVEL lettered in peeling plastic behind the glass. A faded photograph showed towering palm trees swaying over water so blue it seemed like ink. Even the rotting slum had its limits, and somewhere the world was sunny and clean.

Maria wandered down the strip, looking in windows, making plans. With money one had power, power to flee the filth. Her eyes lingered over bright dresses hanging in another window. She would have that, too, and everything else she had ever dreamed of. She had earned it.

Sad but determined, Maria made her way home. The sun was setting, and fall's first chill was in the air. High overhead the first star, her blue star, was there. Vega, they called it. Maybe the men would go there. Then again, with any luck, maybe they wouldn't.

Then two shadows against a stained brick building reminded her where she was.

Maria kept walking, quickly, unslouched. Her legs were too shapely now, her face too clean. She couldn't hide by slouching and shuffling. Her eyes burned. She didn't want to go back to that. It feels good to look nice, she thought. No . . .

"Hi, babe. Where you going?"

Inside she started to crumble. "Home."

"Aw, come on, hang around for a while." They stepped out of the shadows. One was tall and gangly. The other was shorter and had a pocked face. They both looked purple in the cold light of the streetlamps.

Maria kept walking. She passed them, and they began walking behind her. A tear escaped her left eye. It wasn't fair.

They paced her for perhaps forty feet. A black gangway yawned to their right. One boy grasped her arms and dragged her into the shadows. As before, she went limp. She had seen that flash of cold steel.

"What do you say we have some fun, huh?"

"I . . . I've got to go home."

"Home? That's no fun. Come on."

The knife flashed in the open now. Maria leaned up against the cold filthy brick. Screaming would only bury the metal in her throat. The two street-boys stepped back, looked her over critically in the dim light.

"Not bad, this one. You first, Mike."

Mike stepped forward. Maria pushed herself back against the wall. The cold brick touched the tender spot behind her neck.

Act . . . or be acted upon. A tiny glow flashed at the back of her mind. She leapt at the memory, fed it, made it grow. Marlowe's star shone brightly behind her eyes. *Time and space, life and action. That's what matters. The rest is detail.*

"Marlowe," she whispered. Her hands came up from her sides and met in mid-air. The warmth of his star was in them, a glow that radiated to her slender fingertips. It helped her make the absurd motions.

A fountain of strange light leapt from her palm and froze. No life, no energy, nothing but *now*. Maria eased her fingers around it. The pulse of space locked against time flamed in her hand.

"Hey, you . . . you put that away," Mike said, backing up. Maria advanced. *Act.*

"You want me? *You come and get me.*"

CRAIG SHAW GARDNER
NOW! YOU CAN BANISH EMBARRASSING FOOT ODOR FOREVER!

"ut why are you here?" Madge asked them with a smile. They were very polite. And Madge put a big store in politeness.

They flashed their Cheshire cat grins back at her. There were two of them. They always traveled in pairs. More companionable, they said.

"We are here to give our special gifts to Earth," said one of the pair, who introduced himself as Fleep. "And why are we in the Stanley household? That would be your next question, wouldn't it? If you'll excuse me for saying so, Mrs. Stanley, you're very attractive when you laugh. But perhaps, to answer your second question, we should tell you a bit about our homeworld. Do you mind if we sit down?"

Madge insisted that they do just that. In fact, she took the plastic slipcover from our white Barcolounger and insisted that they sit there. And that Barcolounger was reserved for only our most important guests.

She turned to me and whispered, "Fred! Look how clean they are!"

I should have guessed. Madge also put a big store in cleanliness, and she was right about these two. I wasn't as sensitive to these things as my wife, but even I noticed their tidiness, all the way from their pressed black suits to the close-cropped hair on the back of their hands. And those rivetting, immaculate smiles. They had large heads and even larger mouths, so their smiles were just about their most important feature. All in all, they were the nicest aliens you could ever want for house guests.

"Our homeworld, Gleen," Fleep continued, "is far more advanced than Earth scientifically. We have banished all the—shall we say—unpleasantnesses from our lives on Gleen. It is a perfect, happy culture, save for one failing. Once you are perfect, where is your challenge?"

"Exactly," the second alien, who called himself Slarp, chimed in. "So we have decided to visit other cultures, not so scientifically advanced as ourselves, but with a similar distaste for these certain baser aspects of life."

"Not all cultures show our civilized tastes," Fleep added.

"How true! Why, Fleep and I could tell you stories of some planets—those incredibly hairy spider-things on Aldebaran Four, for example—"

Slarp stopped at a sharp glance from his fellow. His big mouth smiled apologetically. "Well, perhaps when we get to know you better."

"As I was saying," Fleep continued, "we of Gleen decided to go out and visit those cultures most suited to our civilized ways. One of those lucky cultures is that of Earth. So, a few prime Gleenians were chosen to visit a few special Earthlings, selected for what we think will be their special receptiveness to the higher purposes of Gleen. And you, Mr. and Mrs. Fred Stanley, are one of the chosen couples!"

Madge clapped her hands. "What have we done to deserve this?"

"Shall we say that we appreciate your viewpoints on life?" Fleep paused, and the two Gleenians looked at each other for a moment. Their smiles faltered a bit.

"I suppose I might as well begin," Fleep said. "It's always difficult to broach this sort of thing, but, once you've been introduced to our culture, I guarantee you'll never be faced with these little problems again."

The Gleenian turned to my wife. "Mrs. Stanley," he said,

"would you mind if I called you Madge? Good. So much friendlier. Madge, are you embarrassed by underarm perspiration?"

My wife colored a bit, then admitted that she was.

"A civilized response!" Slarp cried. "I knew you'd be the perfect couple."

"And we of Gleen have the perfect answer," Fleep added, all smiles once again. He held out a small tube that had somehow appeared in his hand. "Just spread this over your body and you'll never have perspiration odor again!"

Madge was skeptical, but the two Gleenians urged her to try it. She finally agreed and excused herself to go to the bathroom. Five minutes later she returned, ecstatic.

"I never felt so clean!" she giggled. "But will it last?"

"Well, don't take our word for it," Slarp said. "Why not wait and see?"

So we did. And, despite an unusually hot and muggy summer night, Madge awoke as clean and refreshed as the day before. Fleep and Slarp's grins were wider than ever when she reported the results, and, in short order, they introduced us to the Gleenian equivalents of toothpaste, mouthwash, and shampoo. All these worked as well as the Gleenian's first gift, and Madge urged me to try them as well. She also mentioned to Fleep a certain problem I had with my feet. The Gleenians had a short conference on that one, but soon managed to produce another tube, slightly larger than the rest.

It was as successful as the others. Once I had used it, Madge remarked, she almost forgot I had any feet at all.

The Gleenians beamed at the both of us in our new, purer state, though I must admit they spent more time admiring Madge than they did me. But then, the changes they brought about made her look happier than I had ever seen her before. She positively glowed!

"We're so glad the gifts are working well!" Slarp cried. "Now we can move on to the finer points!"

Madge's smile fell.

"Finer points?" she asked.

Even the Gleenian's smile faltered a bit. Slarp looked at the floor. "Yes, I don't like to mention it, but—" He looked back at Madge. "—unsightly nose hair."

Fleep nodded. "And excess ear wax."

Madge was shaken. "Oh, dear! I never realized . . ."

"Of course not!" Slarp cried, all smiles again. "Most creatures wouldn't even notice such small flaws. But then, most creatures have—" He coughed politely, unable to finish the sentence.

"But not you," Fleep added.

"No, indeed! We've seen now that you have the proper attitude to become one of the completely refined."

"An elite state," Fleep remarked, and closed his eyes. It made his smile look even larger.

The Gleenians' approval was beginning to mean a lot to my wife. She plunged onwards towards refinement; nose hairs trimmed, ear wax expunged, even the last stubble of body hair removed. And I came after her. It made Madge happy to think of us as a truly refined couple. I must admit I was beginning to think it was all a bit much, but if it made Madge happy . . .

Finally, the Gleenians gave us tablets to ingest that would insure that no odor would come from any of our bodily orifices.

Madge was rapturous. "For the first time in my life," she said, "I'm sure I won't offend."

"We were hoping you'd feel that way," the Gleenians said. "It's the way we like you best."

When we were alone, Madge raved about Gleenian science. And almost perfect houseguests, too. You hardly even knew they were there.

She was even more ecstatic when they asked us to invite another couple to the house. The Gleenians explained that we were almost perfect now; in fact, Madge approached the Gleenian ideal. There was little more they could do for us. So why not introduce them to another couple that felt the same way about those certain unpleasantnesses that we did. That way, Fleep added, they could make sure more and more people approached the ideal.

So we had the Millers over for dinner. The Gleenians never joined us when we ate. In their advanced scientific culture, they said, they seldom ate anyway, and, when they did, they were afraid that the sight of their large mouths working might prove unpleasant to us.

So polite! Sam and Ethel Miller were just as taken with the Gleenians as we were when we introduced them after dessert. Now that their work was finished with us, they would become the Millers' houseguests tomorrow.

Madge lost her smile for a minute after the Millers left. "But what if one of your products wears off?" she asked. "What will we do then?"

Both Fleep and Slarp smiled at that. "Just about impossible," Fleep said. "But don't worry. We'll keep in touch."

"You have reached the Gleenian ideal," Slarp added. "As you say, there is no way you can offend." He smiled at me. "What do you think, Fred?"

I looked closely at my wife, her gleaming hair and skin, her dazzling white teeth. And no trace of perspiration, no odor of any kind coming from her body.

"Perfect," I said.

"We agree," Fleep said and swallowed her in a single gulp. "Excuse my table manners, but it's not often that we get such delicacies."

I was frozen in shock. My immaculate body trembled, my odorless breath came in short gasps.

"Yes, there's so much preparation involved," Slarp added, "and the final result so often falls short of perfection. Like you, I'm afraid. I think we'll have to add a little whipped cream to make you palatable. I always get the inferior meals."

"It was my turn," Fleep chided.

Slarp sighed. "If you'll please come with me into the kitchen, Fred."

They were always polite. You had to give them that.

DAVID LANGFORD
LUKEWARM

[Warin]

*Trac was very great, and was the first to transcend the Plane, to pass
beyond. Trac, the first.*

I shall be the last. Warin the last: Warin the weak, the feeble.

*Turning in, ever in, seeking the essence, I drift forever between the
heat and the cold. My mind is weak, always has been; but free from
distraction over my cycles, I turn inward once more. Two to the power
of two-to-the-(two plus one) cycles at the least. . . . I will not count
them. There must be no thought of externals. Only thus may I ulti-
mately escape the Plane.*

*Turning in, all my slow energies bending, binding, the circle of
awareness tightening as it shrinks. Almost to the point of no-thought,
unaware of the fires below, the empty chill above: I am not thinking of
these things, I am not, not, not.*

(But negation is a quality. How to shed even this?)

*Time has passed. The circle loosens once more. Again my awareness
snaps out: strange to be so eager for sensation, here in the Middle Plane
between the universe's extremes. I expand myself now in the alternate
form of the Way; if the mind may not sever itself directly from existence,
it is still possible to lose the self in physical infinitude. I have followed
both these ways, many times. The Plane has no boundaries and therefore
is infinite; I extend to fathom its illusory limits, approaching again the
edges of the central essence: not-perception, not-thought, not-being, not
. . . not . . .*

[Mara]

—JUMPSHOCK! And cobwebs of static brush over me. Another Rubicon crossed; surely we should feel more than that tiniest of thrills. The sense of drama demands rending and thunder. The lights come up; pre-jump tension dissipates. We are here, wherever that may be. —Alphecca, they said: a seekerdrone reports a likely world, Mara: come sniff it with your Talent. It is my duty to Probe soon, but there is no urgency. Six hours yet, six hours tumbling through night, before we are close. Moreover, the crew's excitement runs high as a new sun glares. Let it die down, let it sink into calmness, before I peep outside the mindshield. —After Mirfak, there is always the fearful urge to delay. I make the usual bargain: half an hour.

Strange patterns run through every situation. In the hold are racked scatter-torpedoes with their catalysts which, unchanging, will change a waiting world. Centuries from now, our children may thank us. Not mine; a Prober's life has no room for such.

—In the converter, catalysis on the nuclear level. Protons collide behind the webbing fields, becoming helium in half a dozen stages; catalytic carbon drives the process, as it does the greater converter that is Alphecca itself. And so the star and the ship continue their functions; one a simple sphere, the other a jumble of polyhedra looped with straggling tubes.

Last of all, here am I: at my catalytic word, man's interaction with the barren, nameless planet will begin. Shall I, too, remain unchanged?

Lying back, I empty my mind in preparation. (Om mani padme hum) The luminescent seconds flicker by.

The tremor breaks my trance. For an instant it seemed that the whole Plane rippled, was pierced with singularities; this is a thing which cannot be. As I approach withdrawal, my sense becomes paradoxically receptive, so the shiver that ran through the area disturbed me at the core of being. A sign from the Supreme; a thing of my own mind; a chance convulsion of nature? With no data beyond that one experience, I cannot decide. Nor may I continue in introversion, without assimilating and dismissing the distracting fact. So it must, I decide, be a shaping of the mind. Some portion thereof has fallen from discipline. The exercises of Trac must be my lot for half a cycle. It does not matter, I tell myself. When I follow the Race into timelessness, all time will be one. And here between the bitterness and the burning, there is none to mark my progress.

All is well. A likely system, all that the drone's report suggested: so the screen informs. The screen installed since Mirfak. (And a nervous glance to the shield switch.) Alphecca's only offspring: good. Confusion as to the location of intelligence has often arisen in multiple systems. The Talent is not directional, and what's a billion kilometers to a Prober? Very slowly I reach for the switch. The slightest of pressures . . .

(Mirfak. Superior minds or psychic weapons? The switch clicked, my cabin shield collapsed and blazing power came through. Oh yes, there was life! A battering torrent of thought, sweeping the mind from the skull. I stood long enough to reverse the switch and re-erect my defense. The crew had had no chance. Carrying the heavy shieldpack, I stumbled through bright corridors and saw them. Worst, they were not dead. So I wept, and my inexpert hands programmed the jump to safety, whilst all around they lay and would not die. Mindshield generators project a broad and ship-sized field, now. After Mirfak.)

Calmness . . . Detachment . . .

(With steady fusion, the ship and Alphecca continue to function. The question is begged. In the perspective of eternity, a star may have no less purpose than a ship. And my sole function is: to Probe.)

The switch moves. White noise sears my nerves; a hissing confusion, full of half-sensed meanings; this is normal. Here and there I catch unease, resentment: *is that frigid bitch poking in my mind?* One by one I filter out the patterns I know so well, patterns committed to mind over months in the presence of the crew. One by one they are cut from the web, as I tune more and more selectively. The Captain's powerful presence with its hint of hidden weakness, the Pilot's clarity, the harsh Chief Programmer: out they go, and the rest of the forward crew in the bridgeglobe, and then the tech staff—fourteen, fifteen—engineers—twenty-two, twenty-three—is that an overlay on the pattern? Twenty-four . . . the final narrowing takes an age . . . twenty-five. Finis.

And there is an unknown. No room for error; though undirectional, the Talent's range is less than half a lightyear. How annoyed the Captain will be if I must veto his precious catalysts. Unknown, where are you? I flow with your pattern. Probe:

Rebellion! Cancer of the inmost core! A portion of my being spews out irrational thoughts; though I have countered them for the present, I am close to despair. Sickness of the mind has ever been the terror of the Race; it is the only termination they know beyond godlike release from the Plane, and now the fear is in me. To scatter the patterns of the mind until its hold on the physical begins to slip: this is a most terrible end. The ultimate components of body and self are whirled, then, into endless emptiness and cold. Only the willed release from the Plane can achieve the Utter state of heat without pain, fullness without impediment: Oneness. —And it seems I am doomed never to attain it.

Why does my traitor mind whisper within me?

A pattern weak and hesitant, but brilliant in its clarity. A pattern which somehow hides itself at first contact. Is there a technology here that can construct the Shield? I ponder. The shield: Mirfak. A hint there? Am *I* the mind of terrible power, the blasting force that has driven the Contact into hiding? Into amentia? I tap out a message to the bridge: wait. The irritation stings even through my careful filters. But every contact is unique; I am to use my own judgment. We remain in transit, "falling, falling yet, to the ancient lyrical cadence . . . " The catalysts will not be released on arrival, until I give the word. To be sure, it is necessary that I back my decision with evidence—if it is a negative decision. We are not beasts, and little concrete backing is required when once the Prober is convinced of lurking intelligence. Our collective conscience has not forgotten Bellatrix, even as our caution reminds us of Mirfak and Algol. Genocide, it seems, is almost as wounding to the slayer as to the slain. Thrusting all this below the surface of consciousness, I tap the deeper wells and open myself as fully as I may. Probe:

I believe that the madness is past. Where discordant thoughts gibbered, there is only an emptiness and a waiting. The Plane is changeless; no further spasm has convulsed my sense, and I begin to doubt the earlier one. It may be overconfidence, but almost I feel that this mastery of myself was a necessary test, a stage in the Way which I did not know. Still distraction stands always in my path.

To infinity in every true direction: the Plane. There can be no motion, up or down, for only here do the separate vagaries of density and temperature permit existence. From this and no more, Trac once argued the presence of Supreme Benevolence—from the simple fact that parameters coincide at the point where life may be.

Perhaps now I shall sink blissfully into the fire that burns not. Turning in, turning in . . . I fix again on the contemplation of the Cycle of Two plus Two-squared. One / two / two plus one / two-squared / two-squared plus one / two-squared plus two. One / two / —

Do not be alarmed. (Two-squared plus two? Six?) I wish you no harm. Do not be alarmed. Can you sense me? Do not—

Twice! Twice I have been turned from the Way by my sickness. It is an omen; it is the end. I despair.

(A not unfamiliar reaction pattern, I recall) —Do not be
alarmed. I am not-you. Do you understand this? I am Other. I
wish you no harm. Do not be alarmed.

(I pause. Can this be? It would be easy, so easy, to accept this escape.)
How can—*you*—prove this thing?

Nothing may be proved. Nothing. All you sense might be
illusion. It is more profitable to accept reality than to doubt it.

But I do not sense you in the Plane. What remains but to accept the
reality of my madness?

Plane? (I find the underthought of infinite flatness—no, not
precisely two-dimensional, but a narrow zone that is the known
universe.)

Let me enter your perception-space. I must know this delusion fully.
Let me sense with your senses.

(I sigh, allow myself to perceive the polished, aseptic cube
that is the room.) Beyond; beyond your world. (Always the
same. The known universe is the universe.)

This space is more bounded and confined than my own. Subreality?
Existence within existence? —Madness.

Beyond the Plane! Beyond everything you know! (I slide
towards the viewport, touch the polarizer: Stars) —You know
of above and below.

Nothing is beyond the Plane but High Space. The fullness below and
emptiness above. (But . . . what of Rosok's heresy? The cycle of planes,
endless Planes stacked through High Space, forever?)

(The roundabout approach, then. Cosmology is always a
tender area!) Consider this, (what is the name? Probe: it comes
across as) Warin: if you are unsane, what remains? (And a
tentative thought of my own: No infinite plane but a sphere.)

Nothing remains. I anticipate your argument. My only hope, then,
is to assume reality. (If you are fantasy, will you be conjured out by this
approach?) If you are real, then, have pity and leave me.

I must remain, for a little time. Your cooperation will speed
me on my way. Tell me (Probe: no data?) of your surroundings
(incomprehensible data), your race (something there) . . .

There is only the Plane. The Race, apart from myself, has achieved
Oneness, or madness and dissipation. To either side of existence they

scatter, to bask or freeze . . . (And you who are not of the plane, which region of High Space is yours? Are you the husk of insanity or the essence of unity? Neither seems to apply . . .)

(This is the most simplistic heaven/hell system I have ever encountered.) I shall think on this. (Probe: Probe: Probe:) I leave you to do likewise. (Is there nothing? Pro—I am wasting my energies. —And the finger on the switch.)

(Silence)

(Silence)

The alien logic is harsh. To save myself I must admit not only these whisperings, but also, perhaps, the heresy of Rosok. Yet if I convince the other—already I begin to believe—to depart, then whether it is truelife or phantasm, the old stillness will surely return.

Rosok. Many believed him at that time. His mental forces were so great that few wholly escaped the spell. "We are not alone," was the burden of his thoughts: the Believers would flow no more with his being. Still, many were swayed. "We are not alone," they pulsed in unison to their imagined higher planes. —There came a time when they found Rosok sunk in on himself, throbbing "We are not alone." He could not stop. Nor was it a true withdrawing, for the dark message pulsed out for several full cycles, and overrode the weaker minds among us, and it was repeated for a count of many twos and powers of two. Then Rosok departed, swallowed by the cold. The message reverberated long in the Race consciousness, endless, hypnotic, before the madness died. In that time many followed the heretic and shared his end.

Not I! I beg of High Space, not I!

Always I wonder how a new race will interpret the quick thrill of our coming. I was of the first generation to grow up with jumpshock; ten, twenty times a day the shiver might strike down from space, reminding the young girl who was myself of the frontier beyond. (But not the important frontier, my father said. Knowledge is always the challenge. Even then, I heard more from him than he would say . . .)

Warin has no environment. Or rather, he does not perceive his surroundings as such, beyond these most basic and enigmatic rhythms. He is like a fish unaware of its sea. Except why should a fish associate warmth with the downward direction? It should be the other way about. —Would any surface creature think in those terms? It is time to admit, however reluctantly, that I am straying beyond the bounds of my specialty. Still screened from mental interference by the shield, I approach the biotech Lubek.

As do several of the crew members, not all of them male, Lubek lusts after me. (I cannot think why; my thin body has no allure.) It is for this reason, among others, that I keep the mindshield in full operation. Naturally I will not weaken my Talent for the sake of a groping in darkness; better to avoid the very concept. But plump Lubek is skilled in his speciality.

Now, for just a few moments, he considers the slender facts; and informs me that Warin is a deep-dweller. As I had thought, what he perceives as a plane must be a sphere—a layer deep within the planet. Stupid, I am stupid! I thank Lubek, without any show of emotion. If this is so, the changes may begin. Moving now through the bridgeglobe's central level, I see to my surprise (time passes so quickly in linkage) that we are already circling the world they have now called Barathrum. Certainly it is no place for man, not yet: ammonia, and other things.

Above: This ship with its chemical, nuclear, and human catalysts. Assembled from scores of units, it has no unity; the many sections drift sluggishly, linked by their flexible tubes.

Below: Barathrum. A ball of mottled bluegray in three-quarter phase, vaguely iridescent in the screens. No satellites. Arid facts flicker above and below— Distance from primary 8.91 lightminutes, mean surface gravity 1.13g est., period of rotation 16h 38m, mean surface temperature, mean surface pressure est., albedo . . .

Atmosphere: ammonia, methane, hydrogen, water vapor. There is some free nitrogen; gaseous hydrocarbons and hydro-

gen sulphide. A reducing atmosphere, harsh like the young
Earth's; a planet-sized Miller flask where already the first spon-
taneous amino acids could be forming. —And beneath it all,
Warin . . . Augmenting the effects of Alphecca's UV and Barathrum's own thundercells, we shall catalyze the air into mellow
maturity. Someone once asked, is it right for a world's youth to
be compressed into mere centuries? Life comes first: so the
reply has always gone.

But the fining of its potential will leave the deep untouched.
Between crust and core: chill and heat, the "Plane" and Warin. I
retire and relax from my efforts. The strain is considerable;
almost invariably, Probers are thin, bird-thin and undermus-
cled. Relaxation is a discipline. Om mani padme hum: Om
mani padme hum: Om . . .

*I now drift aimlessly. I perceive the Plane in its cycles, changeless and
changing. The other mind will return. There is no profit in the inward
turning, when interruption may come at any time, any moment.*
I am not alone.

Floating up from the crystalline depths of no-thought, I
surface in a splash of renewed awareness. The door-control,
the blank screen, the spare shipsuit hanging on the wall: objects
seem, as always, blindingly sharp and clear to the eyes. It is as
though I have left my plastilenses off for many hours: the shock
of focus on their resumption seems equal to any "heightened
awareness" of the chemical mind-expanders. (These are forbid-
den to me; my mind is a tool.)

—To the screen. The scopes, it seems, show no evidence of
life. A cautious man is the Captain; but the operation will
commence in a few hours, now, unless I pronounce veto. Warin
is safe, safe in the deep. Yet, without rational cause . . . I am
uneasy.

He is so simple and helpless; so like a child.

(Bellatrix. The catalysts dusted insidiously down. No life could be found, not by any physical inspection. They looked so carefully . . . but in those days they did not Probe. —The air burning and condensing, raining down poison on the sentient stones. We could not appreciate ultraslow metabolism, then, until a latent Prober caught the planet's long scream. In half a thousand years, when the changes are done, we may send in the colonists. The remorse now is such that probably we will not; thus even the futile justification of utility is destroyed.)

Distantly there comes the sound of heavy metal. The discharge torpedoes are being made ready. New tension seeps through my mind's protecting field.

Suppose . . . (Om mani padme hum) Suppose the biotech and I are in error? What error? I claw the facts for fresh interpretations. Warm below and cold above. Dense below and thin above. For deep-dwellers, it fits. So take it as Occam's razor slices it, Mara; keep new variables at bay. And yet (the cycle of six?) . . . I flip the switch.

Dully I drift, without purpose, wandering the endless Plane . . .

Warin, I must know more. Tell me how you eat, how you drink, tell me something new.

Ah, you return. Tell me, what is your designation?

Mara. (A crazy thought from nowhere: They could not chat together, they had not been introduced—) I must know more of your metabolism.

I drift. That is all. What else could there be?

All! Oh, what's the use?

It seems you cannot understand me. For my part, I do not find it necessary to understand myself. Or the Plane; or you.

There must be something you have not told me. How are your people born; how do they die?

Die?

Umm—leave the Plane?

The Race was created at the Beginning. When they achieve Oneness, they go, and there is no sign of their passing. They cease to intersect the

Plane, and become free. Trac told us that they find this freedom in the warmth below. Warmth is life, and cold, death.

I—I shall think about this too. May all remain as it is with you until I return.

You wish that I should remain trapped in this existence?

(Silence)

So like a child. He drifts; that is all. The concept, at any rate, is one which my mind interprets as "drifts." Tunnels? Or is Warin a thing of the magma? A blank pause. —A horrible supposition! Imagine a gaseous being (The analysis! Gaseous hydrocarbons . . .) which—drifts—in the middle air. Then his world is denser below and thinner above—warmth of land and chill of space: What have I done? The torpedoes must be nearly ready. The keyboard. Wait! Wait! Wait!

A poisonous reducing atmosphere; and for Warin it could be life. (Om mani padme hum) The catalysts will surely destroy such a being. (Om mani padme hum) I cannot delay forever; I must have a sign. (Signs are taken for wonders) What then may Warin do in the way of physical action? Something that will convince the Captain . . . Not wishing to face the latter's annoyance, I tap out my suspicions from the cabin. In his curt reply I read something very like a snarl.

So I have a day, now. I have a day. He is rigorous but fair: if I produce my data in 23 hours 59 minutes, all is well; a further two minutes' delay and—no, he is not that rigorous, but certainly he prefers to be thought so. To work, then. The databanks show no support, no precedent for what I fear; reluctantly I leave the secure cabin to consult Lubek once more. He can scarcely restrain his smile at the notion of a gaseous Warin: it has not happened before, and therefore it is absurd. I daresay he would have laughed at Bellatrix.

There only remains Warin himself; Warin and my sense of imminent disaster. The solitary cabin; the switch; the opened mind. Again, a phasing-out of irrelevant (yes, Captain, you too are irrelevant) signals:

Mara?
Yes. Warin, I fear disaster unless you can tell me more. You
may be in danger of being . . . of being forced from the Plane.
Such is my desire. You can aid me, then?
No! . . . I meant, there is a possibility of your dissolution
without achieving this Oneness.
*That would be a great evil, of course; but I cannot see how it can
come about.*
I can; but I cannot explain. Warin, can you communicate
other than in this fashion? I urgently need a physical manifesta-
tion—an outward appearance in the Plane. (Earth in upheaval
or turbulent air; the scopes will tell. Which?)
*I am powerless in the Plane. And there is no longer any hope of my
escape. Many cycles I have spent, attempting to transcend the flat and
enter High Space: all, all useless.*
So? I caught some of this before. (I am desperate now)
Meditation is your route, not so?
*Of course. It is the only road to Transcendence. Turning in, turning
in . . . To follow the Way, one requires peace and silence. You under-
stand me?*
Point taken. But—I have had training in one form of the
Way, as practiced by my own kind. Could I perhaps assist you?
The true Way is solitary.
And you have failed in it for—how long? I know you, Warin,
I know your mind.
(Pause)
Very well. Then tell me your Way, if you wish.
First, tighten the link. That's right. Come closer still, and
stay in tune—follow me—
Om mani padme hum: Om mani padme hum:
Jewel? Lotus?
Follow me: Om mani padme hum: *Om mani padme hum:*
Om *mani* padme *hum:* *Om* mani *padme* hum:
Om
    mani
        padme
            hum:

(Time passes. Down and down: the familiar crystal deeps)
  (To the Plane's farthest edge)
(Calm. Calm.)
        (Trac . . .?)
(Still and deep:)
            (The Plane: tilting away: beyond:)
(No-thought . . . . No-thought . . . .)
(. . . .)

                    (O N E N E S S)
(What?)
    (Silence)
        (Silence)
            (Silence and dark)

Warin? Warin? (That this was all folly?) He has slipped away
. . . (Probe: Nothing) Sitting up on the couch, I rub my eyes.
That psychic explosion was like nothing I have ever known.
Warin was real, real! A dream and a legend cannot take him like
this. (Probe:) —I strain to the limit, catch nothing but a wavering heterodyne from the crew. No mental filters are perfect;
also, their tension is very great. Why is this? The pressure on
my consciousness is proportionately painful. Accordingly I
flick on the ship's mindshield, relax in the welcome blankness,
and step uncertainly to the display screen.
    We are leaving!
    The irony of it; there is no bar to standard procedure now. I
am about to tap this to the bridge, when I glance at the screen's
REASONS FOR ACTION paragraph. Many things come together,
then, too many too late: facts assembled into critical mass for an
inner fireball of my own. Heat below and cold above, oh God
. . . He simply drifted . . . He transcended the Plane, having
achieved release. And the Talent is not directional. And even
the hint I caught in his meditations, the cycle of six. Even I, no
scientist, know of the six reactions in the nuclear carbon cycle.

Not plain gas, but plasma. Not the atmosphere, but the photosphere.
Carbon there is an unchanging catalyst; but I, I am not.
Warin . . .
—JUMPSHOCK!

We flee unlucky Alphecca; where the world called Barathrum is scorching in the great flare which burst from the seemingly stable sun. An unfortunate coincidence, says the log. Perhaps they meant well at Mirfak, too.
The last of the Race has passed beyond the Plane; and no one knows or cares to weep, but I.

IAN WATSON
THE ULTIMATE
ONE-WORD
FIRST-CONTACT STORY

...OUCH!"